PRAISE F(

MW01255053

"Hazel Cho…has major league smarts, uncommon ingenuity, charm, and enough humanizing flaws to make her irresistible. So what are you waiting for—go read *The Orphanage by the Lake*."

—**James Patterson**, #1 *New York Times*
and international bestselling author

"Twisting and impossible to put down, *The Orphanage by the Lake* will thrill any fan of psychological mysteries."

—**Darcy Coates**, *USA Today* bestselling author

"*The Orphanage by the Lake* is an intriguing mystery that lures you into a world of secrets and keeps you reading till the last page."

—**Kat Martin**, *New York Times* bestselling author

"Saint Agnes—a sanctuary with a dark secret. When Manhattan PI Hazel Cho is asked to trace a girl gone missing from a revered children's home, it looks like a straightforward case. But nothing in Daniel G. Miller's gripping story is straightforward—not when a respected headmaster, a charming philanthropist, and the girl's own godmother all have something to hide. Top-notch suspense in an idyllic setting makes for great fireside reading. Recommended."

—**G. M. Malliet**, Agatha Award–winning
author of the Max Tudor Mysteries

"Miller is an expert in ratcheting up the tension and deftly scattering red herrings."

—*Publishers Weekly* Booklife, Starred Review

"Miller has crafted a suspenseful tale with quick pacing, naturalistic dialogue, and an endearing narrative voice… A twisty thriller."

—*Kirkus Reviews*

ALSO BY
DANIEL G. MILLER

THE ORPHANAGE BY THE LAKE SERIES
The Orphanage by the Lake

THE
RED
LETTER

DANIEL G. MILLER

Poisoned Pen
PRESS

Copyright © 2025 by Daniel G. Miller
Cover and internal design © 2025 by Sourcebooks
Cover design by Damonza.com
Cover images © David Papazian/Shutterstock, Ana de Sousa/Shutterstock, Ensuper/
Shutterstock, Helena Lansky/Shutterstock, Nik Merkulov/Shutterstock, OokOak/
Shutterstock, Mega Pixel/Shutterstock, Eky Studio/Shutterstock, Here/Shutterstock

Published by Poisoned Pen Press, an imprint of Sourcebooks
1935 Brookdale RD, Naperville, IL 60563-2773
(630) 961-3900
sourcebooks.com

Cataloging-in-Publication Data is on file with the Library of Congress.

Printed and bound in the United States of America.
VP 10 9 8 7 6 5 4 3 2 1

To the Victims

In Memoriam
Tony Ambrose
A friend from the beginning
A friend 'til the end.

1

Watching a man die is a tough way to spend your afternoon. The video plays and I see the inside of St. Patrick's Old Cathedral in Lower Manhattan. The camera shows the inside of a sparse Gothic cathedral sitting dark, silent, and empty. The footage is a little grainy, but it's sharp enough to identify details. Moonlight slips through stained glass, creating a haunting mix of light and shadow. Dark maple pews straddle a long walkway down the spine of the building. Marble pillars stand watch overhead. I've attended this church before, but never at night. It's chilling. Even the silence seems to echo. I feel like I'm watching one of those found-footage horror films where a group of plucky grad students investigate a mysterious haunting and things quickly go awry.

A whining door hinge breaks the silence, followed by shuffling footsteps. Father Kenneally appears and springs into the sanctuary at the front of the cathedral. As a private investigator,

I've learned to note every detail, and he's exactly as I remember him. He's about sixty years old. His red hair recedes from his domed forehead and gray peppers his temples, but his wide, angular face is ruddy and vigorous. The crinkles around his eyes carry the kindness of someone who's smiled and chuckled much of their life. I wish more priests were like him.

He wears all black and a clergy collar. The moonlight glints off the small silver cross around his neck. He walks into the sanctuary with a lumbering, happy gait, whistling "Danny Boy," the old Irish tune. A tan leather portfolio rests in one hand and a Bible in the other. A smile plays on his lips. He sings the words under his breath: "Oh, Danny boy, the pipes, the pipes are calling."

He's enjoying the peace of the empty church.

But something eerie hides behind the silence.

He takes the pulpit and turns on the reading lamp, which highlights his aloneness in the gloomy structure. He rests a pair of frameless reading glasses on a small, slightly upturned nose, then licks his thick fingers and riffles through the Bible. He turns the gilt-edged pages with care, giving the book the respect it deserves. It reminds me of my father when he reads his dusty detective novels. I think it's a requirement when you read old books to lick at least one finger before you flip the pages.

He begins speaking to an audience of none, presumably practicing his homily for the following day. My mind flashes back to those Sundays I visited here, when smiling parents and squirrelly kids filled every seat. It was a happy place then.

"Good morning, everyone. It's so nice to see you all this fine Sunday."

His posture is humble, but his speech booms through the

hollow space with assurance. His voice carries a warm timbre. He's the type of priest you'd confide in over a beer. I've always felt welcome in his church.

"This morning I'd like us to travel to the temple mount and listen to a sermon that Jesus gave over two thousand years ago."

Even in the empty cathedral, his sermon draws you closer, forcing you to reflect on his meaning. He talks about the poor in spirit, the meek, the merciful, about faith, about being a good Catholic, about how church on Sunday isn't enough, about how you must give back to your community. But he does it in a way that's not preachy, more the gentle coaxing of a close friend.

Behind him, moonlight shines through curved stained glass with a cross at its center, forming a perfect silhouette. As he speaks, I perceive that even alone, he can't help but get excited. He adjusts his glasses. He hops up and down on his toes, and his pace accelerates.

And then it happens.

He fumbles a word.

Until now, his speech flowed so smoothly. The error hits like a needle scratch. It catches him off guard. He's a professional unused to making mistakes.

Then he stops speaking.

He retreats from the podium and studies the room, searching for any witnesses to his mistake. His fingertips tremble as he presses them to his lips. Then he licks them as though he's searching for a feeling, but finds nothing. He cranks his head to the side in confusion but resumes speaking, likely hoping it was a momentary glitch.

Again, the words emerge mumbled and slurred. He sounds

like a drunk. Even from the camera's distance, I notice his panicked expression etched into every line on his face. He sidesteps from the podium as if it has infected him and looks around again, searching. He stares at his notes. Then at his hands. He surveys the sanctuary, then the pews. Each head turn, each eye movement more clipped and frantic than the one before.

He looks to the ceiling.

To God.

I lean in closer to the screen and squint my eyes. My mouth dries. I hate watching him suffer like this, but I can't look away. I scan the video frame, searching like he's searching, but the church is as empty as when he began. No one has entered. No item is out of place. Nothing has changed. He's alone.

Father Kenneally brings both hands to his scarlet face, and I watch as the panic metastasizes into terror. He runs his fingers up and down his cheeks and across his forehead as though he's trapped in a mask he can't touch and can't remove. Sweat beads on his brow, reflecting the dim light in sickly glints. He reaches for his Bible, but it slips from his grasp and crashes to the floor with a hollow thud—a symbol of his hope crumbling. He tries to call out for help, but only a weak cry escapes.

No one can hear him.

Realizing his only chance to find help is to run outside onto the bustling Manhattan streets, he descends the steps of the sanctuary and stumbles down the aisle. After a few paces, his feet give way and he falls. The thump of his body against the cold stone echoes through the empty church. He begins crawling, and for a moment, I think he might survive.

Then he vomits.

He retches so violently, I'm afraid he'll break his back, and I can almost smell it through the screen. He collapses onto the floor, writhing in agony, gasping for air. Seconds tick by, and it appears he's found a brief respite from the horror that's overtaken him.

But then his body starts convulsing.

He spasms and tremors like he's possessed by a demon. He cries out again, but this time he can't muster words, only a pathetic grunt.

Father K. heaves one side of his body forward, then the other, losing strength with each thrust. The sound of his failing body sliding along the aisle sickens me. He reaches the middle of the nave, and his strength gives out. He gazes into the camera— directly at me—his desperate stone-blue eyes pleading for mercy.

But there is none to be found in this empty church.

No mercy.

No one to save him.

I wish I could reach through the screen to help him.

He rolls onto his back and gasps for his few remaining breaths, wheezing in and out. First fast, then slow. His body seizes, shaking and trembling as an invisible force grabs hold of his insides. His skull shakes against the floor like a bass drum. Spit and foam spill from his mouth, staining his once-pristine robes. Eventually, the shaking slows, then ceases. His face twists into a horrific expression that mirrors my own.

And just like that, this kind man, this pillar of the community, is gone.

The video ends, and I am left with only one thought.

I cannot be a part of this case.

2

Shavali clicks the off button on the remote and joins us at the oak laminate conference room table. The screen on the wall-mounted television goes black. I look at my assistant, Mary, whose round, rosy cheeks are even more flushed than usual. She crosses herself over her cardigan sweater and spins the cross pendant necklace around her neck. Her husband owns a funeral home, but I wonder if, in her fifty-plus years, she's ever seen someone die before, let alone a priest. We share a moment of silence. I shake the image out of my brain, but it drops from my mind and settles in my stomach.

Shavali leans back in her chair and flips her long, lustrous brown mane over her shoulder. Her orange blossom shampoo scent floats through the room. I shake my head. The woman hasn't changed a bit since law school. She still flaunts a refined British accent from growing up in London. She's still gorgeous with her tall frame, tan Indian skin, and giant brown eyes. She's still flipping her hair from one side to the other like she's posing for unseen paparazzi. She even has one of those cool beauty marks on her upper lip, so perfectly placed that you'd swear she applied it with a pencil. I can't imagine what the rest of her colleagues here at the Legal Aid Society think.

"Quite disturbing, isn't it?" she says.

"Yeah, it is." I swallow the image of Father K.'s contorted face and gaze out the conference room window. It offers a stunning view of an incandescent blue sky against the dark water of the East River. I watch boats putter down the waterway, steam floating into the air on this brisk October day, and think back to when I attended a service at Old St. Patrick's. "I actually met Father Kenneally when I visited his church a few years ago. He was a nice man. I remember when he died last December, but seeing it like that brings it home."

"I'm sure. Unfortunately, I've had to watch it so many times, it's lost its impact." She plays the role of the tough attorney, but I know her too well. When I search her eyes, I can see the video disturbed her.

"He had been the head priest at Old St. Patrick's for years, right?"

She grabs a manila folder from the foot-high stack in front of her and slides it across the table. I trace my fingertips along the coarse paper. Mary pulls out her notebook with the immaculate I ♥ FARGO doodle on the front and prepares to take notes. Having an assistant is the one luxury I allow myself now that our private investigation business has taken off. Mary takes the notes, and I can focus on the client and the case. It doesn't hurt that she possesses the perfect blend of chipper demeanor and steel core.

"Yes. He served as rector for twenty-two years. Before that, he ministered at Saint Mary's upstate, Saint Anselm and Saint Roch in the Bronx, and then finally ended up at Old St. Patrick's. He was a smart guy. Went to College of the Holy Cross in Massachusetts. Then to Yale for divinity school."

"I take it his family was Catholic?"

"Yes. He grew up in New Jersey. Irish Catholic family. Five brothers, four sisters."

"Ten kids?" says Mary, confirming before she writes anything down.

Shavali fires her a wry smile. "Yes, apparently the Kenneallys were not big believers in birth control. Hazel, you and Jack want ten kids, right?"

"Ha, I can barely take care of myself." Merely thinking about having kids freaks me out. Jack's mentioned the idea to me a few times, and I always dodge him.

I try to steer the discussion back to safer ground. "When I was at Old St. Patrick's, it seemed like people genuinely liked him. After Mass, all the parishioners were fawning over him like a celebrity. My ex and I could barely get out of the exit. Is that what you found?"

Shavali nods and flips her hair again. "I would say he was beloved, actually. He was extremely active in the community. On Thanksgiving, he handed out turkeys from the back of a truck. He hosted an Easter egg hunt in the church. That sort of thing. When he died, the bouquets of flowers took up the entire block. It was like Princess Di's funeral."

"And his death. The police determined poison, if I'm remembering correctly?"

"Correct. He died on December twentieth of last year. The cause of death was poison. Tetrodotoxin, which is a devilish neurotoxin. It's what's called a 'sodium-channel blocker.'" She pauses so that Mary can keep up with her note-taking. Mary mouths *sodium-channel blocker* to herself while she writes. "It kills you by blocking signals from the brain to the body, which causes paralysis, respiratory distress, and heart failure, among a variety of other nasty symptoms."

"This is the fish poison we're talking about, right?"

"Yes. It's a poison found in fugu, which is a puffer fish sashimi."

"You're telling me Kenneally was eating fugu before he practiced his Sunday sermon? He doesn't really seem like a sushi guy to me."

Shavali laughs and flips her hair again. Her laugh has always killed me. It's so melodic, it sounds like someone impersonating a laugh rather than genuinely chuckling. In our law school study group, all of us used to mimic her every time she laughed until we were all rolling. I shoot Mary an amused look, and she scolds me with her eyes.

"Of course not. He didn't eat sashimi that night and, as far as we can tell, never ate it in his life."

"Hence the conclusion that someone poisoned him?"

"Exactly."

"So, remind me, why did you drag me down here? It sounds like everything is pretty cut and dried. I mean, don't get me wrong, I love a good hang with my old law school bud, but I'd prefer tacos and margaritas. Or we can skip the tacos and go straight to the margaritas."

She offers a polite laugh and then taps her long, manicured fingers against the conference room table and swallows hard. Her eyes travel along the pigeon-gray walls, past the pictures of civil rights advocates with overlaid motivational quotes, before finally landing on me.

"I need your help."

Her words jar me. I lean back in my chair and put my hands behind my head. My lips curl into a huge smile. This is the first good news I've heard all day. "I'm sorry. Did I hear that correctly? Shay needs my help? The woman who's teased me for years about dropping out of law school to become a PI needs my help?"

Mary stifles a laugh and then says, "Hazel, be nice." I love watching Mary laugh at a sarcastic comment. She chuckles for a few seconds, then an alarm reminding her she shouldn't be laughing must go off in her head, because she stops. Almost like my mother, except she never laughs.

Shavali rolls her eyes at me. She taps her pen on the table and, through gritted teeth, says it one more time. "Yes, I need your help."

"Well, now I am intrigued. How can Hazel Cho, private investigator extraordinaire, help you?"

She gives me another folder, but this time she flings it at my chest instead of sliding it delicately across the table. The stale smell of paper reminds me of my days as a legal intern. I open the folder, which contains a mug shot of a skinny, light-skinned Black kid with Afro puffs. He looks like he's about fifteen, but he could be older. It's a little hard to tell because of his small features. Tiny eyes, miniature ears, a snub nose, a pinched mouth, and a pencil neck. In the picture, he wears a smug smile.

"My client's name is Samuel Sampson. Eighteen years old. From the Bronx. Worked with Father Kenneally at Old St. Patrick's. He's being charged with the murder."

"Oh yeah. I vaguely remember when the police arrested him. You're representing this kid? Why do you need my help?"

She clears her throat. "He wants to plead not guilty. I don't think he did it, but my case is wretched. I need you to do some digging and see if you can come up with something that exonerates him or, at the very least, a plausible alternative suspect I can throw at the jury. I wouldn't ask you to do this, but with all the changes in the discovery rules, everyone in the office is buried, so no one has time to assist me on this case. All our investigators are tied up on other cases, and I can barely keep up with the basic filings, let alone mount a defense. I was hoping you might pitch in out of the goodness of your heart. The trial starts in a week. If I don't get something proper by then, he's going to prison."

"A week? That's not nearly enough time. Why don't you ask for a continuance? This is pretty quick for a homicide trial."

"Because he's at Rikers. It's a miracle he's made it this long. Plus, you understand how it is. If I bump this trial out, it may not get tried for years. Remember Kalief Browder?"

I turn to Mary. "Kalief Browder was held at Rikers for three years without trial for stealing a backpack. Two years after they released him, he hanged himself."

"Oh my," says Mary as she scribbles away. Mary's from North

Dakota, so when she throws you an *Oh my*, things are getting serious. And she's right. Everything about this case seems…off. A dead priest. A young man charged with the killing. A rushed trial. I consider the Catholic Church's previous issues with child abuse. I like to think Father Kenneally could never be involved in something like that. But I've learned that you never know what people are capable of behind closed doors. The face of evil is often the face next door.

My mind flashes to what happened to me behind closed doors a year ago. The Legal Aid Society's Manhattan office is only a few blocks from where I found Mia. Where Andrew…

I shut my eyes, and I'm in that dungeon all over again. Those girls. Those sick, sadistic men. The music. "Time After Time." Andrew's hand on my thigh. Sonia's knife at my neck. I can't go back there.

A faint whining, grinding, buzzing sound vibrates in my ear. I've been hearing that a lot lately since the incident. The room suddenly feels stuffy and warm. My chest tightens. I need some fresh air.

I close the folder, slide it back across the table, and stand up. I want to help this kid, but I'm scared where this case might lead.

"I'm sorry, Shay, I can't help you with this."

I tap Mary on the shoulder to tell her we're done here. She shoots me a confused look but then lifts her hearty Midwestern frame out of the chair.

Shavali stands up from her desk, her eyebrows pinched together. "What? I haven't even had a chance to tell you my client's side of the story. At least hear me out."

I head toward the door. I'm sure Samuel has a compelling

story. And Shavali can be quite persuasive when she wants a favor. If I stay in this room any longer, she'll either convince me or I'm going to have a panic attack. I look back at her. "I...I'm sorry. We've already got too many cases right now. We're expanding our office, and we're hosting a kickoff party tonight—and honestly, I don't think I can handle another case like this right now. Not after what happened last year."

She sets her jaw and glares at me. "You mean because of the priest and the boy?"

Hearing her say it makes my skin crawl. I'm dying to escape this room. I open the door with Mary in tow. "Exactly. And I knew Father Kenneally. I liked Father Kenneally. So the idea of learning something unflattering about him—or worse yet, helping his killer get off the hook—isn't very appealing to me right now."

She lowers her head. I can see that she's desperate. "I understand. But can I at least tell you something that might change your mind?"

I walk out the door and give her a wave.

"If it might change my mind, I definitely don't want to hear it. I'll call you when life calms down, and we can grab drinks."

Mary and I step out into the bustling bullpen, leaving Shavali alone in the conference room with her mouth hanging open. Phones ring and staff chatter in their cubicles. I take long, slow breaths as we stride toward the lobby door.

Shavali shouts something from the conference room.

"What did she say?" asks Mary.

I breeze past the receptionist and fling open the front door. I tap the elevator's down button as fast as I can. Finally, the doors open.

I can breathe.

We step onto the elevator, and I punch the lobby button. As the doors close, I turn to Mary.

"I don't know what she said. And I don't want to know."

3

hustle down Water Street with Mary a step behind me. A delivery truck roars past us, nearly pancaking me, but I keep striding. I want to get as far away from that place as fast as possible. I look to my right down Fulton Street toward the Seaport. Downtown workers indulge in happy hour mojitos on outdoor patios, braving the cold, stealing the last few days of fall. Tourists amble along the cobblestone, wrapped in puffy jackets, window shopping. The sun fades, sprinkling a glitter of light off the river. Yet I can't absorb any of it. I hate being in this part of town. It's one year to the day that I busted up the Dionysus Theater pedophile ring a block from here, but it feels like yesterday.

One good thing about New York, though: the city doesn't give a damn how you feel. People still run past you to catch the subway. Cart vendors still hawk their wares. Drivers still honk and bark at each other. The anonymity calms me.

"Is everything all right?" says Mary, breaking into a mini-jog to keep up with me.

I slow my pace and let her catch up as we turn up Gold Street. I don't need to give my fifty-five-year-old assistant a heart attack on the way to our office-warming party.

"Yeah, I'm fine. That meeting brought back some unpleasant memories."

Her forehead creases. "Oh no," she says with an elongated Midwest *o*. "Anything you want to talk about?"

I look at her sweet face, those gray-green eyes and pink cheeks framed by a dated mop of mousy brown hair with touches of gray. She reminds me of Mrs. Claus. And I don't think Mrs. Claus needs to hear the details of what I've been through.

"No. Thanks for asking, though." I'm walking so fast I'm losing my breath. I smell the skunky stink of marijuana smoke, and that only exacerbates the feeling. I'm fine with marijuana legalization, but can someone please invent a version that doesn't smell like roadkill?

"That video was pretty tough, huh?" she asks.

It's clear she won't let me enjoy this walk back to the office in silence, but that's why I hired her. She's persistent, curious. "Yeah, it was. I met him a few times when I went to church there with my ex. I didn't spend a lot of time with him, but Father K. had this inner peace to him. He stood outside the church at the end of the service and gave everybody hugs or handshakes. He never seemed rushed or distracted. Even if it was for only a few seconds, he looked everyone in the eyes and made a genuine connection. He made them feel special. He was one of those kind, old-fashioned older dudes who makes you feel reassured, like things are going to be all right. I don't meet a lot of them these days. With my work and Jack's work, I feel like I only meet lying, manipulative assholes. Excuse my language."

"That's fine. I get it."

"But what am I complaining about? It was probably even tougher for you. We haven't investigated any murders since you started last year. You probably haven't seen a lot of that."

She nods and swallows. "Yeah, but that's why I work for you. So I can assist with cases like this. Although I didn't expect to watch a priest die."

"You're Catholic, right?"

"Yes, sirree. My family didn't have ten kids, though," she says with a hearty chuckle. "Although my dad would have loved that. More cheap labor for the farm. I actually was a nun once, believe it or not."

"Really? Oh yeah, I remember reading that on your résumé."

"Yep. All of us kids went into different things. One brother became a mechanic. Another went to law school. My sister went into teaching. Broke my pop's heart. He was hoping one of us would come back after school and manage the farm with him. We had this great old Lab named Sarge. So stinkin' cute…"

Mary continues recounting her past while we stroll up Broadway, but I zone out. I'm stuck on the image of Father K. The way he touched his lips. The way his face contorted. The way his broken body dragged against the cold floor. It nags at me. The wind kicks up, and I pull my camel-wool overcoat tighter.

Mary notices that she's lost me to thought. "Listen to me, babbling on about my life. What about you? What do you think about this case?"

"I'm trying not to think about this case."

"Why is that?"

"Because I'm not going to take it."

"Yeah, but why aren't you going to take it?"

I shake my head. Sometimes the simplest questions trigger the most complex thoughts. Why am I avoiding this case? Is it because I liked Father Kenneally and his death saddens me? Is it because I'm worried his murder was revenge for something he did wrong? Is it because of the church's checkered history? Is it because I'm scared to let this Sampson kid down? No. That's not it. There's something else.

I throw up my hands as we walk. "I'm not sure, exactly. I guess...I guess it was the way he was killed. I've seen murders before, and I've seen dead bodies before. But the vast majority of murders are spur of the moment, clumsy. Over 90 percent of murders are spontaneous. A husband gets mad at his wife and grabs a gun, and boom. One gang gets mad at another gang, and the bullets fly. These people know each other. They're close in life and when the murder occurs. These are crimes of intimacy, passion. They're loud, messy."

"Like in *Law & Order*."

"Exactly. You get to the crime scene and it looks like a splatter painting. There's blood, overturned furniture, broken windows. I can't tell you how many times I've assisted on an investigation for the public defender and it's so obvious the accused did it that there's almost nothing to investigate. But this was the exact opposite. You saw the video. The church was silent. There was nobody there. No gun. No knife. No violence. It was like a spirit floated into the room and ripped out his soul."

"I see what you're saying. So what do you think it means?"

"It means that whoever did this is not your typical murderer. They're unusual. And now that I say it, I realize that is what is pushing me away from the case. The sense that something's off here. Like when you're walking home alone at night, and you turn down the wrong street and you know you're not safe."

Mary nods knowingly. It's a feeling every woman in New York has experienced. "So you don't think Shavali's client did it?"

I recall the picture of Samuel Sampson that Shavali showed me. The fragile features. The insecure eyes. I hate that I'm turning my back on him. "No. This murder doesn't fit the profile of an eighteen-year-old kid who's mad at the world. Those boys usually find a gun and go shoot up a school. They don't methodically murder a priest with an obscure poison."

The more I talk, the more I realize someone has to investigate this. I'm just not sure it should be me.

A fierce, frozen breeze rips down Canal Street, and both Mary and I tighten our coats and pick up our pace and race toward the office. Through her rapid breaths, she says, "So what are you saying?"

I put my arm around her as we jog and rub the soft, combed wool of her coat. My body shivers. I'm not sure if it's from the cold or the truth that I've been trying to ignore all afternoon.

"I'm saying that whoever killed Father Kenneally is still out there."

4

When Mary and I arrive at our office on Cortlandt Alley, I banish the dark thoughts from my mind and smile to myself. This place has become a second home.

Kenny, my partner, has placed an easel in front of the steel-framed glass entry to our building with a big sign that says WELCOME TO C&S INVESTIGATIONS HEADQUARTERS and balloons bobbing against the brick facade behind it. We decided on C&S Investigations when a friend pointed out that Cho & Shum reminded them of shark chum; not the image you want when someone's looking to hire an investigator. Other discarded ideas were Hazy K Investigations, K-pop Investigations, and, after a third glass of wine, Hazel and Gretel Investigations.

Mary and I jog up the stairs to our second-floor office. I'm anxious for the party tonight, to see what everyone thinks. The office has come a long way from last year. The only other tenant on my floor moved out, so we took the entire space. It's more than we need right now, and the monthly rent is eye watering, but if we keep growing, we're going to need it.

I open the door and can't help but grin. Kenny is standing in the center of our newly remodeled digs, arms spread wide, glass of champagne in one hand, beaming ear to ear. He decked himself out in a full suit and tie, and gelled his typically fuzz-ball hair for the occasion. He even shaved his patchy, sad attempt at a beard, so his smooth skin is glowing. In the dark-gray pinstripes and red tie, he looks...well, he looks like a man. Like he should have played the lead in *Crazy Rich Asians*.

I can't help but be impressed. The space is pristine. I whiff the sawdust and fresh paint. He designed the office warehouse-style, with an open-concept bullpen that manages to be both historical and hip. Bright red and yellow paint patterns the walls. Mary's desk sits five feet to the left of the door as you enter. An all-glass conference room stands behind it. Straight ahead are a couple of desks: one for Momo, our new intern, and one for the new hire we haven't hired yet. And the pièce de resistance is in the back: my and Kenny's offices, overlooking the street. It's not an ocean view, but it's a start.

And for the party, Kenny set up high-top tables and a serving station with more booze and food than we could ever eat. He's even roped Momo into bartending. I smell a glorious mixture of steak, pasta, cheese, sugar, and spices. My eyes land on a cupcake tower at the end of the serving station. It takes everything in my power not to start picking it apart.

"Well, what do you think?" asks Kenny.

"I think it's incredible. Nice work!"

Mary claps her hands in appreciation. "Kenny, I had no idea you were such an adept party planner."

"What can I say, Mary? I'm a man of mystery." He strikes a James Bond pose and winks at her.

"Oh, Lord," says Mary, blushing and waving her hand at him. After careful study, I've determined that the New Yorker translation for *Oh, Lord* in Mary-speak is *Give me a fuckin' break*. She bends over to move a cooler sitting in the middle of the floor.

"Careful, Mary. That cooler's stocked. It's probably a hundred pounds," he says.

She squats, hoists it up effortlessly, and drops it next to the bar. "Piece of cake. Just like lifting a hay bale."

Kenny and I exchange an amused look. We need to hire more farm people. I inspect the cupcake tower. "Where did you find this?" I say to Kenny.

"I actually didn't find it. That's a gift from Jack."

I put my hand to my chest. My boyfriend is the best. Most men would send flowers, but Jack knows the way to my heart is through a tower of cupcakes.

"Can I eat one now?"

Kenny snorts. "No, you cannot eat one now. Wait until the guests arrive."

"That's just wrong to place a cupcake tower in front of a starving woman and prohibit her from eating it."

"Patience is a virtue," Mary chimes in from her desk.

"Can I get you a drink?" asks Momo in her soft Japanese accent. As always, she's dressed to impress. She wears a form-fitting gray pantsuit on her petite body. Her black hair with caramel highlights frames sharp cheekbones and delicate features, and bangs fall over her forehead. She wears oversize soft-pink-rimmed glasses that are always slightly askew and look like something my grandma would wear but Momo thinks are trendy. A burn scar runs along her neck. I've always wanted to learn how she acquired it but have never found the right time to ask her. It's not something you bring up in a job interview.

But the scar is a red herring. The thing I always notice most about Momo is her intelligent eyes. They're frenetic, always darting up, down, left, and right, absorbing her surroundings. I feel guilty that Kenny's got her tending bar. This is not what she signed up for when we hired her from John Jay's criminal justice program. But that's what I like about Momo Yamigawa. She's a trouper, a grinder—there's nothing too big or small for her.

"I'll have what he's having," I say to her. "How's the Virga Insurance investigation going?"

Momo pours me a glass. "Thank you for asking. I used the pretext trick you taught me and obtained excellent surveillance footage."

"Awesome. I'm so glad that helped." A pretext is an old PI trick where you call someone pretending to be from an agency or utility company and ask questions about their whereabouts, background, or any other information you may need. My personal favorite is to pretend I'm from the power company, trying to send out a refund check. People always dish on that call.

"I have questions about the investigation if you have a moment to discuss them with me," says Momo. Her English is phenomenal, and I have immense respect for her for taking the risk of moving halfway across the world, but sometimes I feel like I'm speaking with a Duolingo bot. And sometimes the bot misfires. She once called Mary a "hefty woman." That was a quiet day at C&S headquarters.

I grab the flute, feeling the cool glass on my skin, and take a sip. The champagne tastes crisp and smooths out my nerves for the big party. "Happy to answer your questions later. Now it's celebration time." I grab the bottle from Momo and pour her a glass, then hand it to her with a grin. I look in Mary's direction. "Mary, can you go into my office, open up Spotify, and play my 'Totally '80s' mix?"

"Now you're speaking my language," she says and hustles back to my desk. Next thing you know, "Africa" by Toto hums through the speakers, and all seems right with the world.

Within fifteen minutes, the guests start showing up. It's the perfect mix of people. My mom, dad, and sister arrive first, followed by Kenny's family. My sister, Christina, dresses so that she's sure to be the center of attention. She wears a tight, slinky red dress, red heels, and a diamond necklace. Thick eyeliner surrounds the top and bottom of her midnight eyes, accompanied by a cloud of charcoal eyeshadow. Whenever I look at her, it's like I'm looking at myself after a few cocktails; the features appear the same, but everything is slightly enhanced. She has the same small nose, but a little narrower. Same black hair, but a little thicker. Same high cheekbones, but a little sharper. Same compact frame, but a little taller.

Other guests start rolling in. Some friends from the old neighborhood where Kenny and I grew up. Some new friends from the city. Past clients. Potential clients. I wish Jack was here. But when your boyfriend's running for mayor, it's hard to complain about him missing an office party. I can tell him all about it when I get home.

To my relief, the event goes off without a hitch. The next few hours fly by. People eat and drink and mingle. I steal about half a dozen cupcakes. The frosting is so fluffy, I tell myself that they're healthy. Everyone's on their best behavior. Kenny busts out the karaoke machine. My sister and I give our most heartfelt performances of Lizzo's "Good as Hell." A few friends even hit the dance floor. I sneak a dance with my dad. As per usual, Christina goes overboard, breaking out every dance move from the last twenty years. There's some Dougie-ing, flossing, and even a Macarena for good measure.

It's an incredible party. It's the first time I've attended an event that was entirely about me and my accomplishments. Christina has always been such a dominant personality in our family that most of my life has been about celebrating her: traveling to *her* graduation from medical school, planning *her* wedding, celebrating the birth of *her* kids. My chest swells from this moment, this one moment, where my family and friends are here for me. As the night winds down, I stand and watch and soak it all in.

Still, I find I can never completely settle into the evening. The thought of Father K. writhing in agony settles in my brain. What kind of sick person poisons a priest? But I keep telling myself, *This isn't my fight.*

As "Maneater" pops onto the speakers, my mom, dad, and sister sidle up to me to say their goodbyes.

Christina gives me a big hug and squeezes me with a mixture of pride and jealousy. My mom and dad aren't huggers, but my sister makes up for it. I think she still sees me as her little toy. "The office looks amazing, Hazel. Am I a talented designer or what?" She can't help but take credit for it. She helped me pick out the conference table chairs and thinks she designed the space. But even she can't irk me tonight.

"Thanks. I couldn't have done it without you."

My dad places a gentle hand on my shoulder. His version of a hug. "It really is very nice, Hanuel," he says, calling me by my Korean name. His narrow, sleepy eyes twinkle, and I catch the pride glowing underneath. "I remember when you and I were painting the walls of your tiny first office. I must admit, I was skeptical about you becoming a private investigator. But you've proven me wrong. You've come a long way."

I brush a tuft of his coarse gray hair off his forehead. "Thanks, Dad." He's always been my biggest cheerleader. Maybe my only cheerleader.

My mom pulls her royal-blue satin jacket tighter over her matching blue dress and screws up her face. "The space is a little cold, though, isn't it? Maybe you should add some plants?"

Only two sentences from my mom, and I can feel my face reddening. And it's not the champagne. Sometimes I wonder if she stirs the pot because she doesn't have a lot else going on in her life. I take a long inhale of her familiar floral perfume and then breathe it out. "Yeah, that's a good note, Mom. Maybe Jack and I will go pick out some ferns this weekend."

Her eyes light up, and she teases her faux-ruby earrings. "Yes, where is Jack, anyway? I was hoping to see him tonight." My mom might have more of a crush on him than I do. But he's the first thing in my life she's approved of, so I'll take it.

"He's got a town hall event in Queens, but I'll see him tonight. He sends his regards."

She twirls her thick black hair in her hand and blushes. "Well, tell him we say hello too."

My dad throws on his sport coat and sighs.

While my mom chatters on about how great Jack is, I scan the room. The party's mostly cleared out, except for Kenny and Mary, who are chatting at one of the high-top tables. Kenny makes eye contact with me and waves me over.

"Sorry, fam, I gotta go talk to Kenny for a second."

Christina puts her arm around my mom and dad. "Mom, Dad, I think that's our cue to leave." My parents nod, and we say goodbye. And that's family for you—the only people whom you love to see arrive and leave in equal measure.

"I'll see you at family dinner next Sunday," I say and saunter over to Kenny, who wears a concerned look on his face. "What's up?"

He gestures to Mary. "Mary was telling me about your meeting with Shavali today."

"Yeah, what about it?"

"That priest—he died of tetrodotoxin poisoning?"

"Yeah, that's right." My mind flashes back to Father K., his desperate eyes staring into the camera.

"Do you remember Fred Tweed?"

"Vaguely. He was the billionaire they busted for defrauding all those investors, right? Didn't he try to hire us?"

"Yeah. He died from tetrodotoxin poisoning. I think it was in March."

Mary chimes in. "I read about that in the *Post*. But he died from bad sushi, didn't he?"

"So they thought," says Kenny. He tilts his head to drive the point home.

Normally, news like this would excite me. A chance to free a wrongfully accused kid? Two deaths from the same poison? A dead priest? A disgraced billionaire? And we're smack dab in the middle of it? Fire up the case management software and let's go!

But right now it makes me nauseous. I'm happy with my life. I have a thriving business. Great friends and colleagues. An incredible boyfriend. For once, I don't crave the action. I want someone else to fight those battles. I want to take boring, high-priced insurance cases, collect checks, and enjoy the little things.

I guess this is what getting older feels like.

My phone buzzes. I've got a text from Jack. **Heading home. Can't wait to see you, cupcake! (Pun intended)**. I drop my phone in my purse and look at Kenny and Mary.

"Guys, I've got to go. Besides, I told Shavali I'm not taking the case, so it doesn't really matter anyway. Let the police and courts handle it."

Kenny puts his hands up and shrugs. "Okay, no problem. I thought there could be something there, is all."

"I get it. Thanks for keeping me in the loop." I give Kenny and Mary a hug. "This was a wonderful night. Thank you both for putting it all together."

I walk out the door of my office, and Kenny's words ring in my ears: *There could be something there.*

The truth is, I'm certain there's something there.

I just don't think I can face it.

5

I love watching Jesus work. He is the perfect teacher.

I love how he sends the Holy Spirit to teach us. To show us the consequences of sin.

I love watching the Holy Spirit float inside someone like a breath. How the Spirit infiltrates their bloodstream, searching for his target. How he coats their nerves. How he blocks their ability to communicate with the rest of the body.

It is a miracle to behold.

You can see him work ever so subtly at first. He tickles their lips, then brushes their face. Eventually he moves to their mouth and grips their tongue, preventing them from speaking their blasphemous lies. Then he chokes their throat and stops them from breathing another sinful breath.

But the real beauty is in what comes next.

He sinks from the sinner's throat down to the belly and boils their insides like the river of fire they will burn in for eternity. Their guts boil and boil until they spew out all the sin that's inside them.

And that's when the Holy Spirit shows his awesome power and delivers the final blow.

He crawls inside their bones, inside their muscles, inside their heart. And he shakes them. He shakes them until their face and body twist so hard that the world sees them for who they truly are. Grotesque, disfigured monsters. Committers of sin. Thieves, adulterers, blasphemers. Masquerading as saints.

I probably shouldn't enjoy watching it so much.

But it truly is a miracle to behold.

6

amble from my office over to Jack's apartment in Washington Square Park under a pitch-black sky. The harsh winter wind has scared all but the toughest New Yorkers off the streets. It's nice to have a little peace after the chaos of the grand opening celebration. Kenny's rendition of "Party in the USA" really sticks with you, in a bad way. As I stroll down Canal, I bask in the emptiness. In a lot of ways, Manhattan is like a living, breathing human being. During the day, it's energetic and talkative. As the sun fades, it becomes quiet and sleepy, and then finally, sometime after midnight or when the weather turns, it drifts away to slumber. A few stray cars putter down the street—no honking, no squeaky brakes. Scattered leaves scutter across the gum-stained sidewalk. The only sound is the wind whining through my ears.

I try to block them from my mind, but I can't stop dwelling on Kenny's words. There was another case of tetrodotoxin poisoning a few months ago. As part of my private investigator training, I took courses in toxicology. We learned about tetrodotoxin poisoning. It's not unheard of. Every year around fifty people in Japan die from it. But that's from puffer fish ingestion, not poisoning. And this isn't Japan.

Two people in New York in one year?

That's more than a coincidence. It's astronomical.

Questions parade through my mind. Where would someone get tetrodotoxin? Are they buying it? Are they making it? It can't be easy to make. Why kill Father K.? What could he possibly have done to warrant that kind of retribution? How is Samuel Sampson associated with this? Was Tweed killed too? Are they linked, or is this an incredibly crazy coincidence?

I try to think about something else, but I can't stop. I have a sickness. What do normal people think about? Parties, shopping, travel? Is this why people have kids? So they can stop dwelling for a minute? My mind keeps returning to the case. The one I'm not accepting.

I reach Washington Square Park, and the wind howls, burning my ears and sending more leaves tumbling from the trees. The smell of a fireplace fire wafts by my nose. A skateboard someone abandoned rolls through the square like it's being ridden by a ghost. Jack's redbrick nineteenth-century townhome rests on the other side of the square. I see a light on in the second-floor window, and I smile. His place is incredible. I don't know how he affords it, but it's a wonderful escape from my and Kenny's Chinatown dump, so I don't ask a lot of questions.

"Honey, I'm home," I bellow as I enter the foyer.

"Bubby!" shouts Jack from the living room. That's his

nickname for me. It makes my day every time I hear it. As I hang my coat, I hear his footsteps padding across the hardwood floors. I step through the foyer, and he meets me and bear-hugs me into the air. He plants a big smooch on my lips and twirls me around like we're slow dancing at a wedding. I'm this close to asking him to hoist me up like that girl in *Dirty Dancing*.

As we're twirling, I look up at his six-foot-two-inch frame and take a moment to absorb his face. I never tire of it. His narrow eyes glint with an icy blue. His small but strong nose cuts a perfect ninety-degree angle. His impish ivory grin forms a kind triangle with polished edges. Thick, hay-like golden hair tops his head over a large forehead that carries kindness but also weight. He straightens the collar of his untucked light-blue dress shirt and grabs my hand.

"I was just working through a bowl of Honey Nut Cheerios and watching the basketball game. Would you care to join me?" he says in a slight Texas twang, which I find irresistible.

"Of course."

Jack is a man of many charms, but a refined food palate is not one of them. His diet consists primarily of cereal and turkey sandwiches. To his credit, he's always willing to try the random dishes I throw at him, and I have been able to hook him on Korean barbecue, a major win for Team Hazel.

We cuddle up on our brown leather sectional couch. Jack's place is a little more traditional and masculine than I would choose—sometimes I feel like I'm at a country club—but it's still cozy. The best feature of the place is the smell. His Versace cologne subtly infuses every inch so that no matter where I am in the house, he's with me. He throws a plaid flannel blanket over the two of us, and we watch the game. He grew up on a ranch sixty miles outside of Dallas and loves Luka Dončić and the Mavericks. At first, I wasn't interested in basketball, but now he's worn me down and I actually enjoy watching hoops with him to wind down—a major win for Team Jack.

He shares a bite of his Honey Nut Cheerios with me. I crunch away, savoring the blend of milk and sugar on my tongue. "How was the office-warming party?" he asks. "I'm really sorry I had to miss it."

"It was great. The cupcake tower was chef's kiss."

"You liked it?"

"Are you kidding? I loved it. Though my mom was extremely disappointed you didn't attend. I'm pretty sure she's ready to leave my dad for you whenever you're ready."

"Aww. Bless her heart."

"And you missed some stellar karaoke from Kenny and my sister."

"There was karaoke?"

"Yep."

"Oh man. Now I'm really upset I missed it. I'm Mr. Karaoke. I do a rendition of 'Friends in Low Places' that will knock your socks off." He takes a break from his Cheerios and then wraps his arm around me and pulls me close. The fresh ocean smell of his deodorant draws me in.

I run my fingers through his luxurious golden hair. "I assure you, there is no version of country music that will knock my socks off."

"How dare you. I'll pretend I didn't hear that."

"So, how did the town hall go?"

"It went really well, actually. Considering it was a mayoral town hall on a Monday night, the turnout was really strong. A bunch of the NYU interns attended, and I think it was good for them to see how local politics works." Jack has a crew of interns that follow him around like the Pied Piper. Half of them have pretty obvious crushes. "The questions were right in my wheelhouse. The only thing…" He swallows for a second, and his Adam's apple bobs. I love a good Adam's apple.

"Yeah? The only thing…"

"It's nothing. The whole Texas thing came up again. A guy asked me how, if I'm from Texas, I'm supposed to run New York City. Never mind that I've lived here for twenty years and served on the city council for eight."

"I told you, you gotta stop saying 'y'all.'"

"I'll die before I stop saying 'y'all.'"

We share a laugh.

"I do have to admit, 'y'all' is better than 'you guys.'"

"I knew you were a woman of reason. Anyway, it's something I'm going to have to navigate for the rest of the campaign. I need to do a better job of explaining where I come from. I need to tell people, 'Look, I grew up dirt poor on a half-assed cattle ranch. I'm in New York because I choose to be here, not because I was born here with a silver spoon in my mouth. And that's how much I care about the people here.'"

He smiles, but his smile drops into a frown when he sees an ad on TV.

A smarmy-looking man walks along the sidewalk of a New York City street in a checkered button-down shirt and khakis. His hair recedes behind a massive pale forehead. His oversize bug eyes stare into the camera, and he speaks through thin lips. As he talks, his hands chop up and down, like a mannequin that's come to life.

"I'm Sandy Godo. I grew up right here in Brooklyn," he says in a high, nasal voice. "I was born a New Yorker, and I've been a New Yorker my entire life. And that's why I'm running for mayor. Because nothing matters more to me than this city and keeping it safe."

Jack puts the TV on mute and shakes his head. He pinches his nose and does a hilariously accurate Sandy Godo impression: "I was born a New Yorker, and I've been a New Yorker my entire life."

I snicker. "That was spot on. Please promise me you'll never do that again. I don't want to have Sandy Godo running through my head when we have sex."

"Ha. Neither do I. But you see what I mean. The Texas thing is killing me. And I love how he says that because he's a New Yorker, he cares about keeping the streets safe. As though because I'm from Texas, I want murder and mayhem on every corner."

I put my head on his shoulder and nestle in next to him. "Yeah, but he resembles a man-size iguana, and you look like... well, you."

"You're too kind." He pauses for a beat and then increases the volume as the game resumes. Sneakers squeak against hardwood in the background. I close my eyes, and my mind frees. That's how you know you love someone—everything else fades away in their presence.

Jack adjusts his position and clears his throat, snapping me out of my trance. "Shavali called me today."

I lift my head off his shoulder and snap upright. "What?"

"Yeah, she said she asked you to help her with the Sampson case and you shot her down."

"Okaaay. Technically, that's true, but why is she calling you about it?" I feel my neck darting back and forth like I'm on a daytime talk show. Shavali and Jack dated briefly a decade ago but are still friends. It shouldn't bother me, but it does.

Jack takes a bite of his Honey Nut Cheerios, crunches for a few seconds, and then swallows them down. He chews with his mouth closed. Another point for Team Jack. "Well, she's been helping a lot with my campaign, and I think she was hoping I'd lean on you a little."

I fold my legs underneath me on the couch and cross my arms. "That sneaky little bitch."

Jack laughs.

I press. "So what did you say to her?"

"I asked her if she knew the same Hazel Cho I know. Because the Hazel Cho I know leans on people; she doesn't get leaned on."

I give him rapid-fire kisses on the cheek. "That's my guy."

He watches the game, but my eyes stay on him, and I see that Adam's apple bob up and down again.

"What?" I ask.

"Well, here's the thing. I was hoping you would help her with the case."

I smack his shoulder. "You gotta be kidding me."

He grabs my hand in his firm, loving grip. "I'm sure there's a reason you didn't want to help her out. But Father K. was a friend of mine and a big supporter of my campaign. And this case could be a problem for me."

"How's that?"

Jack stands up and brings his empty bowl over to the sink. "Sandy Godo's entire campaign is about the city being unsafe. I'm already getting beat up for being soft on crime. Now we have a Black kid being accused of murdering a white priest, and it's going to trial shortly." When he talks, he holds out his over-size hands like he's grasping his ideas. "The last thing I need is a high-profile murder trial before an election. That highlights the very issue that Godo wants to talk about." He grabs three apples out of the marble fruit bowl on the kitchen island and starts juggling them as he walks toward me.

"So, what do you expect me to do about it, show-off?"

He throws one up behind his back. "I was hoping you'd dig into it and find enough evidence in either direction to get a plea deal done."

Blood rises to my face. I want to help Samuel, but I'm not sure this is my fight. "Can't she push for a better plea deal?"

He returns to the couch and continues juggling. "I asked her that. The Sampson kid won't take any deal. The prosecutor thinks they've got a strong case, so they won't offer a good deal, and the kid says he didn't do it, so he's dug in as well."

I rise from the couch and stomp to the kitchen. "I need a drink." I pour myself a glass of pinot noir and take a gulp, my anger building. I can't believe Shavali ambushed me like this. Then again, it wouldn't be the first time. And what is she doing calling Jack at all? Boundaries, girl.

Jack senses my frustration and joins me in the kitchen,

juggling the apples higher, trying to get me to smile. His eyes crinkle and his pursed lips curl upward. I fight it, but eventually my anger dissipates. I snatch an apple out of midair. "You're the worst." He returns the other apples to the fruit bowl.

He drops to the ground at my feet, places his palms together in a begging gesture, and says, "Please. Pretty please."

I shake my head and take another sip of wine. A warm flush rises to my face.

Jack waddles over, keeping his hands in a begging gesture. I'm still mad, but I can't help laughing. That's one thing I love most about him—there's a lightness that keeps me from taking anything too seriously.

"Fine. I'll do it," I gurgle through a mouthful of wine.

He leaps to his feet and gives me a big hug. "Thank you so much. You are the best. I love you so much." He kisses my wine-soaked lips.

"I love you too."

I drag him back to the couch, and we cuddle and watch the end of the game. When it's over, we head upstairs to bed. Jack brushes, flosses, and throws back his multivitamin, and as always, he's asleep in five minutes. How does he do it? He must have a remarkably clean conscience. I watch him sleeping. It's a funny sight. He wears not only a mouth guard to bed but mouth tape as well so he doesn't snore. He looks like someone in a hostage video. I'm not sure he could ever win an election if the public saw that video.

As I'm staring at the ceiling, stewing about Shavali's little manipulation, a creak on the balcony outside our bedroom interrupts my thoughts. When you live in an old townhome, you learn to ignore random creaks, so at first I think little of it.

Then I hear it again.

Closer this time.

I freeze, listening for any other sounds. My breathing hitches, and a chill runs up my neck, causing me to break out into goose bumps.

I listen, but the rustle of leaves and Jack's half snores are the only sounds.

I flip over onto my side. It must have been the wind. A tree swaying against the brick.

A car rumbles by, obscuring the sound. I go back to thinking about a fit punishment for Shavali. Guillotine? The stocks? Throw her in a lake with stones tied to her ankles to see if she's a witch?

Again I hear it.

The groan of metal, like someone leaning on our railing.

I glance at Jack to see if he woke up, but he's lost in his dreams of unicorns and rainbows. I sigh and heave myself out of bed. The ancient hardwood floor groans with each step as I make my way to the balcony doors.

Peering outside, I see nothing but dark trees and swirling leaves in the park. It must have been a falling branch.

Right as I'm about to return to bed, movement catches my eye. A shadow shifts on the corner of the balcony. But just as quickly as it appeared, the shadow is gone.

I press my face against the glass, too terrified to open the door.

A pigeon skidders along the right railing, bobbing its head, trying to stay out of the wind.

I let out a shaky breath and chide myself for being so paranoid.

"You live in New York City, Hazel. There will be noises." I rub my temples. No matter how much I try, I can't fully escape the fear of my past.

I crawl back into bed and put my arm around Jack. The rhythm of his chest moving up and down soothes me. I shimmy my body beside him, enjoying his warmth.

But as I fall asleep, one fleeting thought catches in my mind.

That shadow was too large to be a pigeon.

7

wake in the middle of the night to the sound of footsteps on the staircase. The house is so cold, I can see my breath. Did I leave a door open? A window? With each step, the floorboards creak underfoot.

Creak.

Creak.

Creak.

At first, I assume it's Jack returning from grabbing a midnight snack downstairs, but when I turn to my left, I see he's sleeping peacefully next to me. I watch the back of his head and shoulders move as he breathes, unfazed by the noise. My chest cinches, and I think back to the shadow on the balcony. A stench fills the air. I've smelled it before. It's the smell of corpses and formaldehyde, like what I've whiffed in the city morgue.

I listen again. The creaking continues, closer this time.

Creak.

Creak.

Creak.

Something or someone is climbing our steps. My heart skips a beat, then accelerates. I shake Jack's shoulder, trying to wake him, but he doesn't move. He's out cold.

The footsteps accelerate. They're almost here. "Jack," I whisper. No response. "Jack," I try again. But he remains still.

I roll away from him and reach to grab my gun out of the gun safe.

But before I can enter the code, an icy hand clutches my wrist.

I flinch and lift my head.

The most terrifying visage I can imagine stares back at me.

Andrew Dupont, the man who abducted Mia. The man who kept teenage girls as sex slaves. The man who tried to kill me one year ago today. He's kneeling at my bedside, inches from my face.

"Surprise," he says in a sadistic whisper.

I jump backward, legs flailing, in disbelief at what I'm seeing. He looks like a Frankensteinian version of himself. A zipper scar runs along his neck in the spot where I slashed his throat. His slicked-back hair reveals greenish-yellow skin, like a cadaver. A gray film covers his eyes. His breath smells of rot. I can taste it.

He strokes my hair with his cold, dead hand.

"I missed you," he says and licks his yellow, pocked front teeth.

I'm too paralyzed with fear to move. How can this be? I killed him. I watched him bleed out.

I start to scream, but he covers my nose and mouth with his hand. "Uh-uh-uh." His frozen, clammy palms stink like death. I try to breathe but can't. I feel myself suffocating.

He slithers on top of me and pins me down, his sharp hip bones driving into me. I reach for Jack with my other hand and snatch the comforter, desperate to wake him. I slap his back and legs. Finally, he stirs and I feel him turning over.

"What is it?" he mumbles, half-asleep. But I notice his voice is different. It's not his voice at all.

I scream, but Andrew's hand muffles the sound. I turn to look at Jack, pleading for him to wake up.

But it's not Jack.

It's Andrew again. Another Andrew. There's two of them. Twins.

He sneers with a glistening knife in his hand. The same knife I cut him with. He takes the blade and holds it to my throat. The steel burns as it presses into my skin.

He reaches his arm back, his fangs shining in the moonlight. I'll never forget the malevolent look in his eye.

He slashes with one fierce thrust.

I snap awake.

I bolt upright in bed, hyperventilating. My heartbeat races, a staccato that shakes my whole body. Salty, acrid sweat soaks my tank top through and through. I look around me, still unsure whether it was a nightmare or reality.

The house is quiet.

Jack is beside me.

I lean over to confirm it's him. I see his sandy-blond hair and perfect nose and release a breath.

My body collapses back into bed, my lungs churning and my heart pumping. I run both hands through my soaking-wet hair and stare at the ceiling. Am I losing my mind? My eyes water and my chest heaves. I pull the sheet and comforter up over me, building a cocoon around myself, willing my nightmares away.

My eyes trace the hand-carved crown molding that runs around the ceiling—what I always do when this happens. My version of counting sheep. My vision drifts into the middle distance. I wonder when this will end. When I will stop seeing Andrew in my dreams. When he will stop terrorizing me.

Eventually, I realize the answer and roll out of bed.

The answer is never.

He'll never stop.

8

The next morning—after spending the rest of the night and early dawn watching old movies to shake my nightmares—I arrive outside the Legal Aid Society and see Mary waiting for me out front. I'm still shaken from my dream and the thought of that shadow on my balcony last night, so it's nice to see her sweet, cherubic face. I considered telling Jack about it this morning, but I didn't want to freak him out or sound like the crazy girl seeing things in the night. He's heard enough about my trauma to last a lifetime. It's ridiculous how often we hide our intuition for fear of sounding like we're "crazy" or "overreacting." I'm convinced I saw something. I'm just not sure what.

When Mary and I trundle into the lobby of the forty-floor office building, Shavali's standing in front of security with a box of doughnuts from Doughnut Plant and a Red Bull. Mary serves me a raised eyebrow and a smile. "Looks like she brought you the breakfast of champions." I smell the chocolate, sugary goodness emanating from the box. I've got to give Shay credit. She knows how to ingratiate herself.

She's wearing a black cashmere turtleneck over a black pencil skirt with her espresso-colored hair tied up in a bun. She towers over me in midnight leather boots with four-inch heels. It must be nice to have a trust fund. In that outfit, she looks more like a Bond villain than an attorney. How apropos. Mary and I look more like her victims than colleagues. We're both wearing long cardigan sweaters, pants, and loafers. I remind myself that it might be time to refresh my wardrobe.

"I'm sorry I called Jack," she says, handing me an ice-cold Red Bull, her forehead crinkled and her lips curved down into a maudlin frown. "But I can't do this alone, and you're the best at what you do."

I grab the Red Bull and a doughnut, take a huge bite, and blow right by her, past security and into the elevator. She waves her badge at the security guard and chases after me.

"Apology accepted," I say around a chunk of doughnut as we step into the elevator.

Mary shuffles in behind me and whispers in my ear, "Hazel, be nice."

Shavali can sense that I'm not in the mood for pleasantries, so we ride the elevator in silence and then breeze past the receptionist and main bullpen of cubicles into the same conference room we met in yesterday. But today the room feels different. I look out the window, and furious dark clouds and black, turbid water have replaced the blue sky and glistening river. Even the few ships in port seem rusted over and lonely. The city is a pouty teenager today.

Shavali flips on the lights to counter the darkness. I plop down at the table and stare at the blank television screen. I think of Father Kenneally, dying helpless and alone. I can't believe Shay sucked me back into this. She's like that popular girl who somehow makes people do whatever she wants them to do. One night you're hanging out in her basement watching *Twilight*, and the next thing you know you're toilet papering someone's house and have no idea why. She's a siren of personality.

I crack open the Red Bull and take a long pull. The cough syrup taste sends the neurons firing. I follow it with a glazed-doughnut chaser, and the combination of sugar and fat has me ready for battle. While I don't like Shavali's Machiavellian methods of roping me into this, I am interested in the case. It's not every day you see a death by tetrodotoxin poisoning, let alone one that might be associated with another death.

Shavali sits, a sheepish look on her face. Her confidence from yesterday has been replaced by deference.

"Thank you again for doing this. Where would you like to start?"

I wipe the doughnut crumbs off my pants. "Why don't you start with the police's story?"

"Okay." She pops open her laptop and reviews her notes. I remember in law school she took immaculate notes. She used some type of color-coding system I could never follow. When she was done, it looked like a rainbow had exploded on her laptop screen.

"On December twentieth, at six a.m., a janitor found Father

Kenneally dead in the aisle of Old St. Patrick's Cathedral. He immediately called the police. The police arrived on the scene shortly after."

Mary removes her notebook and begins taking notes. I've tried to get her to use a laptop, but she insists on writing. She writes in a patient, precise cursive that only people born before 1975 seem to practice. And she's one hell of a doodler.

"Who was the homicide detective?" I ask.

Shavali scratches her temple with her pen. "Marcos."

I shoot Mary a glance, and she clucks her tongue. We worked with Marcos six months ago on an arson investigation in which the police originally thought it was a homicide. "Seriously?" I say.

"Sadly, yes."

"Shay, Marcos is the worst. He has no interest in the truth. He picks his suspect and then target-locks on them. He'll manufacture evidence if he needs to."

"I'm aware of that, love. That's why I need your help."

I close my eyes and take another bite of doughnut. The chocolate glaze goes right to my head. If I could have a dozen of these, I might survive this meeting. "Okay, we'll put a pin in Marcos for a second. Continue."

"The police and paramedics promptly reviewed the security footage and found the video of Father Kenneally's death I showed you yesterday. They found no sign of a break-in or theft, so they assumed a heart attack or stroke. Then this came in."

She hands me the toxicology report, which shows tetrodotoxin in the bloodstream but nothing in his stomach that would indicate puffer fish.

"So then they land on poison?" I ask.

"Exactly."

"How was the poison administered?"

"Unclear. There were no needle marks. There was a water glass on the desk, but no traces of poison. By process of elimination, we assume it was a pill of some sort. But Father Kenneally's pill case was empty, so it could have been delivered in liquid form, and the killer could've taken the vessel that Kenneally drank from."

"How did your client become involved? Did they find the poison on him?"

"No, fortunately they didn't, and have found no tetrodotoxin on his person or in searches of his apartment and possessions."

"Well, that's some good news."

"Yeah, but I haven't given you the bad news."

I finish my Red Bull, crunch the can in my hand, and toss it in the blue recycling bin. "What's the bad news?"

"The police found this letter on Father Kenneally's desk." She hands me two pieces of paper. The first shows a photocopy of an opened red envelope. An old-fashioned wax seal, like something you'd receive from royalty, is broken on the flap. The letter *S* is impressed in the wax. The second piece of paper shows a photocopy of a letter. A simple message written in a dated typewriter font runs across the page.

I read it and my breath halts.

FOR WITH WHAT JUDGMENT YOU JUDGE, YOU SHALL BE JUDGED: AND WITH WHAT MEASURE YOU METE, IT SHALL BE MEASURED TO YOU AGAIN.

"Oh my," says Mary, and on instinct, she hands me another doughnut.

The message chills me, but what hovers above it revolts me: a drawing of hell in dark rusty-brown ink. Satan sits at its center, devouring people and excreting them. It's an image I've seen in a painting somewhere before.

I point to the symbol and catch a slight shake of my finger. "Is this...?"

Shavali rests her chin in her hand. "Yes. It's painted in blood. Not human—animal."

"What kind of animal?"

"Unknown. The crime lab didn't test for species. Only whether it's human or animal."

I lean back in my chair and massage my eyebrows. That same sickening sense I had yesterday runs through me in waves. This person—whoever did this—is...different.

"Prior to the police finding the security footage, did they have other suspects?"

She shakes her head and pages through the colored notes on her laptop. "Not really. Before they found the security video, the police interviewed the staff and determined the last point of contact: a Sister Teresa, who met with Father Kenneally earlier that afternoon. She's the archbishop's assistant. Police interviewed her, and she said that she was meeting with Kenneally to finalize Christmas festivities at the church. The archbishop was planning on appearing for the holidays. He confirmed that as well. Apparently, he was close with Kenneally."

She grabs a remote and turns on the television. "But then the police found this footage and ended the search for suspects." She clicks a few buttons on her computer, and a picture casts to the screen. A grainy black-and-white video runs, showing an empty hallway and a closed wooden door with a bronze plate attached to it—Father Kenneally's office. She fast-forwards until we see a small male figure, presumably Samuel Sampson, enter the hallway. He's wearing an oversize white T-shirt, ripped baggy jeans, and vintage Air Jordans. He tiptoes down the hallway, slides something that looks an awful lot like a colored envelope underneath Father Kenneally's door, then slinks away. The picture is incredibly blurry, but he couldn't look more guilty if he tried.

Mary furiously scribbles in her notebook.

I sigh and shake my head at Shay. "How does Sampson explain that?"

"That's the problem. He doesn't, really. He just says he left a different letter."

"What?"

She runs her pointer finger along the bridge of her sharp nose. "Yeah. It's ridiculous. But believe me, I have tried every tactic in the book to get it out of him. I've flattered, cajoled, threatened, withheld—you name it. And the kid won't tell me. Maybe you'll have more luck with him."

I stand up from my chair and start pacing. Never in my wildest dreams did I think the cops would have such damning evidence against her client. I can't believe she can't convince him to take the plea deal. I mean, talk about being caught red-handed. Still, something about the client and the method doesn't jibe. Whoever planned the murder of Father K. was thoughtful, patient, strategic. If this video is any indication, Sampson appears to be a sloppy, amateurish kid. I can't help wondering if someone put him up to it.

I walk past the framed attorney quotes hanging from the wall. A quote from Clarence Darrow catches my eye: YOU CAN ONLY PROTECT YOUR LIBERTIES IN THIS WORLD BY PROTECTING THE OTHER MAN'S FREEDOM. YOU CAN ONLY BE FREE IF I AM FREE.

Even Clarence would be tested by this one.

I turn back to Shavali. "What other incriminating evidence does the police have?"

She drums her talons on the desk. "The good news is, the police searches of his home turned up nothing. No poison. No typewriter. No animal blood. No stationery. No envelopes."

"So they're going to trial based on the video alone? That seems pretty thin."

Her finger-drumming accelerates. "Well, that's the thing. The letter…"

"Yeah?"

"His fingerprints are all over it."

I hang my head. No good deed goes unpunished. But like my grandma always said, *Don't start something you can't finish.* I sigh and toss the photocopies back at Shavali. I walk back to the table and take a bite of my emotional-support doughnut. "Okay. Send me an electronic copy of everything that's in the file. Mary, go to the office and get me all the background you can find on that Bible verse and that drawing: history, context, meaning, if anyone's ever used it in a murder before, et cetera. Shavali, let's go see Sampson."

9

Rikers Island detention center reminds me of the opening scene in a horror movie. The second you see it, a sense of danger and foreboding fills your chest. The jail stands in the center of a man-made island and houses over ten thousand of the toughest, nastiest people in New York. Their presence bleeds into the architecture, all hardness and rage. Twenty-foot-tall black barbed wire fencing surrounds the island. Hulking, gray, windowless buildings cover the landscape. There are no trees. No plants. No animals. The entire place is devoid of nature—devoid of hope.

The only way to access the island is via the Francis R. Buono Memorial Bridge—"the Bridge of Pain," as the inmates call it. Every year, the jail reports thousands of assaults on officers and other inmates. It's gotten so bad that the city plans to close it down by 2026. I'm not holding my breath. As Shavali and I drive over the bridge, the storm clouds darken and the wind whistles through her car. It feels like we're crossing the River Styx.

The inside is even worse.

We park her car and enter the Robert N. Davoren Complex, which houses the younger detainees. "Gladiator School," as it is known inside. As the three of us pass through security and metal detectors, the temperature drops ten degrees. The place is cold and sterile. You know how teachers cover elementary school walls with bright colors and warm drawings? Picture the opposite—white walls and concrete. They should post a sign out front: HAPPINESS DIES HERE.

As we walk, the sounds of every movement echo through the hollow space. Gruff men's voices. A whistle. A howl. The slamming of metal doors. There's a sickness that hangs in the air, like the pathologies of everyone inside have become airborne. The disinfectant aroma only adds to the effect.

Of course, Shavali doesn't notice. She strides ahead, leaving a trail of orange blossom in her wake, oblivious to everything around her, her boot heels banging like hammers on the linoleum. I remember when we would go out for drinks in law school. Her strides were so long that she would be five steps ahead of me within seconds. I had to teach her it's considered rude to leave someone in the dust. Looks like someone needs a refresher course.

I check my pistol in one of the wall-mounted gun lockers. Yes, I carry a gun now. Permitted by the City of New York. I've kept it secret from my family and coworkers, but after what happened at the Dionysus Theater last year, I can't take any more chances. The good news is that gun holsters for women have come a long way. I wear a belly holster—sort of like a fanny pack—that's reasonably understated.

The guard leads us through the lobby toward the visitation center. He opens the door and holds it for us, looking me up and down. That's another thing I notice about jails: everyone stares. Long, appraising stares. It's a power move. Whoever looks away or blinks first loses.

As we're about to enter, I hear a deep, gravelly voice shout from behind me. "Patel, haven't you given up yet?"

I turn and spot a bear of a man with thick chestnut hair and unshaved whiskers. His creased tan forehead hangs over his eyes, casting a shadow over them. A scar shoots out from over his right lip. Detective Marcos hasn't changed a bit. He reminds me more of an inmate than a cop.

Shavali shoots him a snarl. "No, we haven't given up yet, Marcos."

He takes a few steps closer and puts his hands on his hips, making sure we see the badge on his belt and the Marine Corps tattoo on his forearm. DEATH BEFORE DISHONOR, it says. He wears a leather jacket with the sleeves rolled up. It's so thick that it groans with every movement. The room seems to chill from his presence. "Well, let me save you ladies some time. He's guilty."

"We'll see about that," she says.

Marcos moves closer, invading my personal space, and his dark stare slides to me. He smells of cowhide and sweat. He wants me to backpedal. "What's up, Cho? She roped you into this, too, huh?"

I nod but say nothing, holding my ground. I don't want to give this bear any red meat.

"What more do you guys need? We got a death threat. We got video of him delivering the letter. We have his prints on the envelope. Hell, with this trial coming up, he'll probably confess soon. You don't want to embarrass yourselves, do you?"

As frustrating as Marcos can be, I understand where he's coming from. In NYPD homicide, there's only one metric that matters: clearance rate. Of the murder cases they assign, what percentage of them get crossed off as suicide or self-defense or lead to an arrest and, preferably, a conviction? The higher the clearance rate is, the better. If you're a detective, you want murder cases solved, not reopened.

Shavali parts her lips to say something, but I put my hand on her forearm and shake my head. "Thanks for your input, Detective. Have a nice day."

We turn and follow the guard through the door. I look back, and Marcos's shadowed eyes follow me. He twists a ring on his finger and leers.

The guard brings us into a bare-bones visitation room that consists of nothing more than gray concrete walls, a wood-laminate table, and four cheap neon-green plastic chairs. In a strange way, I kind of like it. The subject can't hide here. There's only room for the truth. Shavali and I sit down.

She performs one of her dramatic hair flips and gathers herself. "Apologies. That man gets under my skin." Her fingernails gallop across the table.

"This whole place gets under my skin. Your client won't last long in here—" I'm interrupted by the door moaning as Samuel Sampson enters. He's different in person than in his picture: even younger, smaller, more fragile. He sports the standard-issue

Rikers Island gray jumpsuit on his approximately five-foot-seven, 140-pound frame. His head sits atop a flamingo neck, and I'm not sure they make cuffs small enough to hold his wrists. His smile is the only feature that matches the picture—that smug, know-it-all smile. I inspect him and can't help but wonder, *Does he understand he's days away from going to trial for murder?*

He joins us at the table but doesn't say a word. He slouches in his chair like he's settling in to play video games, except his feet and hands never stop moving. He tweaks a couple of his Afro puffs. Runs his fingers across his eyebrows, one of which has a slash shaved into it. Taps his toes on the floor. Crosses and uncrosses his legs. He holds the energy of a coiled spring.

Shavali clears her throat. "Samuel, I'd like to introduce you to Hazel Cho. She's a private investigator who will be assisting with the case."

He smirks. "I hope you do a better job than she's been doing." His voice carries the arrogance of a New Yorker who's never left the borough but somehow thinks he's seen everything. Is it bad that my first instinct is to punch my client in the face? I don't mean it, though. I've seen young men like Sam before. He's been let down and hurt by adults his whole life, so he shields himself in a veneer of snark.

Shavali ignores the slight. She's used to having clients who've flunked out of charm school.

"Hazel will perform a thorough investigation into Father Kenneally's death to see if she can find any additional evidence that will exonerate you. Given that we're only a week away from the trial, I'd ask you to be open and forthright with her. You can start by briefly telling her your side of the story."

Sam lets out a sigh like we asked him to climb Mount Kilimanjaro. He looks at me for a second, but his eyes can't hold eye contact. Never a good sign.

"Okay, what do you want to know?"

I slide my chair forward and rest my elbows on the table. I force a smile to hide my disapproval of his attitude. "Well, why don't we start at the beginning? How did you know Father Kenneally?"

He bites on the loose skin around his thumbnail and then spits it onto the floor. "I worked for him. I was his assistant, or intern, or whatever. I'd help after school and on weekends."

I sit in silence, prodding him to say more. But he stays still, forcing me to continue. "How did you get the job?"

"My mom said I spent too much time on my computer and I needed to work."

"You like computers?"

"I guess."

"And how did you find the internship?"

"My uncle. He goes to Old St. Patrick's and overheard Father Kenneally talking about how he needed help with computers, and he thought of me."

"How long ago was this?"

His eyes shoot to the ceiling. "Uh, I guess about two years ago."

"Old St. Patrick's is a long commute from the Bronx."

"Tell me about it. Forty minutes on the 5 train. Mom liked that it got me out of the neighborhood. Thought it would keep me out of trouble. A lot of good that did."

"And did you want the job?"

"Did I want the job? Nah. Nobody wants a job. But

sometimes you need a job. My mom wasn't having me sitting around the house all day."

"And did you like working for Father Kenneally?"

"No, I didn't like it. I like playing Xbox. I like hanging with my friends. I like smoking weed. What do you like?" He slides forward and licks his lips. I ball my hands into fists. If this is going to work, I need to penetrate this facade of bravado.

"You know what I mean."

He leans back in his chair and puffs out his cheeks. "It was fine, I guess. I would answer the phone for him. Open the mail. Fix any computer problems. Run interference for him with all the nosy parishioners. You won't believe how many old-ass people bothered Father K. with their problems. The dude was really good about listening to them, but sometimes he needed me to tell them he had another appointment so they'd get the hell up out of there."

"What else did you do for him?"

"I don't know. Standard stuff. I'd keep his calendar organized. Father K. didn't know shit about computers, so I would have to type up emails and stuff. Super easy."

I notice that his eyes never move from the floor. He gives me the bare minimum of information. I look at Shavali, who shrugs as if to say, *You see what I'm dealing with?* I need to shake him.

"Sam, you were about sixteen when you started working at Old St. Patrick's, if I have my math right. Did Father Kenneally ever do anything inappropriate to you?"

His forehead scrunches. "'Inappropriate'? Like touching me and shit? No, Father K. wasn't like that." I notice his legs start to shake faster.

"You never saw him do anything inappropriate with kids? The reason I'm asking is that if Father K. did anything to harm a child, that could be a motive for someone to commit murder. You follow me?"

"No. I didn't see anything like that." His eyes dart toward the wall, as if he's contemplating telling us something, but he stays silent.

"How about the day he died? You mentioned in the report the last person to visit him was Sister Teresa. Is that right?"

"Yeah."

"Did you hear anything that they discussed?"

"No. I was wearing headphones, so I didn't hear shit."

"What about earlier in the day? Did anyone else visit Father K.?"

"No. Only her."

I massage my forehead. I need to switch gears.

"Do you know if Father K. took any pills the day he died?"

"Yeah, he definitely did. He took pills every day. He had one of those old-ass pill kits with the days of the week on them."

"Could someone have tampered with those pills?"

"I guess so. He had them out on the sink in the bathroom of his office."

"Did you ever see anyone in his bathroom besides him?"

He lets out a breath. "I don't know. Maybe?"

I turn to Shavali. "Did the police test the pills that were left in his pill kit?"

"Yes. No tetrodotoxin. But the killer could have substituted only that day's pills."

"Do you have footage of everyone who came into that office?"

She shakes her head. "It resets every twenty-four hours. So all we obtained was from the day of his death."

"Okay. I'll need to see that."

He throws up his hands. "Are we done here?"

"Sam, the police have video of you sliding a letter under Father Kenneally's door the night he was poisoned. I've seen the video myself. It doesn't make you look good."

"Yeah, so?"

Shavali sits up in her chair. "So, we've talked about this. That letter contained a Bible verse that sounded an awful lot like a threat. And your fingerprints are on the envelope."

"I told her this already." He points at Shavali but looks at me. "That's a different envelope that Father K. got earlier in the day. That's not the envelope I dropped off." He takes another bite of the skin on his fingers, and his leg shakes faster.

"Then why are your fingerprints on it?" I ask.

"Because I opened all his mail and put it on his desk as part of my job. My fingerprints are on all that shit."

"So you opened that envelope?"

"Hell yeah."

"What did you think when you read the letter?"

"I thought the drawing was weird, but what did you want me to think? It was a piece of paper with a Bible verse on it. It's not the strangest thing I've seen come across Father K.'s desk."

"So you expect me to believe that you coincidentally dropped off a red envelope the night Father K. died?"

Now he looks me dead in the eyes. "Yes."

I think back to that grainy black-and-white video. I

wonder if Kenny can fire up his ninja video-editing skills to zoom in on the moment Sam slid it under the door. It seems like a long shot.

"In the video, I noticed a stamp on the envelope you slid under his door. Why did you stamp it if you intended to deliver it by hand?"

"Why do you think? I was gonna mail it and then I thought, shit, I might as well deliver it myself."

"The police didn't find any other red envelope. Can you explain that?"

"I don't know. Maybe Father K. shredded it. Maybe he burned it. Maybe someone else took it."

"Okay, fine. Can you tell us what was in the envelope you slid under Father K.'s door? The one from you to him?"

His eyes return to the floor. "I don't know."

"What do you mean, you don't know?"

He chews on another finger and shrugs.

I lean in and grab his hand out of his mouth. His wrist is so thin, I feel like I could break it with a quick twist. "Samuel, what was in the letter you dropped off?"

"I can't say."

"Why? Why can't you say?"

I catch his eye, and for a second the mask of arrogance fades, revealing the scared little boy underneath. I release his hand.

Shavali leans in and does her best impression of a kindly mother. Her voice softens, and she lays her open palms on the table. "Samuel, we can't help you unless you tell us everything."

He squirms in his chair, but his eyes stay glued to the floor.

The silence thins the air. Right when I think he's clammed up, he speaks, barely above a whisper. "All I can tell you is that Father K. wasn't such a good guy."

"What does that mean?" Shavali and I ask in unison.

He makes a lip-zipping gesture and tosses the imaginary key. "That's all I can say. Oh, and he's not the only one."

10

For the next hour, Shavali and I play good cop, bad cop, attempting to pry more information out of Sam. But he's shared everything he wants to for the day. The two of us trudge out to the parking lot. The sky has become even darker, and a cold sprinkle falls. I welcome the rain as it tickles my face. I need a shower after being in that hellhole.

As we drive over the Bridge of Pain back to the civilian world, I ease into the plush leather seat and my mind riffles through the open questions in the case. I almost wish we hadn't visited Sam. I thought he'd give us answers, but instead he handed us more questions. What does it mean that Father Kenneally wasn't such a good guy? What was in the letter that Sam dropped off, if it was a different letter? What is he so scared of? His expression sticks with me. He was elsewhere, probably thinking about what would happen to him if he talked. The question is, Who could create such fear? I look at Shavali and can tell she's running similar questions through her head. The two of us drive in silence, watching the mist-cloaked skyscrapers creep closer toward us.

"What do you think Sam's afraid of?" I say as we roll into Manhattan. I release a breath at seeing the familiar sights of Chinatown, the red lanterns and Traditional Chinese script. The experience of Rikers settles in your chest like a cold. It's good to be home.

She flips her hair over her shoulder, and her fingers tap against the steering wheel as she drives. "I'm not sure. In one of our earlier interviews, he mentioned to me that 'powerful people' were behind this. At the time, I dismissed it as a kid bullshitting his way out of trouble. But now I'm uncertain." She double-parks the Lexus in front of my building and switches on her hazards. "What are your thoughts?"

"I think you're right that he didn't do it. Or if he did, he didn't do it alone. There's no way that kid planned this murder."

"What's your next move?"

I run my fingers through my damp hair. "Given the tight time frame, I think we have to work under the assumption that Father K. died from taking a poison in pill form and that whoever wrote that letter is the same person who gave him the pill. That means that in order to identify someone other than Sam who may have done this, we need to pursue multiple lines of investigation. First, who had access to Father K.'s office in the weeks leading up to his death? Second, who had access to tetrodotoxin, since it's not something you pick up at the supermarket? Third, are there any identifying characteristics about the envelope itself—like stationery type, mailing address, stamps, et cetera—that implicate anyone other than him? Fourth, did anyone else have a motive to kill him?"

"That makes sense. How long will it be till you have some insights?"

"I don't know yet. I need some time to think." A car honks behind us, so I step out of her Lexus and into the drizzle.

Shavali leans toward the passenger side. "Okay. Have a think on it, but not too long. The trial starts in six days, and whatever you come up with, I need time to build it into my defense. Right now, my defense consists of me repeating the word *circumstantial* five thousand times."

"You don't need to remind me." The car honks again. I put my hand up in the New York way that says, *Shut the eff up.* "I'll call you tomorrow." She nods, rolls up her window, and speeds away.

My old mentor, Perry, used to say, *The dimes make the crimes.* He explained that the saying had two meanings to him. People commit crimes for money, and they get away with it because they have money or the folks chasing them don't. In TV shows, the police, attorneys, and private investigators have seemingly unlimited resources—fancy forensic labs, sophisticated legal teams, and an in-house hacker. In the real world, it's usually an overworked cop, an underpaid lawyer with fifty other cases, and there may not even be a private investigator.

I return to the office to find it buzzing with activity. Momo's on the phone, haggling with an insurance company over a bill. Mary's at her computer, humming to herself while doing research. Kenny's drawing one of his illegible mind-maps on the oversize whiteboard in the conference room.

I stop for a second and smile. When I started my private investigation agency years ago, I dreamed of working with a team like this, but over time that dream got buried under the rubble of deadbeat clients and past-due bills. I still can't believe we excavated that dream, dusted it off, and brought it back to life. I take it in, but I remind myself that I can't enjoy it for long. Shavali's deadline and the thought of a scared kid in jail for a crime he didn't commit hang over me like a guillotine.

I watch Kenny scribble away in the conference room. He's really stepped up his fashion game lately. He's wearing black slacks, a button-down shirt with his sleeves rolled up, and a suit vest. He looks like a mixologist at a Brooklyn speakeasy.

He's staring at the whiteboard, rubbing his hand back and forth through his buzzed black hair. He takes a swig of water from his YETI—he's really into hydration these days, like really into hydration—and swishes the water around in his cheeks. He spots me and waves through the glass walls, beckoning me to come in. I pop open the conference room door and return his wave. The smell of whiteboard marker floats in the air. I know it's sick, but I could sniff those all day.

"What's up?" I say.

He pauses his whiteboard jottings and puts a cap on the marker. His face carries a wry smile, and his eyes twinkle. He gestures to the chairs. "Take a load off." I grab a seat, and he joins me at the table. "Mary tells me Shavali conned you into taking the Sampson case."

"Emphasis on 'conned.' Yeah, she even called Jack and asked him to persuade me. He gave me the full Texas charm, and I was toast."

"Texas toast? Ooh, she pulled the boyfriend card? That's cold. But that's Shavali for you. It's not all her fault, though. I knew you would take the case."

"Oh, did you, now?"

His round cheeks rise like dough. "Are you kidding? Dead priest, mysterious poison, might be more than one murder... This has Hazel Cho written all over it."

"I don't know. I think *that* Hazel Cho might be dead. The older I get, the more I like the idea of chilling with Jack, watching basketball, and taking insurance cases."

Kenny raises an eyebrow. "That might be the most ridiculous statement you've ever uttered. If you did that, you'd throw yourself out the window after three months. And I'd be right behind you."

I laugh. The truth hurts. "Is that why I see 'Old St. Patrick's Cathedral' in bold letters on your whiteboard here?"

"It is, indeed. While you were off with Shavali, I did a little more research on the Archdiocese of New York and Old St. Patrick's, more specifically."

"This whiteboard is great, but I wish you had put together one of those cool corkboard dioramas you see in movies with the photos pinned to the board and the red string connecting them."

Kenny laughs. "You're right, boss. I totally blew it."

"Opportunity missed. Next time. So tell me, whatya got?"

Kenny's smile drops and his forehead creases. "Long story short, there is more to this case than the poisoning of a single priest."

"I agree. But why do you say that?"

"One word: money. A few years ago, the Archdiocese of New

York agreed to a settlement with the victims of child abuse committed by priests and other employees of the diocese, including at Old St. Patrick's."

"Yeah, I remember that. The settlement was for like fifty million or something. But that was a while ago. What's the connection to Father K. being murdered in December?"

"It was actually sixty million." Kenny points to a barely legible SIXTY written on the whiteboard. "And here's where it gets interesting. It turns out that the archdiocese hasn't paid up yet."

"Really?"

"Yes, they've been arguing that their insurance company should foot the bill."

"And I'm guessing the insurance company is saying they aren't responsible for insuring pedophiles."

"Correct. And a judge ruled on December tenth that the archdiocese needs to start paying regardless of what happens with the insurance. That same day, the archdiocese appealed the decision, preventing the victims from receiving the funds they deserve."

"That's one week before Kenneally was killed."

"Exactly."

"That's curious. Sam said something interesting to me today that may tie into this."

"What?"

I raise my fingers and make air quotes. "He said Father Kenneally 'wasn't such a good guy, and he's not the only one.'"

Kenny taps the tip of the whiteboard marker against his teeth and then swigs his water. More mouth-swishing. I really need to knock that habit out of him.

"Do you think Kenneally could have been molesting kids?"

"I hope not, but I can't say for certain. I asked Sam about it today, and he was confident that Father K. never touched a kid. And that matches my take on him. And I know Jack wouldn't visit that church if he heard even a whisper of impropriety. But you never know with these things. Maybe he wasn't involved in abusing kids but covered for someone who was? He was also pretty well respected in the church hierarchy, so maybe he was a part of the legal effort to deny the payout? Shavali mentioned he met with the archbishop's right-hand woman, Sister Teresa, the day he died. Maybe that meeting had something to do with his death?"

Kenny writes the questions I'm asking on the little white-board space that remains and puts a box next to each one of them. "We've got a lot of boxes to check."

"You don't know the half of it. I've got about ten more unanswered questions I haven't even told you yet. But in the meantime, this makes sense as a theory of the case. Someone found out that the victims of church abuse were getting stiffed yet again and sent a message by killing Father Kenneally. The question is, Who?"

"It sounds like you need to visit Old St. Patrick's and see what the hell is going on over there. Maybe they've received threats about the court decision."

I get up from my chair and groan. "It sounds like I do." I open the door and shout to Mary. "Mary, can you call over to Old St. Patrick's and tell them I'm working with Shavali Patel and need to have a look around?" She nods and waves.

I swivel back to Kenny. "In the meantime, will you start a

case file and find out everything you can about that billionaire who died, Fred Tweed? How he was poisoned. Where did he eat? Who was with him at the time? Are any of those people affiliated with Old St. Patrick's? Or Father Kenneally? Or the archdiocese? How did the police determine fugu killed him versus a manufactured version of tetrodotoxin? Or did they assume it because he ate sushi?"

Kenny makes more notes. "I got it. Will do."

"Thanks. I'm sorry to bark orders at you, but Shavali's on my ass. Her trial starts in six days."

Kenny drops his marker onto the whiteboard ledge. "Six days? Hazel, this could take six weeks."

"I know, I know, but we don't have six weeks, so you better get started."

"Ugh."

I open the conference room door to leave for the church but then stop. "Before I go, did you find any information about Old St. Patrick's I should know about?"

Kenny pauses and looks at his whiteboard. "Hmm. Not much. Oh, there's a graveyard on-site and catacombs that run beneath the building. Thirty-five family crypts and five priests buried right underneath the cathedral, a bishop and some corrupt politicians. There's a local rumor Pierre Toussaint, a freed Haitian slave said to have cured a boy of scoliosis, haunts the church at night. So you got that going for you." He raises his hands up in the air and makes a scary face. "Mwwwaaahhhhh."

"Perfect. Just perfect. Okay. I'm leaving now."

I grab my coat from my office and stop at Mary's desk.

"I called over to St. Patrick's, and they're expecting you," she says.

"Good, let's go."

"Oh, you want me to come too? I was just finishing up my research on that Bible verse."

"You can brief me in the Uber. You're always telling me I need to go to church. Well, now's your chance to join me."

11

Mary and I hop into the Uber and zoom to St. Patrick's. The cherry car freshener smell really hits in this one. Rain slams against the windshield, and the wipers squeak with every wipe. The driver plays "Alone" by Marshmello in the background, and I'm tempted to ask him to turn it up, but I'm guessing Mary hasn't caught the electronic dance music bug yet.

She sits next to me in the back. I catch a hint of her soft floral perfume underneath the car freshener. She clutches her oversize purse in her lap like she's poised for a burglar to rip it from her hands, which is hilarious because I'd bet on Mary in a showdown with a burglar any day. I don't know how she finds anything in that bag. But, to be fair, I can't tell you how many times I've asked her for something—a piece of gum, ChapStick, a Band-Aid—and she's produced it instantly. Part of me wants to test her someday and be like, *Mary, do you have an original signed copy of* Macbeth *in your purse, by any chance?*

Our Uber driver weaves up Broadway, judiciously using his horn to keep us alive. I turn to her.

"So, what did you find about that Bible verse?" Honestly, I'm not expecting her to find much, but she's always so excited about our work that I like to keep her involved.

Mary sits up straight in her seat and removes her notebook. She places her tiny, frameless reading glasses on the tip of her pixie nose and clears her throat. I think she still gets nervous around me because I'm her boss, even though I'm over twenty years younger.

"Nothing particularly interesting. The verse is from the Gospel of Matthew. Chapter seven, verse two. Specifically, the Douay–Rheims Version, which was the standard English Catholic translation until the mid-twentieth century."

"Hmm, that could be something."

"Why do you say that?"

"It would suggest that whoever wrote it is probably an older Catholic. I'm guessing fifty-plus, since most people my age would be used to a new version of the Bible. Obviously, a kid like Samuel could look it up online and quote the Douay–Rheims Version because it sounded badass, but I doubt it."

"Oh, I never thought of that. Good to know."

"I interrupted. Continue."

She peers back down at her notes and runs her index finger along the page as she reads. She reminds me of the school librarian back in middle school. "The verse is part of Jesus's Sermon on the Mount: 'For with what judgment you judge, you shall be judged: and with what measure you mete, it shall be measured to you again.' It follows the more famous 'Judge not, that you may not be judged.' Some people would disagree with me, but I believe it means that whatever standard you judge others by will be the standard by which you are judged by God." She removes her glasses and bites the tip of the earpiece to ponder.

The Uber driver looks in the rearview mirror at the two of us, probably wondering if he's picked up two religious fanatics. Hearing those words, I can't blame him. I picture that letter with the demonic painting in blood, and it sends a chill through me. Does the killer see themselves as God, or merely as an instrument of God? I put it aside and focus on the meaning behind the words.

"The question is, What standard was Father K. judging by that he failed to meet himself? If we find that, we find the killer's motive. We find the motive, we find the killer. What about the Gospel of Matthew? Anything unique to Matthew that might give us any insight? I haven't visited church for a while."

"Oh, you must go to church, Hazel. It's good for the soul."

"We're headed there right now, aren't we?" I laugh, and Mary scowls. "I know, I know. My mother tells me that every Sunday. But in the meantime, what can you tell me?"

"There's nothing unique to Matthew that jumps out at me. It was written in the first century, following Jesus's death. Matthew was Jewish, and the gospel was directed toward other Jews who doubted the divine nature of Jesus. The only aspect that could be relevant is that it's the first book of the New Testament. I don't know. Maybe first murder, first book?"

"It's possible."

"The drawing was more interesting."

"Really?"

"Yes. It is a rough copy of the lower-right section of Giotto's *The Last Judgement*, painted in 1307."

"I knew I had seen that image somewhere."

"The painting depicts the moment when Jesus renders his last judgment on humanity. I'd say, given the choice of Bible verse and painting, whoever did this is rendering the Lord's judgment."

I feel a chill run through me. This killer is a special type of deranged. I picture him in a basement somewhere, dipping a paintbrush in animal blood and tracing it across the letter, storing up puffer fish poison to deliver it to Father K., smiling at the thought that he's doing God's work.

"If that was his first judgment, I'm guessing it won't be the last."

The Uber pulls up in front of the cathedral entrance on Mott Street. The rain falls faster now, and thunder rumbles across the river in the distance. The city has gone from sad to morose. Mary pops open her green-and-yellow North Dakota State Bison umbrella, and we both crouch under it as we exit the car. I squint, and my gaze falls on the graveyard adjacent to the cathedral. Round gray headstones stand in neat rows. Raindrops splatter against the ancient graves. A mist settles on the ground, hemmed in by the mildew-covered brick wall that surrounds the property. I can almost picture Pierre Toussaint rising from the grave. Lightning flashes in the sky, followed by a crack that sounds like a gunshot. Mary and I run to the entrance, throw open the thick rosewood doors, and scurry inside the red-stone cathedral.

The doors slam behind us, and an echo vibrates through the church. I flinch, expecting someone to shush us, but there's no one here.

We're alone.

I scan the space. The only light flows through the stained glass, creating a haunting blend of light and darkness. A few candles flicker near the front of the church. It's eerily similar to the night Father K. died. I place my hand on one of the dark-wood pews. Goose bumps run along my skin from the damp chill. I take a long breath through my nose and catch a hint of mold. I smell the death in this place.

I tiptoe forward to see if someone is here and I'm just not seeing them. Each step sounds like a thump in the space. But there's no one. I turn back to Mary, who's twirling her pendant in her hand, eyes wide open. She's as creeped out as I am. I flash back to the video of Father K. exiting the side door left of the sanctuary.

A door squeaks from that same spot and groans as it opens. I know it's ridiculous, but a small part of me expects Father Kenneally's ghost to emerge. Footsteps pad down the hallway. I hold my breath as they come closer.

An elderly nun comes into view, and I sigh and wipe the rain from my forehead. She nods her acknowledgment and makes her way down the aisle but says nothing. As she approaches, I see she's even smaller than me, but there's a compressed power in her. A stiff chin anchors a hard face run through with creases. Her bottom lip juts out, and her mouth turns downward as if it has never smiled.

"Hazel Cho?" she asks. Her voice sounds worn but firm.

"Yes, I'm Hazel Cho."

She extends her bony hand and gives my fingers a crushing shake.

"I'm Sister Teresa. I'm Archbishop Dinwiddie's assistant. I was told you were coming. How can I help you?" Her words are kind, but her tone is ice. She stands with her hands crossed, blocking the aisle like a bouncer at a nightclub.

"Oh, does the archbishop have an office here?"

"No, our offices are on First Avenue in Midtown. The archbishop requested I greet you in person." She eyes me with distaste.

It's odd that the archbishop even heard I was coming, let alone sent his assistant to meet me. I reconsider what Sam said about powerful people.

"Oh, that wasn't necessary, but that's very kind of him."

She nods and clears her throat. "What can I do for you?"

"We're working with the defense team in Father Kenneally's homicide case. We believe that the police have the wrong man, and I'm conducting a supplementary investigation to ensure whoever murdered Father K. is brought to justice."

"I see," she says. She swallows and her mouth twists.

"Maybe we could start with you showing us around? This is a beautiful church."

"It's a cathedral, actually."

"Yes, excuse me. It's a beautiful cathedral. May we see it?"

"Of course. Follow me."

She turns, walks back down the aisle, and, without looking at us, recounts the history of the cathedral. Lightning cracks, and thunder shakes the structure, but she doesn't acknowledge it. I pull out my phone and start recording.

"Old St. Patrick's was built between 1809 and 1815 and was the cathedral of the Archdiocese of New York prior to the construction of the new St. Patrick's Cathedral in Midtown." She gestures to the stained glass and the gold sculpture of Jesus on the cross that hangs over the sanctuary.

"How long did Father Kenneally serve as head priest here?" I ask.

Mary pulls out her notebook and begins jotting down notes while we walk.

"I'd have to check, but at least twenty years."

"How did you two meet?"

She keeps walking toward the front of the church, head forward. I speed up to get beside her and make eye contact, but she stares straight ahead, ignoring me as though I'm a fly buzzing about.

"I met him before I came to the city. I was a nun at Poor Clares in Wappingers Falls and he was a priest at St. Mary's."

"What did you think of him?"

We arrive at the front of the church, and she stops in front of an ancient oak door. "What did I think of him?"

"Yeah. Did you two get along?"

"I suppose so. He was a kind man. A loyal servant of God."

"Did he have any enemies that you know of? Anyone who wished him harm?"

"You mean besides the Sampson boy?"

"Do you believe Samuel wished him harm?"

"He's in jail, isn't he?"

I stifle my desire to argue with her. It never pays to bicker with a witness. "Yes, besides him."

"No."

"One of my colleagues noticed that Father Kenneally was murdered shortly after the church appealed a court decision that would have paid the victims of child abuse. Do you know of anyone who was particularly upset about that decision?"

"How would I know what someone was thinking?"

"I don't know. Maybe letters or emails the church received. Any public outbursts. Visitors to Father Kenneally?"

"No. None that I can recall. Of course, we received letters, but none that would imply something so awful as murder."

"May we see those letters?"

"I'm sorry, we don't keep our parishioners' mail."

She opens the door and holds it for us, revealing a curved staircase spiraling downward. A gust of frigid, moist air rushes over us. I look at Mary and gesture with my hand. "You go first." Her eyes widen, but she leads us across the threshold.

I trail Mary, and Sister Teresa follows me.

She throws the steel slider and locks us in. I shoot her the side-eye.

"To keep any stray visitors from coming down," she says.

As we descend the frigid staircase, Mary says, "Sister Teresa, if you don't mind me asking…where are you taking us?"

We reach the bottom, and she splays out her hand. "The catacombs. I assumed you'd want to see them. They're the only ones in New York City, and one of a few in the United States."

I actually had no intention of seeing the catacombs, but if this gives me a chance to interview Sister Teresa, I'm in. Mary appears less enthusiastic. We step from the stairs into a long, dark tunnel. The mustiness is so thick, it sticks to my tongue.

Small white lights line the floor but provide only the faintest glow. Every bulb illuminates a stone slab with the names of families buried there. At the end of the tunnel, a red light shines over a doorway.

My mind flashes back to the Dionysus Theater. To the red light over its entryway. To what I saw inside. I feel my pulse rise and sweat bead in my underarms, the terror from that night creeping up inside me. The grinding, buzzing sound in my ears returns. People think of trauma as a moment, a temporary visitor. But it's not. It's a lifelong companion.

I try to block the thoughts from my mind and focus on this investigation. "It's my understanding that you met with Father Kenneally the day he died. Is that correct?"

She disregards my question and keeps walking through the catacombs. "Each one of the stones you see marks the entrance to a family crypt. Husbands, wives, daughters are buried here."

The old nun seems to derive pleasure in spending time among the dead. I don't. I feel my breath become shallower, and my chest tightens. It feels like an invisible hand is squeezing my heart and lungs.

"That's very interesting, but can you answer my question, please?"

She pauses, leans over, and inspects one of the crypt stones, running her crooked finger over it. "Yes. We met. To review the schedule for Midnight Mass."

"And did anything about him seem different? Off?"

"No."

"Are you aware of anyone else who met with him?"

"No. I do know that I was his last meeting, because he told

me he was going to work on his Sunday sermon after I left. He was struggling to decide what his theme was going to be. As far as earlier in the day, I couldn't say. I didn't keep his schedule. Samuel did."

"Do you have a sense of how many people Father K. would see on a typical day? I'm trying to understand how many individuals would have access to his office."

"I couldn't say for sure since I spend most of my time in the archbishop's office, but no more than four or five people a day. And no one would have access to his office without him there. Except for Samuel, of course."

She straightens up and keeps walking toward the red light. I look at Mary and roll my eyes.

"Where does this tunnel lead?" I ask.

"It leads up to the back offices, one of which was Father Kenneally's."

"Question: If someone had access to the catacombs, could they reach Father Kenneally's office while still avoiding the hallway camera?"

We approach the red light at the end of the tunnel.

"It's possible, but the other cameras in the church would still see them. Much like they saw Samuel."

"But the cameras reset every day, right? So, theoretically, someone could break into the catacombs, wait overnight, and then strike."

Her face puckers. "I suppose. But they would have to possess a knowledge of the catacombs and know the cameras reset daily."

"And who would know that?"

"No one besides me, the archbishop, Father Kenneally, and Samuel Sampson."

She raises a dagger of an eyebrow at me and opens the door beneath the red light to reveal pitch black. The way this interview is going, part of me wonders if Sister Teresa is going to throw me and Mary into our own crypt and destroy the key. It's absurd, but the thought of it sends a burst of anxiety through my chest. Sweat pours down my face.

I need to get out of here.

I walk through the door. For a moment, I can't see anything, and panic takes hold. My heart thunders in my chest, and my lungs search for oxygen. Then my eyes adjust, and I spot stairs and the glint of light from above me. I race up the steps, leaving Mary and Sister Teresa behind, and burst through the door into the clergy offices. I inhale and close my eyes. My heart slows. I look down at my hands. They're shaking.

"Are you okay?" asks Mary as she follows me out of the catacombs. She places a steadying hand on my shoulder.

I rub my temples. "Yeah. Since what happened last year, I get a little claustrophobic sometimes."

Sister Teresa looks at me and smiles. I can't help feeling that she did this on purpose. A power play to knock us off-balance. "This is the office where the head priests and staff work."

"Where was Father Kenneally's office?" I ask.

"Right here." She walks over to a closed wooden door with a bronze nameplate that reads FATHER RICARDO, HEAD PRIEST.

"I'd like to tour the office, if that's all right."

"I'm sorry, that's not possible."

Mary and I shoot each other confused looks. "Why is that?" I ask.

"The archbishop has forbidden any outside investigation."

"Ah, there must be some confusion. This isn't an outside investigation. This is part of the legal defense. The defendant has a legal right to inspect the crime scene."

The old nun stiffens. "Yes, I'm aware, and the defense attorney, Ms. Patel, has already done so. And given that Father Kenneally's passing was ten months ago and this is now Father Ricardo's working office, the archbishop feels it would be inappropriate."

"Look, I'm sure Shavali can get a court order to give us access to the office, but wouldn't it—"

"Then she should do so." Sister Teresa's bottom lip sticks out even farther than normal.

My fists curl into balls. I doubt I have time to get a court order, and she knows it. It looks like another case of the unstoppable force meeting the immovable object.

"All right. Then may I speak with Father Ricardo? Where is he?"

"He's out. I asked him to give us privacy. I'm afraid the archbishop feels it would be inappropriate for you to interview him as well."

I feel the veins rising underneath my eyes. What is the archbishop so afraid of? "I would think the archbishop would want to know who killed one of his priests."

"We do know. His name is Samuel Sampson. He is in jail."

I cross my arms and rock on my heels. Mary wraps an arm around my waist and practically drags me away from her. I paste a fake smile onto my face.

"Thank you for your time, Sister Teresa."

"You're very welcome."

Mary and I walk outside. The storm roars overhead, and she opens the umbrella.

"She was not the nicest," says Mary. Translation: She was a bitch. Whenever Mary says something's "not the [fill-in-the-blank]," it means it's terrible. If she ate garbage, she would say, "That food was not the best."

"No, she wasn't the nicest."

"So, what do we do now?"

I flag down a cab. "We visit the archbishop."

Mary's forehead creases. "But she said that the archbishop doesn't want anyone talking about the investigation."

I open the cab door for her. "And that's exactly why we have to talk to him. It's like my old mentor, Perry, used to say: 'The lies are in the streets; the truth hides behind closed doors.'"

12

The Archdiocese of New York is everything Old St. Patrick's is not. The black steel and glass structure looks like any other Midtown office building. There's no religious iconography. No Gothic spires or marble carvings. Old St. Patrick's is a place of worship; this is a place of business. The only hint the building is home to the archbishop of New York is a small crown of thorns resting on a royal-purple pillow in the center of the atrium.

As we cross the lobby, I catch a whiff of my sweater. The moldy reek of the catacombs stays with me. I get chills picturing that creepy old nun. There was something not right with her. Something sadistic. Mary makes a move to the security desk to check in, but I grab her arm and tug her closer to me.

She looks at me, confused. "Where are we going?"

"I don't think the archbishop is going to welcome us with open arms. This needs to be a sneak attack."

"Oh, Hazel," she says, but I can tell part of her likes the adventure.

We slide in behind a group of priests as they amble across the shining marble-tiled floor to the elevator banks and pretend to be part of the group. It helps that Mary looks like an Irish Catholic nun. I'm pretty sure if I were trying to sneak in by myself, this wouldn't be going so smoothly.

We board the elevator, and the priests hit the button for the seventh floor. I realize I don't know what floor the archbishop's office is on. Without hesitating, Mary hits the button for the top floor. I raise an eyebrow.

She crinkles her nose and whispers, "The boss is always on the top level."

The priests exit on seven, and we shoot up to the thirtieth floor. The doors open, and I expect to see an ornate, awe-inspiring office. This is the archbishop, after all. But it's the reverse: a typical floor in a typical office building. Beige carpet. Styrofoam ceiling tiles. White walls with meaningless modern paintings with simple brushstrokes. Dull fluorescent light that lulls you to sleep. This could be an accounting firm or a law practice.

To the right, across the hallway, a gold plaque outside a manufactured-wood office door reads ARCHBISHOP MILTON DINWIDDIE. I freeze as a couple of office workers in business-casual tromp down the hallway, expecting them to call us out. But they smile and breeze by, talking about their weekends. Barbecues and Little League.

I open the door to the archbishop's office to reveal a luxurious reception area with a lustrous leather couch and chair, and a marble coffee table with a vase of blue hydrangeas sitting in the center. The faint scent of incense clings to the space. A reception desk stands watch in front of the archbishop's private office. But it's empty. Fortunately, we beat Sister Teresa here.

I take a second to look around. A massive picture of Jesus draped in blue hangs from the left wall, and a bookcase lines the right side of the room. The smell of potpourri drifts through the air. Bibles and other religious books line the bookshelf, along with pictures of the archbishop with presidents, popes, and other dignitaries. He clearly enjoys the privileges of his position. I notice from the pictures that he uses a wheelchair. He hides it well. The few times I've seen him on television, he's always behind a desk, so I never knew. Mary taps her foot on the floor, reminding me I need to get on with it.

"Wait here," I whisper to her, pointing to the couch.

"What do you want me to say when Sister Teresa gets here?"

"Tell her the truth."

Mary sits and watches the door while I tiptoe across the plush dark-green carpet. As I get closer, I can hear Dinwiddie talking to someone. It sounds like he's on the phone given the one-sided conversation. I raise my fist to knock.

A firm voice stops me.

"What do you think you're doing?"

I turn and my face drops. Sister Teresa stands in the doorway. She's out of breath, like she rushed over here. She's a pit bull, this one.

I throw her my best smile. "Oh, hello. I was stopping by to introduce myself to the archbishop and ask him a couple questions."

Her strong chin gets even stronger as she charges toward me. She grabs my shoulders and moves me away from the door like an oversize chess piece. I'm shocked by the strength in her grip. I guarantee those hands have whacked a few kids with rulers in her day. "The archbishop is very busy. If you'd like to see him, you must make an appointment."

I straighten up and lean into her. It's so rare that I get the chance to look down on someone. I'm not letting this opportunity pass me by. "Okay, then. I'd like to make an appointment to see him now."

She narrows her eyes, and the creases in her face deepen. "I'm sorry, but he's booked all day."

"Tomorrow, then."

"He's booked all week."

I spy Mary out of the corner of my eye. She hates conflict, and I can see her pupils sliding back and forth between us, willing us to find common ground. I know her approach is probably better, but Dinwiddie is hiding something, and there's zero chance I'm backing down. I raise my voice. "Look, I'm not leaving here until I talk to the archbishop."

"Fine, I'll call security."

The door opens, and Dinwiddie's face pokes out, covered in a frown. "What is all the commotion?" he growls.

In one glance, I can see why he's risen to the heights he has. His face rings with power. An enormous head sits atop wide, rectangular shoulders. The weathered dark-mahogany skin on his face pops against a statesmanlike receding salt-and-pepper hairline and a mustache to match. And his voice sounds like the voice of God himself, a rich warm bass.

Sister Teresa's face flips from an icy frown to an obsequious smile. "I'm so sorry, Archbishop. I was telling these... ladies...that if they want to see you, they need to make an appointment."

Dinwiddie's face softens as he assesses me and Mary. Surely not the most intimidating duo he's ever seen. His eyes meet mine, and he smiles. "And who are you?"

I reach out to shake hands. "I'm sorry to drop in on you like this, Archbishop Dinwiddie. I'm Hazel Cho. I'm a private investigator who's working on Father Kenneally's murder. This is my assistant, Mary Donahue."

Mary gives a warm nod.

Dinwiddie assesses the two of us, then turns his wheelchair back into his office. Sister Teresa moves toward the door to close it behind him. My shoulders drop, and my brain fires with other angles to crack these two. Then, over his shoulder, the archbishop says, "It's all right, Sister Teresa. She can come in."

She pauses and glares at me, then holds the door. I suppress a smile. "Wait out here for me?" I say to Mary. Maybe Mary can soften her up while I work on the archbishop.

Sister Teresa closes the door behind us. Dinwiddie wheels his chair behind his timeworn walnut desk and gestures to one of the two purple velvet chairs across from him. I swipe my palm across the crushed velvet as I sit and take in the tranquil view of the East River.

"Thank you for seeing me. I'm sure you're very busy."

He smiles, and I'm struck by the mix of warmth and steel behind it. "I am indeed a busy man, but Father Kenneally was a close friend."

"Thank you. I—"

"I read about you, you know."

"Is that right?"

"Yes, I saw what you did for those poor children at St. Agnes. It was quite the news story." He speaks slowly, every word chosen with care.

I can't help blushing. I still haven't adjusted to my fifteen minutes of fame. "Yeah, it was a terrible thing, but I was happy I could help."

"Yes, awful. There seems to be no limit to the evil that we are capable of doing to each other. 'And God saw that the wickedness of man was great in the earth, and that every imagination of the thoughts of his heart was only evil continually.'"

He quotes scripture. Kenneally's killer quotes scripture.

He catches the quizzical look on my face. "Apologies. An old priest's habit. I would imagine the St. Agnes case was good for your career, though."

"I guess so."

"And you're married to Jack Powell, the candidate for mayor, if I recall correctly."

"Not married. Dating. You've really done your research."

"No, no. But I do like to keep tabs on the major players in my diocese. I've known Jack for a while. He's a good Catholic. Are you Catholic?" He speaks so slowly, I feel like I could run errands between each sentence. I glide my fingers across the velvet chair arms to soothe my impatience.

"No, I'm not really religious."

"That's a shame. Well, there's still time."

Sister Teresa opens the door and enters with a tray carrying a water glass and a bottle of aspirin. She places it on his desk and waits.

The archbishop grabs a couple of pills and tosses them back with a sip of water. "I apologize, it's that time of day. Need to take a couple of baby aspirin every day to keep the old ticker going." She takes the tray and exits. "I find the body is like a car. The older it gets, the more maintenance it requires."

I curve my lips upward but keep them pressed together, wondering when we're going to get down to business.

"Enough chitchat," he says, as if sensing my impatience. "What can I do for you, Hazel?"

I pull out my phone and place it on his blotter. "Do you mind if I record our conversation?"

He looks at the phone like I placed a snake on his desk. "As a matter of fact, I do. I'm happy to talk with you, but I won't have you recording me like I'm some common criminal."

"I'm sorry, but it's standard practice. I want to make sure I get the details right."

He stiffens in his wheelchair. "I'm sure it is, but you'll have to make do with your memory."

He ends his statements with a period. He's used to giving orders. No debate. I consider calling Mary in to take notes, but I'm already on thin ice. He doesn't need to talk to me at all. I press record anyway and put my phone in my pocket.

"Well, regarding my investigation—"

"Yes. What exactly is there to investigate? It was my understanding that the police found the killer. That Sampson boy." He rubs his mustache.

"We believe the police may have the wrong man."

"Hmm," he says, and continues stroking his facial hair. He pauses so long between statements that I wonder if I'm supposed to keep talking. "Why is that?"

"I can't go into the details of the case, but let's just say he doesn't fit the profile."

"Hmm." Another long pause. "You may want to look at your profile again."

"Why do you say that?"

A clock ticks on the wall, and he looks at it. I wonder if he's counting the seconds of his pauses. "I can't go into all the details," he says, parroting my phrase with a smirk, "but I assure you that Samuel Sampson is not the choirboy he has convinced you he is."

"Do you know Sam?"

"No, I don't know him, but if you speak to people in the diocese as much as I do, you learn these kinds of things."

"That's actually one reason I'm here. When we were at Old St. Patrick's, Sister Teresa informed us you had ordered her and others in the diocese not to speak to us."

"That's correct."

"As I'm sure you understand, that makes it difficult for us to investigate the murder of Father Kenneally."

"I understand, but *you* must understand the police have already investigated this matter, and they arrested your man, Sampson. In addition, your colleague—Ms. Patel, I think her name is—also visited the scene and spoke with the relevant folks. It's been nearly a year since Sean died. I think we've been more than accommodating. I can't have church business interrupted ad infinitum by investigators. You can see that, can't you?"

"I do, but the trial starts in less than a week, so I would only be around for a few days, and then you'll never hear from me."

"I'm sorry. I must say no. That said, I'll be happy to answer your questions." He flashes a bold white-toothed smile. He's not budging. He enjoys his position of power.

I consider threatening a court order like I did with Sister Teresa, but if I do, he'll clam up and kick me out.

"That's fine. Maybe we can start with the day Father K. died. Can you tell me about that?"

"Of course. I was here at the diocese. I was meeting with Sandy Godo, your boyfriend's opponent in the mayoral race. He wanted my support. Don't worry, I didn't give it to him." He winks at me. "Sister Teresa knocked on my door. The instant she did, I knew something was wrong. She rarely interrupts a meeting once it has started. She told me Sean had died."

"What time was that?"

"Approximately nine a.m."

"And what did you do then?"

"At first, I did nothing. I was so shocked. Sean was a dear friend of mine. I spoke to him on the phone the night before, and it seemed inconceivable that he could be dead." He massages his hands and watches the boats float down the river. "But then I made my apologies to Sandy and went directly to Old St. Patrick's."

"You spoke to Father K. the night before?"

"Yes, I've already told the police this."

I flash back to the case file. There's no easier way to catch a liar than by reading their previous statements on record. So far, everything matches what he told the police. Yet he seems uncomfortable. Why?

"What did you discuss?"

"Nothing important. I wanted to know when specifically he wanted me there for the Christmas festivities."

I hold his gaze for a second. I note the way his bottom lip curls. He's hiding something. "Was there anything else you discussed?"

"No, not that I can recall."

That seals it. He's definitely lying. If you're interviewing a person in a position of power and they use the words *I don't recall*, it's a guarantee that they're lying. Tacking on the phrase gives them enough wiggle room when you later catch them dissembling. I shift to a more innocuous question to keep him talking.

"What happened when you arrived at the church?"

"The police and paramedics were there. As was your boy, Sampson. The officers had taped the aisle off, but I remember seeing Sean lying there, lifeless." His eyes drift past me as he conjures the scene in his mind. "The expression on his face... It was awful."

"Did you talk to Sam at all?"

"No. I wanted to, but I couldn't. The police kept him separated so they could interview him."

"The killer left a letter. Do you—"

"Ah, yes. The infamous red letter. Too clever by half, don't you think?"

"I'm sorry. What do you mean?"

"The red letter?" He stares at me and leans his head forward like a teacher prodding the class for an answer. "The verse on the letter?"

"Yes, from the Gospel of Matthew. But I'm still not following."

He sighs and grabs his black-rimmed eyeglasses off his desk and puts them on his face. He opens a desk drawer and withdraws a gorgeous leather-bound Bible. I notice DOUAY–RHEIMS VERSION embossed in gold on the bottom. He flips to the chapter and verse. Red text covers the page.

"Hazel, you need to start going to church." I laugh to myself. Thank God Mary wasn't in the room to hear that. He pushes the Bible across the desk to me and points at the red text. "In the Bible, the verses spoken by Jesus are often printed in red. We call them 'the red letters' for short." He lets the implication sink in. "Your man, Sampson, inserted a red-letter verse from Jesus in a red letter before he killed my friend."

"Someone, Archbishop. Someone inserted a red-letter verse. We don't know it was Sam."

He shuts the Bible and pulls the glasses off his face. "I suppose that will be for a jury to decide."

"Yes, it will. You mentioned Father K. was a friend. How did you two know each other?"

"Sean and I went to seminary together. We did a missionary trip to Japan together. We served in the same church together. I loved the man." His lip quivers and his voice drops. He takes another sip of water and turns his wheelchair. He grabs a photograph off his shelf and hands it to me.

From the multiple fingerprints on the frame, I know this isn't the first time Dinwiddie has held it since his friend died. The picture shows a group of young priests, with Dinwiddie and Kenneally in the center. In the picture, Dinwiddie is standing. He must have become paralyzed later in life. The two men wear broad grins, chests out, proud and hopeful.

"That's a nice picture. I went to Father K.'s mass a few times. He seemed like a wonderful man."

"He was. Many priests speak the calling, but Sean truly lived it." Dinwiddie's mouth curves upward at the memory of his friend. "He used to challenge his congregation. He would always say coming to church on Sundays wasn't enough. He would browbeat his parishioners into working at the food bank or picking up trash in the streets." A wistful smile crosses his face. "And he would never ask anyone to do anything he wasn't willing to do himself. I often wished I could be more like him."

"Do you know of anyone who may have wanted to harm him?"

"Besides Sampson?"

I decide not to argue the point. "Yes."

He fidgets in his chair, and I observe his eyes. His gaze drops to the floor. He opens his mouth to speak and then closes it.

"No, I can't think of anyone," he says. The second he says it, I know he's lying.

I lean forward and place my hands on his desk. "Are you sure? I understand you think Samuel is responsible for Father Kenneally's death, but I'm telling you there's a strong possibility he's not, and if someone else could be involved in this, I need to know."

This time, his voice resounds with authority. "No, there's no one." He clamps his lips together as if forcing himself into silence.

I pull back to give him breathing room. "Understood. What about acquaintances? Was he close with anyone who wasn't as popular?"

"How do you mean?"

"Shortly before Father Kenneally was murdered, the archdiocese appealed a judgment that would have compelled you to pay the victims a sixty-million-dollar child abuse settlement."

In a swift move that catches me off guard, Dinwiddie swivels his chair ninety degrees and wheels himself out from behind his desk. He rolls past me to the window and looks down at the cars navigating First Avenue. Before he speaks, his jaw clenches. "I know where you're going, and I don't appreciate the implication."

I stand up from my chair to face him. "I'm not going anywhere. I'm merely wondering if you or Father Kenneally received any hate mail or angry phone calls or social media posts or any communications that could give us a lead. Usually, these types of killers show signs before they act."

"Sean would never harm a child."

"I never said that he did. But could someone have killed him in anger at the church's position on the settlement?"

"Our position? Our position is the victims deserve to be compensated for the abuse they suffered. But we believe the insurance policy we paid for decades should cover those payments." His face reddens, and spittle follows his words.

"I know, but you can see how someone might be angry that the archdiocese stalled the payments and could exact retribution on Father Kenneally, can't you?"

"What I see is you are not here in good faith, Hazel. I invited you into my office because I thought you were seeking the truth. But you're yet another nonbeliever trying to destroy the church."

"I'm not trying to destroy the church. I'm trying to get to the truth."

"I'm afraid that's all I have to say on this matter. I'd appreciate it if you and your assistant would leave my office now."

"May I ask one more question?"

"No, I think I've given you more than enough of my time at this point. I'm not here to be a punching bag for you and your boyfriend to score cheap media points against the Catholic Church."

"That's not what I'm doing at all. And Jack has nothing to do with this. I'm trying to find out who killed your friend."

Dinwiddie's kind face twists into a scowl, and he slams his fist on the desk. "We know who killed my friend. Samuel Sampson killed my friend, and he deserves to burn in hell."

13

return to Chinatown that evening, exhausted from the day. I exit the Uber and breathe a sigh of relief. I watch the steam from my breath rise into the chilly night air. Mrs. Yu is out front of the Yu and Me bookstore below my apartment, closing up shop. I wave limply as she locks her door, and she waves back with equal enthusiasm. We've both had a long day, and the unseasonable cold isn't helping. As I slog up the stairs, my brain grinds through the strangeness of this case. I rearrange the pieces around in my mind, but nothing fits. The accused is young, but the actions of the killer—the physical letter, the Douay–Rheims Bible verse, the poison—are those of an older man. The evidence against Samuel is thin, but everyone—the DA, Marcos and the cops, the archbishop—seem certain he's guilty. The style of the killing appears serial, but there's only one dead body, unless you count the Tweed death, which could be an accidental poisoning.

I reach our floor, and the scent of Kenny's cooking gives me a jolt of energy. From the smell of it, he's preparing his famous jjigae, which is a Korean stew, perfect for a cold fall evening like this one. I can almost taste the fatty pork meat sizzling in the pot. God bless that man. He knows when I need a good meal.

I open the door, and the sound of K-pop music fills my ears. This is the devil's trade-off you make when Kenny is cooking. You're going to eat great food, but you're also going to hear whatever bad K-pop song he's listening to on repeat for an hour. Right now, he's into a song called "3D" by Jungkook. To make matters worse, he listens to it on YouTube on the television. Shirtless Korean men in white suits performing coordinated dance moves bombard my vision.

"Not '3D' again," I say as I throw my bag on the worn brown carpet and shut the door behind me.

Kenny gives the stew a stir and taps the jumbo wooden spoon on the edge of the pot. He's rocking his standard post-work gray sweatsuit. He thinks it makes him look like a cool celebrity, but in reality, he looks like the kid who failed gym class. The suit was a much better look.

"Well, it's nice to see you, too, Hazel. My day has been wonderful. Thank you for asking."

I smile and grab the remote and turn the volume down. Kenny frowns.

"C'mon. You know that's my cooking music."

I shrug. "From the smell of it, it seems like the food is about ready."

"Fair point."

"Thank God. Big Mama H is hunnngry."

I pull up a seat at our new white Scandinavian-designed kitchen table. We actually have a kitchen table now, and swoop-arm chairs to boot. We finally broke down and got rid of the old secondhand card table we'd been using. Of course, everything else in the apartment is still either a donation or a discount Goodwill purchase, but we're making progress. With the new hires and office renovation, Kenny and I have drained our savings, so the home reno is on pause. Baby steps.

"You seem awfully cheery today," I say.

Kenny grabs spoons out of our peeling '70s-green utensil drawer and drops a couple of steaming bowls of jjigae on the table. I salivate at the smell of onion and pork. I debate whether it's worth burning my tongue off to take a bite without waiting for it to cool down. I decide for now it's not, but reserve my right to change my mind at any moment.

"I am," he says. "You know how you asked me to review the Tweed case of tetrodotoxin poisoning?"

"I do."

We both blow on our spoonfuls of stew, desperate to take the first bite.

"Well, I dug into it today and got some good dirt."

"Really?" I can't wait any longer, so I take my first slurp. It scalds my mouth, but I do that trick where you hover food back between your tongue and the roof of your mouth, creating a zero-gravity hot-food environment. Totally worth it.

"Yes. You're going to like this. Your old friend Bobby Riether is the detective assigned to the case." He raises an eyebrow and watches my reaction.

I nearly spit out my stew, and I can feel my face reddening.

Bobby worked on the case of girls missing from St. Agnes Children's Home. He's a good cop, whom I may or may not have had a slight crush on. "What? Bobby works for Warren County. What's he doing in Brooklyn?"

"Is that a blush I see?" says Kenny with a smirk. "I'm not sure exactly what he's doing. But he transferred to Brooklyn PD about six months ago. He's over at the Seventy-Eighth Precinct. Maybe he missed you."

"I'm sure." I take another bite of stew. "Did you talk to him?"

"Yeah, he says you should call him."

"Call him? I can't believe he didn't call me. What else did he say?"

"He gave me an update on the case. It's basically closed now. People weren't exactly falling over themselves to investigate Tweed's death. They were happy he was gone. However, Bobby gave me a few nuggets I thought you might find interesting."

"Like what?"

"He said before Tweed died, he attended church at Old St. Patrick's and was a major donor to the archdiocese."

"The plot thickens. I wonder how well he knew the archbishop."

Kenny's eyebrows curl like caterpillars. "Why do you say that? Something you found when you went to Old St. Patrick's today?"

"Basically the opposite. Mary and I got stonewalled by this creepy nun. She gave us a tour of these macabre catacombs but wouldn't even let us see Kenneally's old office. She said the archbishop ordered her not to give us any access, so afterward we paid him a visit."

His forehead jumps to his hairline. "You crashed the archbishop of New York's office?"

"Yep. He wasn't super excited to see me."

"I'm sure he wasn't."

"He didn't give me much, but a couple of things stood out. First, he admitted he spoke with Kenneally but withheld something regarding what they discussed. Second, he got really defensive when I mentioned the sixty-million-dollar child abuse payment. Then he implied I was investigating to create more headlines for me and Jack."

"Sounds like a nice guy. By the way, where is Jack? Should I save him some stew?"

"No, he had another fundraising dinner. He asked me to go, but I swear if I go to another political mixer, I'm going to blow my brains out."

Kenny takes a slurp of his stew, and I see his eyes watering from the heat. "So, do you think the archbishop is hiding something?"

"He's definitely hiding something, but I don't know if it has anything to do with Kenneally's death. I mean, it's not exactly surprising that he wouldn't want me dredging up the child abuse settlement."

"Yeah, it's not a good look for a guy whose office resides in one of the more expensive properties in Manhattan."

"Exactly. But either way you slice it, we now know the archbishop knows both Kenneally and Tweed. I'm getting more skeptical that Tweed died from a bad piece of sushi."

Kenny takes a big gulp of water from his two-million-ounce Stanley cup. "You're going to be even more skeptical when you hear my last piece of info. It turns out that Tweed also received a letter shortly before his untimely demise."

I drop my spoon and perk up. "Please tell me it was red."

"It was."

"Did it have a wax seal?"

"Yeah, how did you know?"

"Never mind. What was the letter on the wax seal?"

"F."

"F for Frederick. S for Sean. And what did it say?"

Kenny's smile drops as he pulls up his phone and reads the text from the letter. "It was another Bible verse. It said, 'The fearful, and unbelieving, and the abominable, and murderers, and whore-mongers, and sorcerers, and idolaters, and all liars, they shall have their portion in the pool burning with fire and brimstone.'"

I grab my spoon and lean back in my chair, tracing the warm metal along my lips.

Kenny leans forward with a grin. "What do you think of that?"

"I think we might have a serial killer on our hands."

14

The next morning, I head over to the Seventy-Eighth Precinct to pay Bobby Riether a visit and learn more about the Tweed case. The seventy-eighth is one of my favorite police stations. It patrols Park Slope, one of the wealthier and safer neighborhoods in Brooklyn, and Prospect Park. The building stands a modest four stories tall, and a beautiful stone runs across the exterior. The sun hits it just right, and the structure almost glows. Blue-and-whites stand at attention out front, and a group of cops trade stories and chuckles on the sidewalk. Someone has decorated the entrance of the station like a jack-o'-lantern, so the front door resembles the mouth of a giant pumpkin. It feels like a station from the old days, when everyone knew their local officer.

On a day like today, when the sun is shining and the streets are bouncing, it's easy to forget why I'm here. There's a psychopath out there poisoning people, and based on how meticulous and methodical he's been thus far, I'm almost certain he will kill again.

Bobby Riether stands out front, smoking his trademark Parliament Lights, laughing with a couple of other cops. He's the only guy I know who somehow still makes smoking cool; there's something in the way he takes a long drag, like he's inhaling enhanced oxygen, and then shoots it out of his mouth like a blow dart. He's sporting charcoal slacks, a gingham shirt with the sleeves rolled up, and one of those overly skinny ties that hipsters wear. It fits the Brooklyn milieu. I take it all in—his rugged vibe, tightly cropped dark hair, firm chin, five-o'clock shadow, and hawk nose—and wonder why I never went out with him. He did ask, after all. Then I remind myself that I have Jack now, so I need to stop thinking these thoughts.

"Look who the cat dragged in," says Bobby as I approach. His lips part, and I see that he still has that endearing chipped front tooth.

I shoot him a smile and give him a hug. "It's good to see you, Bobby." He squeezes me tight against his crisp cotton shirt. I smell his familiar scent of smoke and sandalwood cologne. He's holding a manila folder, which I pray is the Tweed case file.

"It's good to see you too."

We both pause and look into each other's eyes as the dark memories come roaring back. It's funny—when you've been through the fire with someone, it welds you together permanently. You don't need to say anything. You're connected for good or ill.

I clear my throat and inspect the ground so he can't see me

blush. "So, are we going to stand on the corner all day, or are you going to invite me in?"

He takes another drag of his cigarette. "I was actually thinking we could take a walk."

"Trouble at the station?"

"No, nothing like that. I love the guys here. But it's been so cold lately, and we finally got a beautiful day…and I just started this cigarette." He shoots me a mischievous wink.

"All right. Lead the way."

We head south down Sixth Avenue. Brooklyn has changed so much in my lifetime. It's almost like walking through the suburbs now. Kids roll by on bikes, laughing and chomping on gum. Squeals from a nearby playground meander through the air. Disheveled parents push strollers to the neighborhood coffee shop. Trees dotted with orange and brown leaves line the sidewalks. Today, New York is a folksy parent. We amble and enjoy the day for the first few minutes.

Bobby breaks the silence. "How have you been?" His voice still carries a hint of smoker's rasp. He fidgets with his cigarette.

"I've been good. Things have really taken off at my private investigation agency. I've got an actual business now."

"I'm glad to hear it. How did you get involved in this case?"

I put a hand on his bony shoulder and stop walking. "Wait, I'm not letting you off that easy. First things first. How the hell do you move to Brooklyn and join the NYPD and fail to tell me?"

He bends down and picks up a piece of loose trash as we walk. Another one of my favorite things about New York: the sidewalk trash. There is no limit to how bizarre it can be. One time, on the same block, I found a one-hundred-dollar bill, a baby bottle from the '50s, and a porno mag. Hopefully not all dropped by the same person.

"Yeah, sorry about that," Bobby says. "I planned on calling you, but after you shot me down when I asked you out, I didn't want you to think I was stalking you, so I kept procrastinating."

I give him a gentle shove and start walking again. "I didn't shoot you down. It was two weeks after I found out that my boyfriend was a child sex trafficker, so I'm sorry if I wasn't up for dating."

I leave out the part about how Andrew tried to rape and murder me, but the image flashes through my mind like a strobe. I still haven't learned how to talk about it.

"Is it my fault you have such poor taste in men?" he says.

I bust out laughing. "Oh, ho, ho, that is a dark joke."

Sometimes that's the only way to survive in this business.

Bobby twists the cigarette butt in his fingers so that the cherry falls to the ground and then puts the finished butt in his pants pocket. I give him the side-eye.

"There has to be a better way to do that."

"I'm sure there is, but here we are." He grabs a Listerine strip, drops it in his mouth, and clears his throat. "So, I'm assuming you didn't come here to discuss my smoking habits."

"No. I want a status update on the Tweed case. Kenny told me he spoke to you and you said it was closed."

Bobby takes a long breath of the crisp autumn air like he's trying to repair the damage he inflicted on his lungs. I inhale, too, and enjoy the scent of dried leaves. "Yeah, it was closed until Kenny told me about the connection." He opens the manila folder and flips through pages of scribbled pencil notes.

The text is pure guy-writing: straight, firm strokes that look like they were carved into stone by a caveman.

"May fifteenth, Tweed's wife, Arika, calls 911. Says her husband is having some type of seizure. By the time the paramedics arrive, he's dead. Autopsy reveals he died of tetrodotoxin poisoning."

"Kenny mentioned you attributed it to puffer fish?"

"That's right. He ate fugu that night. The medical examiner determined the cause of death as food poisoning. That turned out to be a huge mistake, because we entered the case into CompStat as food poisoning."

"So nobody connected it to the Kenneally homicide?"

"Exactly. If we would have input *homicide by poison*, we might have pinged the Kenneally case. But the Kenneally murder took place in Manhattan months earlier, so it wasn't really on our radar."

"But what about the letter?"

"Yeah, we found the letter, but you got to keep in mind that the medical examiner ruled it food poisoning and the letter contained a Bible verse, not a murder note. Plus, these days it's all about the statistics, so nobody wants an open homicide case unless it's definitely a homicide. That, and everybody was happy to see Tweed gone, so there was no incentive to pursue it."

I think about when Jeffrey Epstein hung himself in jail. Few people were interested in investigating that either. "I get it. Where did you find the letter?"

"It was on his desk, buried among a stack of papers. There was no sign that he ascribed any significance to it."

"Kenny told me about the Bible verse. It was typed, I assume?"

"Correct. I read the thing and I got goose bumps."

"Did it have anything else on it?"

"It did. "

He flips the case file to the picture of the letter and hands it to me. The upper third shows a blood-brown drawing of naked sinners falling into the fires of hell, being speared by demons as they fall. My palms sweat as I picture this psychopath dipping a paintbrush in animal blood, smiling while he paints agony, typing the letter with bloodstained hands. "I assume you tested the envelope and the letter?"

Bobby raises an eyebrow. "Now you're insulting me. Yes, we tested the letter. No conclusive DNA besides the mail carrier and the victim. The blood was animal blood. Not sure what animal."

I flip the page to the picture of Tweed's body. His three-hundred-pound frame slumps on the floor. Vomit covers his beard and designer button-down shirt. His facial expression matches Father Kenneally's: a ghoulish mixture of terror and pain.

"What about the envelope and paper? Anything unique?"

"No, both the envelope and the paper are common. You can find it at any stationery store or online. The only thing vaguely interesting is that the envelope was red and secured by a wax seal."

The pace of our walking and talking picks up as we dive into the case. We're both junkies for this stuff.

"The type?"

"That was a dead end too. They were typed with a typewriter, though, not printed on a printer. I talked to my buddy who owns a print shop, and he told me, based on the typeface, it was likely a Brother Charger II model from the eighties. It's in the file."

"Man, you're full of bad news, aren't you?"

Bobby shrugs and hooks a left at the end of the block. "Yeah, that's why I was telling Kenny that we chalked this up to food poisoning and moved on. There wasn't much there."

"Was the letter mailed or dropped off?"

"It was mailed."

"Could you research where it was mailed from and see if Marcos can do the same?"

"Yeah, that might take a few days but should be doable. I wish I had checked it then—but until Kenny called, I didn't know the letter was related to Tweed's death. He was a serious Catholic, so I thought it could be a modern piece of art or something."

My mind flashes to Sam, to his DNA on the letter to Father Kenneally.

"Did the name Samuel Sampson ever come up in the Tweed investigation?"

"No, why?"

"He's my client. He's the one about to be tried for killing Father K. at Old St. Patrick's."

"No, I never heard that name, but…" Bobby lights another cigarette and takes a pull, smoke billowing out of his mouth while he speaks. He waves his pointer finger in the air and talks in that weird tone smokers use where they're both inhaling smoke and talking at the same time. "Old St. Patrick's. That's the other item I wanted to discuss. When I interviewed Tweed's wife, Arika—who's a real piece of work, by the way—I noticed she became irate when talking about Old St. Patrick's and her husband's relationship with the diocese. She was not a fan. I wonder what she knows."

"Did she inherit his money when he died?"

Bobby's mouth breaks into a wry grin. "She did, but because of the fraud, she mostly inherited a bunch of lawsuits. So I don't think money would be her angle. We looked into her but found nothing tying her to the letter or poison. I never looked into a connection with Kenneally because at the time, I didn't have any reason to associate the two. Still, there's something about her that was…off."

"Any interest in paying her another visit?"

"You took the words right out of my mouth."

15

Bobby and I lock down a time to visit the widow Tweed, and later that day, I return to my office. As I'm about to turn onto Cortlandt Alley, I spot Yanush, my local hot dog vendor. He gives me a gold-toothed smile that sparkles in the afternoon fall sunlight. I wave, and the smell of hot dogs pulls me in like a tractor beam. I'm forming a love-hate relationship with Yanush, like an addict with her heroin dealer. I stop at the stand and buy four loaded hot dogs. I really just want one for myself, but giving one to everyone at work gives me cover and makes me look generous.

I enter the office, hot dogs in hand. "Hot dog time!" I shout.

No response. Kenny, Mary, and Momo are all at their desks, eyes glued to their computer screens.

"What kind of greeting is that for the hot dog queen?"

Momo raises her head from her computer and removes the

grandma glasses from her face. I notice that she's striking with her glasses off. Her dark eyes are set off perfectly against her dyed auburn hair. "Sorry, Hazel, I'm watching this security video for the Virga Insurance case."

I hand her a hot dog and pull her out of her chair. "No more security footage. I've got something much bigger than insurance for you. I'm officially ordering you to take a break and come eat hot dogs with me in the conference room."

She smiles and follows me into the conference room. I think this is the first time I've had the opportunity to be the cool boss. It feels good. I turn to Mary and Kenny. "You two. Get in here. It's hot dog time."

Kenny and Mary reluctantly rise from their desks and shuffle to the conference room. I don't know why, but I take perverse joy in interrupting people at their work. I think it helps remind me not to take life too seriously. I slide the hot dogs across the table and take a big bite of mine. I know it's terrible for you, but you can't beat the taste. Mustard and relish spill down my lips and chin, and I couldn't be happier. I can tell from Mary's, Momo's, and Kenny's faces that they're enjoying the treat too. Hopefully, this will make what I'm about to tell them go down a little easier.

"Mmm," says Mary. "I haven't had a hot dog in forever. Reminds me of when my dad used to grill on the farm. Hot dogs, burgers, a little sweet corn. Can't beat it."

Kenny wipes his face with a napkin. "Yeah, these are great, Haze. But did you call us in here for a reason? 'Cuz I got work to do."

"Geez, you're no fun," I say. "What happened to the guy

who played Call of Duty in his sweatpants until four a.m.?" Momo stifles a giggle with her hand over her mouth.

Kenny frowns and takes a vicious bite of his dog.

"All joking aside, I called you guys in because I need you to drop everything else you're doing and focus on the Sampson case." My smile fades as I consider what I'm about to say. I clear my throat.

"Why? What's going on?" says Mary.

"It's become obvious that the person who killed Father Kenneally and Fred Tweed are one and the same."

The room goes silent.

"Both men ingested poison. Both men received a letter containing a Bible verse and an image painted in blood. I think it is safe to assume that the suspect is currently planning their next victim."

"Oh my," says Mary.

"The good news is, this likely means that our client Samuel Sampson is innocent, since he was in Rikers when Tweed was murdered. But the Sampson trial is in five days, so I need your help proving that Tweed was murdered and finding out who killed Kenneally and Tweed before a jury convicts Sampson or someone else dies."

Everyone puts their hot dogs down on the glass conference table. I write notes on the whiteboard as I speak.

"Here's what I need from you all. First, I need to know more about tetrodotoxin." Momo raises her hand, her frenetic eyes jumping between me and the whiteboard. "You don't need to raise your hand, Momo, you can speak." Someday I'll be able to beat that Japanese politeness out of her.

"I can look into that for you. In Osaka, my mom had a puffer fish license. She makes fugu all the time." Her voice is as gentle as birdsong.

"You need a license to buy puffer fish?"

"In Japan, you do. She taught us how to prepare it so that we didn't kill ourselves. You skin the fish and remove the innards. Most of the poison is in the skin and liver."

"Okay. Momo, you are officially our tetrodotoxin expert. I want you to find out everything you can about how someone can obtain the fish or commercially produced tetrodotoxin."

The corners of her lips slide up, and her high cheeks redden. I'm guessing this is a major step up from watching security footage of a yacht accident.

I spin the whiteboard marker in my fingers and point it at Mary. "Mary, I need you to research the Bible verse and drawing on the Tweed letter. I assume it's more of the same, but see if you can find information that leads us to the killer or gives us an indication of the next victim. I also want you to search social media for any mentions of the church child abuse settlement. Our working theory is that whoever did this was disgruntled about the church stiffing the victims of abuse. I want you to find anyone who might fit the profile."

"On it." She nods and makes a note in her notebook.

"And I take it you want me to look into the letters themselves?" asks Kenny.

"Exactly. Bobby said that, in both cases, the killer used a Brother Charger II typewriter to write the letters. I want you to visit every typewriter shop in the city and talk to any online typewriter sellers to see if they've sold that model to anyone suspicious.

It's a long shot, but you never know. Bobby also said the killer mailed the letters, and he's working with the post office to find out where they were mailed from. I'll let you know what I find out."

"The killer mailed the letters?" says Kenny. "Why would Sampson mail a letter and then drop it off under Father Kenneally's door?"

"My thoughts exactly. Unless he was trying to mislead people, but that doesn't make much sense. We also need that footage of him dropping off the letter. Sam claims it was a different letter. I watched it once, and it's super blurry. See if you can get a better look at it. Also, he says there were no other visitors besides Sister Teresa that day, but will you watch the whole video to make sure he's right?"

"What about the previous days?"

"They only have twenty-four hours of storage."

Kenny shakes his head. "I'll never understand why people get security cameras and cheap out on storage. It's like they've never heard of someone casing a job." Everyone at the table nods in agreement.

I massage my temples. "I know. It kills me because I guarantee that whoever sent that letter has been to that church before. I'll pursue the stationery angle."

Momo starts to raise her hand again but then checks herself. "When do you need this by?"

"As soon as possible." I envision the shadow I saw outside my window. The blood painted on the letters. "The clock is ticking, and none of us will feel safe until we find the person who committed these murders."

16

I often wonder why Jesus chose me to be his partner.

Why he asked me to deliver the Holy Spirit to those who have sinned.

But then I observe and I see what has become of the world. The world that God gave us, that Jesus and I must save.

I see whores lurching around the street in broad daylight, their vile figures on display for everyone to see. I see diseased drug addicts, bodies like corpses, screaming to ghosts at the tops of their lungs. I see debased pedophiles posing as men of God, molesting God's children with no retribution. I see the sweaty, gluttonous politicians give to the rich and steal from the poor. I see godless murderers roam free, smug smiles pasted on their evil faces. I see degenerate thieves celebrated as saints, and saints mocked and ridiculed. I see dirt and filth and grime on every corner. Hate spewing from every mouth.

I see all these things.

And I realize Jesus chose me because I'm the only one who sees. The world has been awash in so much sin for so long that people don't even notice it. In fact, they celebrate it and reward it. Like children swimming in a pool of feces, oblivious to the disease surrounding them. But Jesus knows that I still see. I have a gift.

I am like Abraham living in Sodom and Gomorrah.

And if they will not hear me, much like Sodom and Gomorrah, God will destroy them for their wickedness. I will rip their lives away one by one until they learn. I will coax the Holy Spirit into their homes and watch them twist in agony until they learn. I will watch them flinch, and spasm, and vomit until they learn. I will melt their skin and devour their insides.

I am the brimstone and the fire.

17

spend the rest of my day researching stationery, and yes, it's as boring as it sounds. It's funny, in all the old detective movies I watched with my dad, I don't recall one stationery-research scene. That's the bizarre paradox of investigative work. You're facing down a homicidal maniac, and the best way to find them is by studying the differences in paper fiber, pulps, coatings, and dying methods. Did you know that paper was originally made from hemp?

To make matters worse, my research only confirms everything Bobby told me. The red #10 envelope the letter came in is extremely common. As is the 80-lb. eight-and-a-half by eleven inches paper that sits in the envelope. You can buy them both on Amazon or any stationery-supply store. I spoke with an Amazon rep who sells hundreds of thousands around Mother's Day. The wax and stamps aren't any better. Apparently, brides-to-be use them on invitations all the time. They sell little wax balls you can heat on a specialized spoon and then drip onto the envelope to seal it. Is it just me, or are we moving backward in time with wedding paraphernalia? Pretty soon, brides will make invitations out of papyrus and deliver them on horseback.

Once I feel my eyes rolling back into my skull from boredom, I close up shop and head over to Jack's place. I open the door to his town house expecting to hear the squeak of basketball sneakers, but instead I hear a song that makes my blood run cold: "Time After Time" by Cyndi Lauper. The song Mia—the abducted girl I located a year ago—sang. I freeze in place, too overwhelmed with memories to step forward.

I absorb my surroundings. Darkness envelops me, except for a flicker of light in the dining room.

Cyndi Lauper's voice echoes through the air. I creep through the living room, sensing that something's off.

The old floorboards groan as I step. I peer around the corner.

A single long-stemmed candle sits on the ebony eight-person dining room table, the flame swaying, casting shadows on the ceiling.

My eyes catch a rectangular bloodred object on the table next to the candle, and my heart skips a beat.

I freeze in place and squint.

Is that…?

I release a breath.

It's not an envelope. It's a jewelry box.

"Surprise," a voice whispers in my ear.

I flinch, and my bag goes flying out of my hand, sending lip balm and pens across the floor. I turn to see Jack backpedaling in response to my flinch. "Oh my God," I say. "You scared the shit out—"

As he retreats, he steps on my lip balm, and his socks slip on the polished hardwood. His feet fly up from under him, and he crashes to the floor, splashing the Lone Star Beer in his hand all over his sweater and face.

I place my hand to my mouth, half recovering from the scare, half stifling a laugh at the sight of my boyfriend on the ground, covered in foam. After a few seconds, I burst out laughing.

Jack doesn't even try to recover. He just lies there, his arms above his head like he's been shot, and licks the beer pouring down his face. He snorts, then lets out a high-pitched Texas laugh. His chest shakes.

"And that, my friends, is how *not* to surprise your girlfriend." He picks up the beer bottle and sits up. I reach out my hand to lift him off the ground. The song switches from "Time After Time" to "One Night in Bangkok."

"That's what you get for sneaking up on a girl," I say, planting a long kiss on his plush beer-scented lips.

He straightens up and wipes a tear from his eye, still chuckling. In the candlelight, I take a moment to savor his tanned skin and the fine wrinkles from too many days in the Texas-summer sun. He's wearing a hunter-green crew-neck sweater, light jeans, and a checkered apron that says KISS THE CHEF. Don't mind if I do.

He grabs a roll of paper towels off the counter and soaks up the beer from the floor and his sweater. "I'm so sorry, bubs. I was trying to be all romantic and sophisticated and serve you a candlelit dinner, and I ended up scaring you half to death."

He gives me a big hug and a kiss. I rub my cheek against the cashmere. He's the best hugger. When we embrace, it's like two puzzle pieces sliding together perfectly. Sometimes I hold him and squeeze tighter as he tries to escape because I'm enjoying it so much. He releases me, and I flip my hair out of my eyes. He rolls up his sleeves, bends over, and gathers my ChapStick and pens. I admire the sinews of his tanned forearms.

I take my coat off and throw it, along with my bag, onto our leather sectional. "No, don't apologize. I totally overreacted. That song you were playing?"

"'Time After Time'?"

"Yeah. Mia was singing that song when I found her at the Dionysus Theater. I should have told you. It never came up."

"Oh, I'm so sorry. I had no idea. I know how you love eighties music, so I threw on the first eighties playlist I found on Spotify."

"It's not your fault. It brings back a lot of terrible memories."

"I hear you."

"Plus, this case has me spinning in circles." The oven beeps in the kitchen.

He raises a finger to pause me. "I want to hear all about it, but first let me grab our supper."

He glides into the kitchen, and for the first time since I arrived, I inhale through my nose. The smell of sweet barbecue sauce rushes to my brain. I do a little dance in place. Jack cooked his famous barbecue ribs tonight. Being scared half to death is a small price to pay for this meal.

On cue, he comes back with two steaming plates of barbecue ribs slathered in sauce and places them on the table.

"Sit, sit, sit," he says, pulling out one of the tan-cushioned rattan dining chairs.

I sit down and gawk at the glistening ribs and smile. "This looks spectacular," I say, placing my napkin on my lap.

He raises a finger and winks. "I'm just getting warmed up." He runs back into the kitchen and returns with three plates balancing in his muscular arms: mashed potatoes, homemade mac and cheese, and corn on the cob. Jack has managed to drown all my anxiety in a sea of Southern cooking and carbs.

He places the plates on the table and pulls up a chair for himself. The table is dressed with a seasonal table runner, gold chargers, and gold-rimmed plates to match. An orange-stemmed candle resting in a gold candlestick flickers in the center of the table.

I raise my eyebrows. "My, my. You're really laying it on thick tonight."

He flashes a smile that feels like it should come with a *ting* sound.

"They canceled my fundraising meeting, so for the first time in this damn campaign, I had spare time on my hands. I know you've been killin' yourself with the office reno, and you're really doing me a solid with the Sampson case. I wanted to show you some appreciation."

"Well, it's working. What's this?" I ask, pointing to the red box at the center of the table.

"Geez, I nearly forgot the crown jewel. It's a small thank-you gift." He hands me the red box, which still looks eerily similar to the red letters in the Sampson and Tweed cases.

I untie the red bow and pull apart the box, and my breath

catches. A stunning gold-and-diamond tennis bracelet rests on a velvet pillow. I'm far from a jewelry expert, but this can't be less than ten thousand dollars.

I look up at Jack, who wears a proud smile on his face.

"Jack, this is beautiful."

"Isn't it?"

"Yeah, but this is too much. This must have cost a fortune."

He grimaces but then covers it with a heavy smile. He grabs the bracelet and places it on my wrist. It's so delicate that it lies on my wrist like a breeze. "Don't worry about the cost. I'm glad to do it. When I was younger, I had no money for gifts. I swore to myself that if I ever made a few bucks, I would spend it on the people I love."

"Yeah, but I've seen what you make on the city council."

He laughs, but I think I catch a flicker of hurt. "I'll grant you that. But you know, I did pretty well in consulting before I took this crazy public servant gig. Plus, it looks damn good on that wrist of yours."

I look down. I don't know how, but this ridiculously expensive bracelet makes my wrist appear more refined and dainty, like I should be enjoying gin and tonics at the club after a long day of doubles.

"Well, thank you. It's gorgeous." I remove the bracelet and put it in the box. "But I don't want this anywhere near these ribs."

He laughs. "Agreed. Speaking of, let's dig in."

We dive into the ribs, which taste as good as they look. Jack's sauce strikes the perfect blend of tang, sweetness, and spice. And he doesn't overdo it. It feels like every taste bud on your tongue is singing.

He puts down his ribs for a moment and grabs his fork to test the mashed potatoes. "I realize I cut you off earlier. You were saying the Sampson case has you on edge?"

I reluctantly put my ribs down and wipe a stray dot of sauce off my cheek. "Yeah, it looks like there's more than one murder."

He drops his fork and runs his fingers through his sandy locks. "What? You mean Sampson killed two people?"

"No, somebody killed two people. It can't be Sam, because he was incarcerated when the second victim was murdered."

"Who does your gut tell you it is?"

"I'm not sure yet. But I spoke to the archbishop yesterday and—"

"Wait." His forehead creases and his eyebrows pinch together. "You saw Archbishop Dinwiddie?"

"Yes, and I think he's hiding something."

Jack pushes out his chair and crosses his legs, biting his bottom lip repeatedly. He scratches his stubble, and I can hear the sound from across the table.

"Is something wrong?" I ask.

"Yeah, this night is a disaster."

My eyes soak in the spectacular spread and candlelight. "How is this a disaster?"

He keeps scratching his chin but raises the thumb of his free hand in the air and counts with his fingers. "Well, let me see... First, I scare you half to death and then spill beer all over myself. Second, I give you a gift and you basically ask me how I can afford it. Third, I ask you to make the Sampson case go away, and you expand the investigation. Fourth, you go to visit the archbishop without asking me and tell me he's hiding something when you know I need his support in this election. Finally, I have a mayoral debate tomorrow, and if this leaks to the media, I'm going to be answering questions about a murderer on the loose and why my girlfriend is attacking the Catholic Church. The *New York Post* lives for that shit. Wouldn't you say that qualifies as a disaster?"

He takes the napkin off his lap and throws it on the table like a petulant child.

"Are you serious?" I say, a scowl crossing my face. I know that's not the right reaction, but I can't believe how overdramatic he's being.

He purses his lips, rises from the table, and storms into our living room overlooking the park. He opens the door to the balcony and steps outside. Jack has a short fuse, so this isn't the first time I've seen him cool off on the balcony, literally and figuratively. I take a bite of my mashed potatoes. If he wants to pout, he can pout.

After a few minutes, I cave. I shake my head and put my fork down. I don't know if I'm more upset about Jack's outburst or walking away from the ribs.

"Hey," I say as I join him on the balcony. "I don't know why you're blaming me for this. I turned down the Sampson case. This was your idea."

He gazes at the glowing night sky. Steam from his breath floats over the balcony. He turns and gently grabs my shoulders, then brushes a few stray hairs from my face.

"I'm sorry. I'm not angry at you at all. And I don't blame you for this. I know you're trying to help me. I don't know what I was saying. I'm just frustrated. I feel like I can't catch a break. I try to plan a romantic dinner for you and mess that up. Godo's kicking my butt over this crime stuff. I'm begging people for money all day long. I haven't slept in two weeks. I don't know. Can we forget everything I said and start over?"

I peer into his sky-blue eyes and note the bloodshot in the whites. I give him a deep kiss and put my arms around his waist. I can feel the weight of his body.

"How about this? I'll run to the bedroom, change out of my work gear, and find a good mystery film. You grab the food and we can share a little dinner and a movie in bed."

He smiles his perfect triangle grin. It's somehow both honest and mischievous at the same time. "Are we at all worried about spilling barbecue sauce on the sheets?"

"I'm not. I might enjoy a little barbecue sauce on my pillow. Or I might pour some on you."

"Ooh, ma'am, things just got interesting." He pulls me close and kisses me, hard.

I push him off me and slap his butt. "Okay, get out of here. I'm going to go change."

He goes to the kitchen, and I make my way to the bedroom. I hang my coat up beneath Jack's endless collection of University of Texas hats. Before I change, I trod past Jack's seersucker bedspread, open the sliding glass doors, and take a moment to look out at Washington Square Park. The fresh air braces me. It's stunning on a cold, clear night with the lit-up arch overlooking the rustling trees. I can even glimpse a few stars.

But then I see it.

A dark figure standing on the sidewalk in the park. Wearing an ankle-length parka, a New York Yankees baseball cap, and a black respiratory mask.

Staring at me.

He's standing in the shadow of a lamppost, so I can't make him out, but I can definitely tell he's staring at me. Is it the same person from the other night?

Then I hear a faint whistle.

It's a familiar tune, one I've heard recently. A haunting, grief-filled melody.

My heart stops.

It's "Danny Boy."

The song Father Kenneally was humming before he died. The tune winds its way up my spine and tickles the hairs on my neck. Is this the man who killed Kenneally? Who killed Tweed?

I watch to see what he'll do next. But he stands there, stiff and straight, whistling and staring at me. His posture matches the style of his killings: still, composed, unhurried. I stand frozen, looking back at him. The images of Kenneally's and Tweed's contorted corpses run through my mind, and goose bumps crawl up my arms.

I hear Jack tromp up the stairs. As nonchalantly as I can, I turn and step inside, whisper-shouting to Jack. "Jack, Jack!" Finally, he hears me. He scampers into the room, holding two loaded plates of ribs and sides.

"What?" he whispers back.

I make a face and call him over with my finger. He places the plates down on the entertainment center and follows me onto the balcony. I point to the park, but the figure is gone. The park is silent.

"What am I looking at?" asks Jack.

I drop my head. Maybe I need some sleep. "It's nothing. Somebody in the park was watching me."

Jack puts his arm around me. "Really? What did they look like?"

"I couldn't tell. They were in the shadows."

Concern washes over his face. "Should I call the cops?"

I walk inside and plop onto the bed. Jack's got enough on his plate without worrying about being stalked. "No, it's probably nothing. Let's enjoy our night."

"Okay. But let me know if you change your mind. I want you to feel safe. In a month, I'll be mayor and we'll have our own security detail."

"Thanks. I have a feeling we might need it."

Jack returns to the kitchen to grab silverware and napkins while I change and settle into bed. I try to relax, but I can't. Too many questions swirl in my mind. What is the archbishop hiding? What was in the letter that Sam dropped off in Kenneally's office? Where is this killer getting the tetrodotoxin?

And now a much bigger question has landed in my lap.

Who is stalking me?

18

That night, I toss and turn, fading in and out of dreams, drifting into nightmares. By 5:30 a.m., I relent and slide out of bed. Per usual, Jack purrs away peacefully. They say if you want to know if someone committed a crime, you check their jail cell at night. The innocent ones can't sleep because they're trying to figure out how they got there. The guilty ones sleep soundly because they know how they got there. Somehow, I don't feel like the innocent one.

I shower, get dressed, and pitter-patter out of the bedroom, down the stairs, and into the kitchen. I open the stainless steel fridge. Great. It's stocked with fruit, vegetables, eggs, fresh cuts of meat—but not an ounce of Red Bull. I seriously consider digging through the recycling to find an unfinished can but decide that's one step too far, even for me.

Before I leave for the day, I pull up the Nest app on my

phone to see if Jack's security camera captured footage of my masked stalker last night. I scroll through a few hours' worth of footage but find nothing. He never walked in range of the camera. Begrudgingly, I throw on my coat and open the front door of Jack's apartment to reveal a rainy, misty darkness.

Of course it's raining.

I feel like 75 percent of the time I wake up in a foul mood, some type of rain is falling. It's as though God is up there watching me, sees my facial expression, and is like, *Cue the rain*. I grab the umbrella from Jack's antique stand and march out into the abyss. As I walk down the street, rain tapping my umbrella, I look over my shoulder. It's a habit now. I doubt I'll ever stop looking behind me.

Once I'm confident nobody is following me, I put in my earbuds and walk south on Wooster Street. I play my "Sad Mix," which is a heavy blend of Radiohead and Lana Del Rey, and embrace the misty air running across my face. My theory is, if you're in a dark mood, lean into it. I walk for a bit, pouting, and then the sweet glow of neon from a doughnut shop catches my eye. I tell myself that I deserve a treat on account of the rain. I'm the master of treat rationalizations. I closed a case today. I deserve a treat. I walked a lot today. I deserve a treat. I got out of bed today. I deserve a treat.

I order a dozen doughnuts—a perfect mixture of glazed, fritters, twists, and bear claws—and the baker gives me an extra strawberry frosted and a sugar-free Red Bull for the road. They invented the baker's dozen for people like me.

By the time I arrive at the office, my mood has upgraded from sour to serviceable. I scan the key card, open the external door to my building, fold up my umbrella, and smile to myself. I love getting to the office early. It rarely happens, because I enjoy sleeping in way more than getting to the office early. But on the rare occasion it does happen, I soak it in. Nothing beats the silence and emptiness of an office before the chaos ensues.

I trundle up the worn stairs and remove my obscenely crowded key chain. As I pull it out of my pocket, the keys slip from my fingers and clang onto the floor. I bend down to pick them up.

That's when I hear a second sound. And it's not my keys.

This one is coming from inside my office. It sounded like a chair sliding.

My neck hairs stand on end.

It's six in the morning.

Kenny, Momo, and Mary never arrive before seven.

Who is in my office?

I recall the watcher in the park from last night. The dark coat, the Yankees hat, the black face mask. The whistling hums in my ears: "Oh, Danny boy…the pipes, the pipes are calling…"

I remove my pistol from its holster and flip the safety.

I check the door handle, but it's still locked. Could I be imagining it?

Crouched against the doorframe, I slide the key into the lock, holding my key chain with my other hand to prevent it from clinking. It goes in smoothly. I turn the key and rotate the brass doorknob one millimeter at a time.

Once it clicks, I ease the door open but stay crouched behind the frame. The door squeaks as it moves. I listen for any activity.

Silence.

I keep the gun at my side in case someone's waiting next to the entrance. I stay low and peer around the corner.

There's no one.

I open the door farther.

Nothing.

The office is empty.

I step into the space with my gun raised, half expecting someone to jump up from behind a desk. The ghosts of my past flash through my mind. I check behind Mary's desk, in the conference room, in Kenny's office…

There's nobody he—

My phone rings, and I flinch so hard, I nearly pull the trigger. I put my hand to my chest and look at the screen.

It's Shavali.

Of course. Who else would call me this early? I safety my pistol and place it back in the holster underneath my sweater.

"Good morning," I say as I pace back into my office, my eyes still scanning the room for anything I've missed.

"Ah, Hazel, my love. You're awake."

Two seconds in, and she's already condescending to me. That's got to be a record.

"Yes, I am. At the office already, actually."

"My, my, my. My little Haze is finally growing up."

I flop down in my new ergonomic desk chair and fire up my computer. "All riiiight. Take it easy. I remember a couple of mornings I had to hold your hair back over a toilet bowl."

"Touché," she says with a melodic laugh. "I was calling to get a status update on how things are coming along. I've got a meeting scheduled with opposing counsel tomorrow, and I want to know if you've been able to strengthen our hand at all."

I pull up our case management software and scan the file to see if Kenny or Momo have added anything since yesterday. Momo's entered a few more notes about tetrodotoxin, but that's about it. "Yes and no. You remember Fred Tweed? The billionaire who died of food poisoning?"

"Yeah?"

"It wasn't food poisoning. He received a red letter and was poisoned in the same manner as Father Kenneally. Not only that, but Samuel was already in prison when Tweed died."

"That's spectacular news! Well…sad about the murder and all, but good news about the killer, yeah."

As she's talking, I notice Kenny and Momo slinking through the door. Kenny's eyes pop when he sees me, and they both give me an awkward wave. I guess everybody's working early today.

I return my attention to Shavali. "Yeah. Of course, this doesn't clear him of the Kenneally murder. The DA could argue that Kenneally was a copycat killing, or someone on the outside assisted Sam. But it might give you enough to make the DA wobble."

"Perfect. I'll set a meeting with Sam for today straightaway. He's going to be quite pleased."

"Okay, but there's one minor issue." I grab a pen and chew on the end as I say it.

"What's that?"

"Tweed was a big donor to Old St. Patrick's, so he may have had contact with Sam, which could actually make things worse for your guy."

I can hear Shavali's sigh through the phone.

"Jesus, Hazel."

"What?"

"I asked you to find evidence to exculpate the boy, not incriminate him."

I feel the blood rushing to my face. Ungrateful b... I'm doing her a favor, and she complains about how I'm doing it. I spin the pen in between my fingers.

"I'm not incriminating him. I'm telling you the facts so you don't get ambushed. Your job is to defend him. My job is to investigate and report on what I find."

"Yeah, but I don't want you wasting your time and mine chasing down leads that implicate my client."

I look at the ceiling and bite my knuckle. "Wasting your time? I'm doing this as a favor for you. You don't think I have better things to do? You're not even paying me."

Silence. I can't tell whether I struck a chord with her or she's remembering that she needs me. "I'm sorry, Hazel. I'm under a lot of pressure on this, and I'm taking it out on you."

"Why do you care about this case so much, anyway?"

She pauses again. I feel like I'm talking to Archbishop Dinwiddie. "This is between you and me, but I'm currently being considered for Attorney-in-Chief of the Legal Aid Society. Obviously, there's some resistance because I'm young for the job, but if I win this case, I'm a lock."

I take a pull from my Red Bull. No surprise, this is about her career. I love Shavali, but there's always an angle with her. Now I have not only my boyfriend's political campaign on my conscience but also my friend's legal career. I don't know why part of me thought she might care about this case because it's a poor, innocent, messed-up kid. But that's Shavali for you. She's a roller coaster ride that takes you where she wants to go. I never liked this job, and I like it even less now.

As if sensing my hesitation, she says, "Please, Hazel. I'm sorry I got snippy. Let's visit Samuel and share the good news and then cut out early and celebrate with apps and cocktails. Then, as far as you're concerned, the case is over."

I groan. "Fine. I'll meet you at Rikers in two hours," I say.

I hang up the phone and look out my office window, shaking my head.

The image of Father K.'s pale face and the bloody depiction of hell flash through my mind. Regardless of what happens with Sam, I know this case is far from over.

19

step out of my office, still stewing from my call with Shavali.
Mary hangs her coat in the closet, whistling the song "Whistle
While You Work." Sometimes I think she'd be much more at
home in Mayberry than in New York City. She turns and sees the
look on my face and immediately stops whistling.

"Oh dear. You look like you had a rough night. I don't think
I've ever seen you here so early."

I've never heard Mary say *Oh dear* simply from looking at
me. That's the equivalent of any other New Yorker eyeing you
and saying, *Oh shit.* Tough way to start the morning. I snatch a
bear claw from the box and take a bite.

"I don't want to talk about it," I say as I grab the box of
doughnuts and bring them to the conference room. "Everybody
in the conference room."

Mary follows me, grabbing some plates and napkins on her

way. I think the trail of doughnut crumbs I'm dropping on the floor is giving her anxiety. Kenny and Momo slink in with frazzled looks on their faces. I bet they thought they were going to have a nice, quiet morning of catch-up work, like I did. They join me and grab doughnuts while I stand at the whiteboard. The board shows a checklist of the information I asked them to gather. I tap the first item on the list, *tetrodotoxin*, with my marker and point to Momo. "Momo, what did you learn about tetrodotoxin?"

Momo fires up our CROSStrax case management software on her laptop.

"Tetrodotoxin is a guanidinium compound synthesized by bacteria in animals such as puffer fish. Its molecular formula is $C_{11}H_{17}N_3O_8$."

"Carbon, hydrogen, nitrogen, and oxygen," says Mary, like the class know-it-all.

"Teacher's pet," Kenny says to her with a smile.

Momo ignores them and keeps her alert eyes locked on me. "It is highly poisonous, but in extremely small doses is used clinically for pain relief for cancer and migraine patients. I spoke with the major tetrodotoxin vendors. All U.S.-based tetrodotoxin orders this year have been submitted by professional labs."

"How do they know?"

"To purchase tetrodotoxin, the buyer must complete an end-user certificate, which is verified by the seller."

"Could someone fake it?"

Momo pauses and shifts left and right. Her words are halting, matching the cadence of her native Japanese. "Possibly, but they would need to have access to the labs and intercept the shipment before it arrived, because the manufacturers won't ship to a residential address."

"Okay, I want you to talk to the labs an—"

She lifts her hand again. I cock my head and shoot her a raised eyebrow. She puts it down. "Sorry. I spoke with the labs this morning. I obtained an order list from Hello Bio, Biotium, and others, and verified with the universities and labs. They confirmed they had placed and received these orders."

My eyes widen at Momo's zest for casework. She reminds me of a younger version of myself. I decide to test her. "Nice work. What about black market purchases?"

She shifts in her seat and traces her fingers along the scar on her neck. "What do you mean?"

"I mean, not all murderers follow the rules, Momo."

Her cheeks flush. "I…I'm not sure."

"Okay. Look into it."

"How?"

"Kenny can show you how to access the few dark web markets that the Feds haven't shut down yet. We use Tor and a surveillance account you can borrow." She puts her head down and nods. I keep rolling. "And what about the puffer fish?"

"What about them?"

"Could someone have purchased puffer fish and then stored the poison?"

Momo freezes up, her face scarlet. I don't think she's used to being questioned. "I guess so. But they would have to remove the poisons and convert it into pill form. That would be extremely difficult."

"I understand that, but we can't take anything for granted. Reach out to every puffer fish seller and see what they know."

She nods. "Yes, I will do that."

I take another bite of my doughnut. I can feel the sugar kicking in now. I'm on a roll. I'll probably collapse into a heap around two p.m., but that's a problem for another time.

I tap the next item on the whiteboard, *Bible*, and then point to Mary.

"Mary, what do you have for me?" Mary straightens in her chair. "Oh, not much. The verse in the second letter. That was also a red-letter verse. Something Jesus said."

"Not a surprise."

"No. This verse is from Revelation. But it is also from the Douay–Rheims Version of the bible. The drawing is a copy of *Casting the Damned into Hell* by Hans Memling. Another painting from the late Middle Ages."

I think of the Douay–Rheims Bible Dinwiddie removed from his desk. "More backing for our theory that the person is older."

"Yes, and probably a man."

"Why do you say that?"

"Well, I think I read once that most serial killers are men."

Kenny leans forward in his chair. "That's true, but not all of them."

I put my hand on Kenny's shoulder. "Easy, big fella. Nobody's attacking men, even though you all are serial killers." Momo and Mary laugh. Kenny takes it, knowing he's outnumbered. I turn back to Mary.

"Is that the only reason, Mary, or did you discover something else?"

She sighs and plays with her pendant. "Well, I had a hunch, so I called a bookstore yesterday and asked them who buys Douay–Rheims Bibles?"

"Look at you, crushing detective work. I love it."

Her smile widens. "Thanks. Anyway, they all said mostly men buy Douay–Rheims Bibles. One even said he'd never seen a woman buy a Douay–Rheims Bible."

"Hmm, did he say anything about age?"

"Oh yeah, one guy said something funny I remembered. He said it is either young men buying their first or old men buying their last."

I make a couple of notes on the whiteboard. None of this is rock-solid, but it gives us a profile. "What about social media? Did you find anything?"

"I did, but unfortunately it contradicts everything I just said."

"How's that?"

"Well, a bunch of people posted angry messages on social media about the church's refusal to pay the settlement, but nothing that seemed extraordinarily angry or pointed. However, I did notice that Arika Tweed posted."

"Really? What did Mrs. Tweed have to say?"

Mary puts on her glasses and reads the post on her phone. "'This is despicable. After all the money that Fred and so many others have given to the church, it's outrageous that they won't compensate these poor people. @archbishopdinwiddie, make this right. God will judge you.'"

"Interesting. That will be a spicy topic of conversation for my interview with her tomorrow. Great work, Mary."

She blushes and smiles.

I point my marker at Kenny. "Last but not least."

Kenny does a fake bow in his chair and runs a hand back and forth through his tennis ball haircut. Is he wearing the same outfit as yesterday? I'll have to make fun of him about that later.

"You want good news or bad news first?"

"Bad news."

"The bad news is, Bobby was right. The typewriter was a complete dead end. The Brother Charger II was the most popular model in the U.S. from 1985 to 1988. Whoever was using it has probably owned it for years or purchased it online."

"Yeah, I hit the same dead end with stationery."

"Also, Sam was right. Kenneally didn't have any visitors to his office the day he died other than Sister Teresa. I watched the video of her entering and exiting, and the exchange appeared perfectly pleasant and normal."

"There's nothing pleasant and normal about that woman. I thought she was going to lock Mary and me in the catacombs. Will you do some more digging into her background?"

Kenny makes a note on his laptop. "Sure, no problem."

"So, what's the good news?"

"The good news is, I had some time to tinker with the security-footage video in IVE. I zoomed in on the envelope at the moment he's dropping it off. There's no wax seal."

He stands and spins his laptop screen so we can see it. The black-and-white video shows a close-up of a hand holding an envelope, fold face down. Kenny has clearly adjusted the contrast to brighten it, but it's still barely visible through the grain.

Momo, Mary, and I all lean in to see what Kenny's talking

about. He hits play, and the screen shows a hand flip the envelope underneath the door.

"Did you see it?" he says, cheek balls pushing his eyes into a proud squint.

The three of us stare at each other, confused.

"Ah, no," I say.

"I know. It's grainy. I wish I could do that 'enhance' thing they do in the movies. Let me slow it down." The video starts again in slow motion. It's only for an instant, and it's incredibly blurry, but that envelope is definitely not wax-sealed.

Momo claps, but her eyebrows bunch. "I don't understand. Why didn't the police find this?"

"Because they didn't want to find it," I say. "Marcos has his guy, and he's going to ignore anything that doesn't serve his purpose." I smack Kenny on the back. "Man, talk about burying the lede! I'm over here talking about tetrodotoxin, and Kenny's found some actual evidence that could clear Samuel."

"Maybe," says Kenny. "But we're not any closer to finding the actual killer."

"One step at a time, my son. One step at a time." I shoot Mary a wink. "As a wise woman once said, 'Patience is a virtue.'"

20

As I drive across the Bridge of Pain to Rikers Island, my mood fades back to gray. There's something about this place that wriggles inside you. All the dysfunction, all the rage, sticks in your gut when you arrive and follows you home when you leave. I observe the dull concrete wasteland and am reminded of the expression *Prison is an expensive way of making bad people worse.*

I enter the building and meet Shavali at the security entrance. She's wearing a navy-blue pin-striped pantsuit that makes her look like the prime minister of India. I bury my negativity and force a cocky smile onto my face. "Who's your favorite PI?"

She gives me one of her stiff British hugs, squints, and twists her mouth. "You are?"

"That's right." We pass through the metal detector, and I

hand her the blurred screenshot of Sam sliding the letter under Kenneally's office door. Without context, it's indecipherable.

She peeks at it and furrows her brow. "And remind me, why are you one of my favorite PI's?"

"Because we can prove the letter that Samuel dropped off wasn't the threat letter."

"How?"

"I'll save you the gory details, but long story short, we found a section of video where you can see the underside of the letter for a split second, and it doesn't have the wax seal."

Shavali hugs me again, but this time it's a real, hearty American hug. "Hazel, you're brilliant."

"Kenny's brilliant, actually, but I'm happy to take credit."

She pauses outside the entrance to the inmate meeting rooms and rubs her hands together like an evil billionaire. "This is fantastic. This will be enough to convince the DA to fold."

"It should." I nod absentmindedly and run my fingernail across my lip. The footsteps and chitchat of lawyers, security guards, and administrators echo through the lobby.

Shavali scowls. "What?"

"What?"

"I know that look, Haze. What are you thinking?"

"Nothing. I'd still like to know the contents of that letter he delivered. I have a feeling it might lead us to whoever killed Father K. and Tweed."

Shavali crosses her arms and straightens on her four-inch heels. She leans over me so I can feel her height. "Who cares what was in the letter? There's probably a reason that he doesn't want to talk about it. Maybe it's a love letter. Maybe it's a confession about something embarrassing. Maybe it's a list of his favorite video games. Whatever it is, I doubt it's going to help Samuel, so I'd rather not know."

"Shay, two people were murdered, and Sam might have information that could help us find their killer."

"I understand that. But that's not your job, and it's certainly not my job. That's Marcos and the NYPD's job."

I open my mouth to respond but then reconsider. "Fine, let's go talk to him." I gesture toward the interview rooms.

She nods triumphantly, and we head inside the secured area. A security guard escorts us into the interview room—the same one where we last met Sam. We take our seats at the laminate table. I spot a crack that wasn't there the last time. Someone must have lost their temper.

The guard ushers Sam into the room. He's not the same boy I met last time. A bruise marks his right cheek, and a fresh cut hovers over his left eye. The other inmates have beaten the bravado out of him. I feel for the kid, but I can't say I'm surprised. Scrawny smart-asses don't do well in jail. Shavali was right not to delay the trial. He could be dead before he ever gets there.

"Did you two figure out how to get me out of this shithole? I can't take it in here no more," he says as he sits down. He tends to his hair, and his foot taps furiously against the floor. The hurt vibrates from him.

"It's lovely to see you, too, Samuel," says Shavali. She reminds me of those British nannies from the show *Nanny 911*. They'd enter houses filled with screaming kids and broken-down parents but never lose their cool, always keeping a stiff upper lip and perfect manners. "As a matter of fact, we did discover a way to spring you from this 'shithole,' as you call it."

Sam leaps forward in his chair like a kid who's found out he's going to Disneyland. For a moment he's forgotten his laid-back, too-cool persona. His voice jumps an octave. "Really?"

"Yes. My colleague Hazel here and her team analyzed the security video and found that the letter you dropped off didn't have the wax seal that was on the threat letter."

Sam slaps the table and smiles, then winces and rubs his cheek. "See, I told you that shit wasn't mine."

"Indeed, you did. We also may have found something else that might help your case."

"Really?"

"Have you ever heard of Fred Tweed?"

As she speaks, I watch his facial expressions and movements. Does he shift? Does he make eye contact? He stays still—or at least, relatively still; the legs are always shaking—and meets Shavali's eyes.

"Yeah, the rich guy? Why?"

"He died while you were in jail. He received a red letter and was killed by the same poison that killed Father Kenneally."

Sam's eyes widen as the realization dawns. "Wait, you mean this is some serial killer shit?"

Shavali raises a hand to calm him. "Possibly. And that's what we'll contend to the DA."

"So, you'll get me out of here?" His voice cracks, and his eyes shine with hope, reminding me he's still a kid.

"I'm not making any promises, but I'll do my best."

"How long will it take?"

"I'll talk with the DA today, but I don't want you to get your hopes up. There's no guarantee that he'll agree to drop the case. And even if he does, it could be weeks or months."

Sam slumps in his chair, and his lower lip trembles. He's put up a good fight, but Rikers is finally breaking him. "Is there anything I can do?"

She shakes her head. "Not right now. For now, I need you to hang tight."

I raise my index finger. "One second, Shay, I actually think there is something he can do." Shavali coughs, as she knows what's coming.

Sam leans forward in his chair, mouth open wide. "What? Anything."

"I need you to tell me the contents of the envelope you gave to Father Kenneally."

His face drops, and he stares at the floor. He scrapes at a hangnail on his thumb. "Why? I thought you said you had enough evidence already."

"We said we *might* have enough. But the best way to exculpate you is to identify an alternate suspect. There's someone walking the streets who killed two people. They're going to do it again. It's only a matter of time. If you have information that could help us find him, you need to produce it. Then I guarantee you'll walk."

He slinks in his chair and puts both hands over his face. "I told you, I can't talk about that."

"Why?"

"I just can't."

"Was it a love letter?"

"What? No."

"Are you sure? Red envelope. Under a door…"

"No, man. What, you think I'm gay? Believe me, I'm not gay."

"I don't care if you're gay or straight. I'm trying to under-stand why you won't tell us."

"I can't."

I feel my voice rising and my eyebrows pinching. "Sam, I see the cut on your face. The bruises on your arm. How much longer do you think you'll last in here? Do you want to die in jail or tell us the truth and live your life?"

He stares at the ceiling, weighing his options. I see my chance to break him.

"And even if Shavali works her magic, the police may let you go now, but you're still in their sights. They'll keep coming after you. And that's the cops. What about the other people? Until this is resolved, they're going to make up their own theories. They're still going to think you did it. They're going to wonder what was in that letter. Do you want that?"

He digs at his hangnail harder. His knee pops up and down like an oil derrick. His eyes water with fear. "No."

"Do you want people saying you're a murderer?"

"No."

"That you had an affair with your priest?"

"No."

I see he's losing his cool. I slam the table. "Then tell us. What was in that letter?"

"I was asking him for money!" he shouts.

I freeze, afraid that if I move, he'll stop talking.

I watch his shoulders rise as though the weight has literally been lifted. I lean back to give him space to speak.

A pregnant pause fills the room.

After several seconds, he lets out a heavy sigh, rubs his drooping eyes with the palms of his hands, and slumps his elbows onto the table.

"A few months before Father K....before he died, I came back to the church late because I left my phone in the office."

"What time was that?"

"Probably ten o'clock. When I got there, I heard music coming from the catacombs. It was weird because it was hip-hop, a Drake song, and no one ever goes down there except the tourist groups. It's creepy as fuck."

I nod, remembering my visit with Sister Teresa.

"I went downstairs and turned the corner, and that's when I saw it."

"Saw what?"

"Father K. and some other dudes with some girls."

My heart drops, and I think back to Mia and the St. Agnes girls. A wave of nausea washes over me.

"Young girls?"

"Nah, nothing like that. Older girls like you two. Except professionals, you know."

"Prostitutes."

"Yeah."

Shavali stands up and leans on the table. "Wait, I want to make sure I'm understanding you correctly. You're saying that Father Kenneally and other men hosted a party with prostitutes in the catacombs?"

"Yeah."

"How did you know they were prostitutes?"

He raises an eyebrow and curls the right side of his lips. "You could tell. They was wearing leather skirts, and fishnets, and bras and shit."

"Okay. Go on."

"Yeah, it was crazy. They had it all tricked out. They had candles lit all over the place and some cots on the floor. One girl was dancing. It was like a freaky club down there."

"And what about the men? How many were there? Did you know any of them?"

"No. It was dark. I could barely see. And I was focused on the girls. I know there were four of them. A bunch of old dudes—I assumed they were priests, but I don't know. Three white dudes and a brother in a wheelchair."

Shavali and I shoot each other a look, eyes bulging out of our heads. She sits back down, unable to resist what she's hearing. "What did you do then?"

"What do you think I did? I got the fuck out of there."

"And then what?"

"Then a few days later, I started thinking, Father K. definitely doesn't want people knowing about this. So I thought I could probably make a little extra cash."

I lean back in my chair and run my fingers through my hair. "Let me get this straight. You were attempting to blackmail him?"

"I guess you could say that. I thought I deserved over fifteen dollars an hour for keeping that shit secret."

"But, to be clear, the letter you delivered the night Kenneally died said what?"

Sam takes a long breath and shakes his head. I can see his time in jail weighing on him.

"It said, *'Give me five G's, or I tell everyone about the sex parties'*, with an address and time to deliver the money."

Shavali taps her long nails on the table. "I don't understand. Why couldn't you tell me this from the beginning?"

He crosses his arms and looks up at the ceiling. For once, the fidgeting stops. It's as though he's accepted his fate and is ready to face it. He fears what will happen if he talks, but he's more afraid of another month in Rikers.

"Because I was scared, okay?"

"Of what? Being charged with blackmail?"

"Yeah. That and…"

"And what? I know that's not all you were afraid of Samuel."

His mouth dries and his voice shakes. "The day Father K. died, I found a note slipped in my desk."

"What did it say?" Shavali asks.

His eyes fall to the floor. He picks at his nails, and I see a tear roll down his cheek. He sniffs and swallows hard.

"It said, *'One word about this, and you're next.'*"

"Do you know who wrote it?"

"I think so."

"Who?"

"Archbishop Dinwiddie."

21

That was interesting," I say to Shavali as we step outside the detention center. I tie my hair into a bun to keep it out of the wind. I'm conflicted. I'm glad we found something that will free Sam from this hellhole, but I'm devastated about what he said about Father K. I'm still hoping it's not true, but I've found when someone dies the way he died, there's usually a reason.

A frosty wind whips through the Rikers Island parking lot as we stroll to our cars, reminding me that winter is right around the corner. It's the kind of wind that cuts through you no matter how many layers you're wearing. The sound of I-278 sharpens in the dry air.

Shavali throws her camel coat on like a countess with a cape. "Yes, that was quite interesting, indeed." She surprises me by giving me a big hug and holding it for a few seconds. "Haze, I can't thank you enough for everything you've done. I haven't been much of a friend to you, but you were there for me when I needed it, and I won't forget it."

I extricate myself from the hug and blush and punch her on the shoulder. "It was nothing. I was happy to do it."

"Nothing? You proved that the envelope Samuel delivered wasn't the threat letter. You identified a second murder. And you got Samuel to share a potential motive for the killer. Because of you, the DA will probably drop the prosecution. You saved a kid's life, and you got me a promotion. Not a bad week's work. You've earned as many tacos and margaritas as you can handle."

As she's talking, I throw my coat on in a much less dramatic fashion, getting one arm stuck in an armhole as I put it on. Within ten seconds, I'm cooking in my jacket. It reminds me of another thing I hate about winter: my underarms are in a permanent state of sweat. I'm outside in a down coat, then inside in overheated conference rooms, then back in a coat. By day's end, it's like a Louisiana swamp in there.

"Don't thank me yet," I say. "There's more where that came from."

"What do you mean?"

"The archbishop. We need to nail his ass to the wall."

She looks out at the choppy gray-blue river and flips her hair from one side to the other. Then she turns to me, sighs, and grabs both my hands. "Please don't do this to me?"

"Don't do what? The archbishop could be behind these killings."

"Hazel, please. We don't even know if what Samuel is saying is true. He could be besmirching a powerful person to protect himself. Even if it is true, it doesn't mean he murdered Kenneally."

"I agree. But don't you think we owe it to society to investigate?"

"No. Maybe the police do, but we don't. He's an extremely powerful man with powerful friends, and the last thing we need is to alienate powerful people. And it's probably the last thing Jack needs as well."

Hearing her mention Jack's name sends me off the edge. I rip my hands out of hers and point a finger at her. "Thanks, but I'm pretty sure I know what Jack needs better than you." I turn and open my car door.

"Hazel, I didn't mean it—"

"Don't worry about it. You worry about you, and I'll worry about finding this killer. You're welcome." I slam the door and grab the wheel.

She says something more, but I don't hear her over my car's music.

I peel out of the parking lot and speed toward Manhattan, fuming at Shavali's audacity. After all I've done for her, that she has the gall to ask me to stand down blows my mind. There's a murderer out there, and she couldn't care less.

I pick up my phone and search for the number to the archbishop's office. I know I shouldn't do this. I should take a moment and consider my actions. Part of me knows Shavali is right: investigating the archbishop isn't a stellar career move. But another part of me knows that is why I must do it. Because powerful people count on the Shavalis of the world. Too selfish, too greedy, too ambitious, too poor, too powerless, or too scared to hold anyone's feet to the fire. If I don't do it, no one will.

I find the number and dial, taking out my anger on the gas pedal. As I do, another frigid gust of wind blows across the water, and my car feels like it's going to be thrown into the river. The phone rings and my hands shake, but I don't know if it's from the cold, my frustration, or the looming confrontation with Dinwiddie.

A voice answers as I merge onto the Williamsburg Bridge. I can tell from the frigid tone that it's Sister Teresa, the archbishop's assistant. Somehow, her iciness crackles through the phone. I summon my kindest inflection and prepare to be stonewalled.

"Hello, Sister Teresa. This is Hazel Cho, the private investigator. I met with you the other day."

"Yes, I know who you are."

I swear my phone just got colder. "Yes, um, I was wondering if the archbishop is available. I have a few follow-up questions for him."

"Hold, please."

Handel's *Messiah* plays in the background, a welcome change from the instrumental versions of Michael Bolton songs that I'm used to. The music stops, and the line picks up. I brace myself to argue with Sister Teresa about why she should put me through, but to my surprise, it's a man's voice on the other end.

"This is Archbishop Dinwiddie."

I notice that his voice carries none of the deep confidence of yesterday. Today it shakes. I was prepared to bust him for cavorting with prostitutes and threatening a teenager, but now I'm off-balance.

"Oh, Archbishop. This is Hazel Cho. Thanks for taking my call."

"No thanks needed. As a matter of fact, I was about to call you."

His words sound cheery, but there's a sadness buried beneath them. Something's not right. I change lanes to exit and nearly collide with a car in my blind spot.

"Really. Why were you going to call me?"

"I…uh…I realized I may have been a little rough on you the other day."

I jerk my car into the parking lane of Delancey Street, nearly causing a five-car pileup. A chorus of honks sounds outside my window. I hit the brakes and let traffic whiz by.

"I appreciate you saying that," I say. But in my mind, I'm thinking, *You're damn right you were.*

"And there's some information I'd like to share with you that may be of use in your investigation. If you're available, I'd like to meet with you tomorrow at nine a.m."

"I can make that work. Is there something in particular you'd like to discuss?" I'm hoping he wants to come clean about his activities with Father Kenneally and the note.

He pauses. His breaths come in fast succession. I want to reach through the phone and slap him and shout *Hurry up!* Finally, he speaks. "Yes, but I'd rather not talk about it on the phone. Better to discuss in person."

I flip on my turn signal and ease back into traffic. One of the golden rules of being a private investigator is, when someone wants to talk, you don't wait. You move heaven and earth to interview them, because you need to prevent anything or anyone influencing them before you. Not a friend, not an enemy, not even their conscience. "I'm actually in my car, heading back into the city. I could come to your office now if you'd like. What's the saying... 'Don't put off for tomorrow what you can do today'?"

"That is the saying—but in this case, it's unnecessary. Besides, I'm walking out of the office as we speak. I have a fundraiser this evening that I must attend. Come by my office tomorrow."

"Are you sure? I have a couple of items I'd like to discuss with you."

"Yes, I'm sure. Duty calls. There will be plenty of time to speak tomorrow."

I groan and slam my palm on the steering wheel. Cars rip by me, offering me middle fingers and horns for my indecision. "Understood, but I need to ask you one quick question. It's about something that Samuel Sampson saw. You and Father Kenneally—"

"Come by my office at nine a.m. tomorrow. We'll speak then."

"But—"

The line goes dead.

22

After cursing the archbishop out in my mind, I park my car a couple of blocks from my place and then march to the Franklin Street subway station. Jack's debate starts in an hour, and I don't want to be late. Commuters jam the station, heading home after a long day at the office, but I don't notice them. I'm in one of those trances where my mind is somewhere else but my body keeps moving toward its destination. Next thing I know, ten minutes have gone by and I have to double-check the subway map to make sure I didn't miss my stop.

I board the 1 train and wedge myself next to a woman in a McDonald's uniform on her way home from work. I can smell the fries and grilled onions on her, but for once, I'm not thinking about food. A weathered man in a stained gray T-shirt sings an off-key rendition of "(Sittin' On) The Dock of the Bay" by Otis Redding, but I don't hear him.

The archbishop's words echo in my ears.

There's some information I'd like to share with you.

I run through the case in my head to distract myself from the thought, although the case isn't much better. We have almost zero hard evidence. No fingerprints, no DNA, no purchase records for the letters, typewriter, or poison. No video. The thought stops me. Video. I make a note to myself to check the video at Tweed's house. The killer or an accomplice had to visit him to deliver the poison. Maybe something will jump out on camera. But unless we get something on video or Momo digs up a tetrodotoxin buyer, we've got squat for hard evidence.

What about the softer stuff? That's not much better. We know this is a serial killer. We know that the method is poison, likely delivered in pill form. We know that the first killing occurred right after the church's refusal to pay the child abuse settlement, but I'm suspecting the timing of that might have been a coincidence given Tweed's death months later. We know that Kenneally and maybe the archbishop were involved in illicit sexual activities, and that they, along with Tweed, are all linked to Old St. Patrick's. We know the killer is a religious zealot, likely an older man, based on the typical profile of murderers and his use of the Douay–Rheims Bible. The only flaw in that logic is the poison, which is typically used by women.

In summary, we don't know shit.

The train car screeches to a halt, and I snap out of my trance. Lincoln Center. My stop. I take a deep breath and steady myself. Jack doesn't need a paranoid Hazel right now. He needs a rock.

I enter the studio, which is much smaller than I would have expected. I guess it's true that everything looks bigger on TV. A nervous assistant guides me back to the green room where Jack is getting ready. This is another disappointment. *Green room* sounds cool, but really it's a small, dumpy waiting room with a stained couch, makeup chair, and mirror.

"Speak of the devil," says Jack with a boyish smile as I enter. "I was telling Sheila here about my smokin' hot girlfriend. I'm so glad you made it." Sheila applies foundation to his face. He looks like a blonder Kennedy. He's wearing a white shirt, bloodred tie, and navy-blue houndstooth suit pants. I know the election is close, but how can anyone vote for another candidate, if for no other reason than if Jack wins, you can stare at him for four years?

"Of course I made it. I wouldn't miss this for the world." I give him a kiss on the top of the head. "I'd kiss you on the lips, but I don't want to ruin your pretty makeup job."

"Just puttin' a little lipstick on this pig."

The makeup lady releases a fawning laugh. I bet she was done with his makeup fifteen minutes ago and is now stalling so she can drool over him.

"And a damn fine pig you are," I say. "I'll let you focus. Good luck. I know you're going to crush it tonight."

"Thanks, bubs. I appreciate you being here. I saved a seat for you front and center so I can look at your gorgeous face the whole evening."

"You sure that's a good idea? You might get distracted by my beauty and forget your talking points."

"True, but it's a risk I'm willing to take." He shoots me a wink.

Sheila finishes her work and removes the tissue from around Jack's collar. He stands and stretches his back.

I grab his suit coat off the door hook and hand it to him. "All right, don't say I didn't warn you. Do you need anything?"

He puts on his suit coat and looks around the room. "No, I think I'm all set. How do I look?"

Sheila blurts out, "You look amazing," and then catches herself.

I laugh. I'm used to other women embarrassing themselves in front of him.

"I couldn't have said it better myself. You look amazing. I'm so proud of you." I lean in and give him a delicate kiss, careful not to touch his makeup. Then I give him a slap on the butt. "Now, go kick Godo's ass."

He gives me another kiss. Ugh, I wish we could skip the debate and have some fun in the green room, but duty calls. "Thanks, bubs," he says. "I'll see you after the show."

I exit the green room and take my seat in the audience. It's a small space with approximately thirty chairs set up for friends and family. I say hello to Jack's mom and a few acquaintances, then sit.

The lights drop in the audience section and rise on stage, and the debate begins. Jack mouths the words *I love you* and gives me a thumbs-up from the side of the podium. I glance at Sandy, who wears a suit two sizes two big and a clashing striped shirt and plaid tie.

An overly tanned news anchor with silver hair and face makeup that looks like the makeup artist applied it with a putty knife introduces the candidates. For the next hour, the debate proceeds similarly to the other two debates that preceded it. Sandy, with his salamander face and bug eyes, attacks Jack for being soft on crime, and Jack, with his movie-star looks and glib charm, prods Sandy about how he made his money over-charging for pharmaceuticals. Forty minutes in, I'm struggling to keep my mind from drifting to the case. But then, with one phrase, the tone of the debate changes.

Sandy says, "Folks, Jack Powell talks a lot about public safety, but how is he supposed to keep us safe when he can't even keep his own supporters alive?"

Jack's mouth drops open. "What are you talking about?"

Sandy smiles, and his tongue darts out to his lips again. "I'm talking about Fred Tweed, the Ponzi-scheme billionaire and donor of yours who is now dead. I'm talking about Father Sean Kenneally, another supporter of yours, who is now dead."

Rage flickers on Jack's face, and his hands clutch the lectern. Then he gathers himself. "Sandy, that's low, even for you. To use the tragic death of two people for your own political purposes is beyond the pale."

It's a solid answer, but judging from Sandy's face, it's the answer that he was expecting and hoping for.

"You're right, Jack. Those deaths were a tragedy. But, folks, what Jack Powell isn't telling you is that these weren't accidental deaths; they were murders. An eye for an eye, tooth for a tooth." An audible gasp comes from the audience, and Godo can barely con-tain his glee. Even the debate moderator is speechless. "Not only that, they were murdered by the same man. A man who sent each of them red envelopes containing threats days before they died." Godo holds up a prop red letter in his hands for effect. "That's right. The Red-Letter Serial Killer is on the loose in our city, and Jack Powell and his cronies in city hall have been covering it up."

I sit with my jaw on the floor, watching this train wreck, unable to do anything about it. How could Sandy know all this? I just learned it myself. Could he have a contact in the NYPD? The archbishop's office? This case was hard enough before the media knew about it. Now this will be front-page news.

Phone screens light up around me as the spectators text the news. Journalists sprint up the aisles to call their newsrooms. The chatter becomes so loud that the moderator pauses the debate and pleads for silence. The Red-Letter Serial Killer. I can see the Netflix documentary now.

I look at Jack, and my heart breaks.

The spotlights burrow down on him, and camera flashes shower him in a flickering light. He looks at Godo, who is sneering and posturing, and his jaw clenches, and a resigned expression marks his face. I expect him to yell, to gesticulate, to bicker, to explain how absurd these accusations are. But he doesn't. He stares deep into my eyes for five seconds that feel like an hour and gives me a pinched smile. Then he simply folds his notes into his suit coat, widens his stance at the lectern, and grips it tight, bracing himself for the moderator's next question.

He sees the tsunami coming, and he knows he's powerless to stop it.

23

The rest of the debate goes from bad to worse. Regardless of the question, Sandy hammers Jack about the Red-Letter Killer.

"What's your approach to tax policy?"

"My approach is that we have to first focus on keeping the streets safe from Jack Powell and this Red-Letter Killer, and then we can lower taxes for our residents."

"How would you improve city parks?"

"I'd make sure the Red-Letter Killer is behind bars so that our families and children can play safely."

The only positive is that the crowd and the media members are so flummoxed by the news that they're barely paying attention.

After the debate, Jack tells me he needs to stay and do damage control with his team. I don't blame him. I'm not much use when it comes to politics, so I head back to his place solo. It's an epic journey, but I decide to walk so I can process what happened. I exit the studios and head south on Columbus. The sun has set, and the energy of New York City vibrates like a teenager on Friday night. The frigid breeze bites my cheeks, a welcome refresher after the stuffy studio.

As I pass tourist couples on romantic holidays and single yuppies out for a big night, my mind flashes back to the debate. How did Godo know about the red letters? How did he know about Kenneally and Tweed? No one in my office would have told him. They all love Jack. He must have an informant in the police department or Dinwiddie's office. It wouldn't surprise me if that bulldog detective, Marcos, was a big Godo fan. You can always count on him to make the wrong decision. But I don't think he even knows about the link between the Tweed and Kenneally killings yet. Maybe the DA? By now, Shavali has probably told him to pressure him to drop the case. Could the DA have leaked it? Or could it be Dinwiddie?

Regardless, this case is a mess and is about to get downright filthy. The media loves a good serial killer story, and Godo gave them the perfect headline: "Red-Letter Serial Killer Terrorizes Manhattan." I can't wait to see what witty pun the *New York Post* comes up with tomorrow morning.

The wind whips down Ninth Avenue. I flip my coat collar up and curse myself for not trusting my instincts and turning down this case. I knew something was wrong from the moment I watched that video. I saw it in Father K.'s eyes, his face twisted in agony. He knew he was dying, but he didn't seem surprised. It was as if he felt he deserved it. That was the sign.

After another half hour of walking and pondering, I hook a left on Greenwich and meander through the Village. The streets are quiet on account of the cold. It's amazing how quickly a New York side street can go silent. The few remaining leaves on the trees rustle, and suddenly I'm alone.

Except, I realize, I'm not alone.

Someone is following me. I can feel it. Something about the light, the shadows.

I look back and see a shadowy figure a little less than a block behind me by the corner deli, wearing an oversize ankle-length parka, a New York Yankees hat, and a black respiratory mask.

My blood freezes.

It's the same guy I saw standing beneath a streetlamp in the park, watching.

I listen, but the only sound is my footsteps.

I cast my eyes left, then right, assessing my surroundings. My skin prickles, every instinct screaming for me to run. But I don't. I force myself to keep walking, keep my steps steady. A brick townhome fifty feet to my right has the light on. A family sitting down to dinner. Could I get to them in time? The rest of the block is dark.

I slow my pace and glance behind me. I notice he slows down as well. My mind jumps back to the Mia Thomas case, when two thugs attacked me in the alley in front of my office. I still have a mark where the blade touched my neck.

I rub my fingers along my throat and feel the raised scar tissue.

I wasn't prepared that time.

I will be this time.

As I quicken my pace, I subtly reach under my shirt and place my hand on the gun in my belly holster. I slide the pistol into my coat pocket. Face Mask should be gaining on me, but he's not. He's still following me but keeping a greater distance. A tingle runs up my neck.

He's not trying to attack me.

He's watching me.

I walk faster, my hand sliding across the cold steel of the gun.

Then it starts.

The whistle. The song.

"Danny Boy."

It soars through the empty block and lands in my chest.

The lyrics play in my mind. *Oh, Danny boy, the pipes, the pipes are calling.*

The tune bounces off the buildings and surrounds me, choking me. I don't look back again—I don't want to tip him off that I know he's there. But the whistling. That eerie, slow melody continues, cutting through the air like a knife.

I'm one hundred feet from the corner of Greenwich and Sixth. Pedestrians, bars, and restaurants line Sixth Avenue, but right now it's the two of us, alone. I should be relieved to be steps away from safety, but I'm not. I'm angry because I know the stalking won't end here.

It won't stop until I'm dead or he is.

The whistling pauses. The rage bubbles up inside me, and my cheeks flush. Ever since I was alone with Andrew in that basement, I've been afraid. I've been a hollowed-out outline of the woman I was. I'm tired of being afraid.

I turn on my heels.

"Why are you following me?" I shout, my voice riding the wind. I clutch the gun in my pocket.

But there's no one there.

I search the street, wondering if I'm losing my mind.

The block is empty.

I spin around.

The only sound is the hum of streetlamps.

Then I hear it.

The whistling resumes, but it's a decrescendo, as though whoever's doing this is down an alley or walking away from me.

I walk toward the sound, but it dissipates.

Without thinking, I bolt forward, my boots pounding against the pavement, the cold wind cutting through my jacket. I chase in the direction in which he vanished, darting past a row of parked cars. I know it's crazy. Running after your stalker is not a best practice. But sometimes avoiding the terror is worse than confronting it.

The whistling fades but continues. The sound reverberates off the buildings, making it difficult to hear where it's coming from. As I approach Perry Street, over my quick breaths, I catch it.

I break into a sprint, fueled by the realization that this may be my only chance to catch this psychopath. I skid around the corner onto Perry Street, passing a hand-holding couple, post-date, doggie bag in hand, but no whistler. They shoot me a confused look as I sprint by them.

I hear the whistle from an alleyway and dart to the right. My eyes search the alley, from the brick walls to the beaten-down asphalt.

But there's no one.

I check behind a dumpster. Then I see something—a shadow. Movement behind a pile of garbage bags, down in the basement entry of a town house. My heart leaps into my throat. He's hiding. Waiting. I pull the pistol from my holster, the cool metal solid in my hands. I hold it low, ready, as I tiptoe toward the garbage pile.

The whistling has stopped. It's dead quiet now, so quiet I can hear the blood rushing in my ears. I move closer, every nerve on edge. Something rustles behind the bags. My fingers tighten around the gun. I crouch down, the pistol raised, ready to fire.

And then...a low growl.

A dog—a scruffy, mangy dog—scurries out from behind the garbage, looking at me with wide, scared eyes before bolting down the street. I run my free hand through my hair.

"Seriously?"

Before I can get to my feet, I hear it again.

Oh, Danny boy, the pipes, the pipes are calling...

Closer this time, but still faint, as if it's slipping through the cracks in the air itself.

I slide the gun into my holster and jog back into the street.

I still hear the whistle, but I'm losing it in the New York din. It sounds like it's coming from Bleecker.

I run onto Bleecker Street, ready to meet my stalker, but I'm blocked by a herd of bodies. NYU students and partygoers pack the sidewalks, and side streets branch in every direction. My ears strain for the whistle.

I dart through the clouds of perfume and cheap cologne, shoving people out of my way, shouting, "Move!" at the top of my lungs. But as I push through the late-night crowd gathered outside the bars, I lose it. The tune fades into the night, and all I'm left with are the faces of people who aren't him. The sidewalk swallows me up, the strangers surrounding me, unaware of the chase I'm in.

I lunge back into the street, running with traffic. It's faint, distant, but there's no mistaking the whistle. He's there. He's close. I can feel it in my bones. Halfway down the block, as the traffic thickens and the chatter grows, I realize I'm screwed. I've lost the whistle. Face Mask is a ghost.

I slow my pace and stop in the middle of Bleecker, then spin in circles, hoping to catch a glimpse. A cab hammers its horn, and I move to the sidewalk. My heart slams in my chest like I just finished a marathon. I wait on the corner of Bleecker and Thompson, holding on to the icy metal street pole, waiting and watching, hoping he'll come back out of curiosity, out of some sick desire to watch me. But he doesn't.

I raise my hands to my head and catch my breath. The sound of live music from Wicked Willy's and the Red Lion thumps through the night. A dreadlocked guy passing by offers me cocaine under his breath. Do I look that tired? I politely decline.

As the crowds flow around me, I try to digest the last few minutes. I hate that Face Mask got away, but strangely, I feel... invigorated.

I inhale another deep breath of crisp air and realize how afraid I've been. And for how long. It hasn't been an explicit fear, but something prodding my subconscious. And that's been the worst thing about it. It's been ephemeral—behind me when I walk home at night, in basements, around dark corners of quiet streets, in the unexpected ring of a phone, in an elevator full of drunk men when I'm the only woman. I've carried this fear deep in my gut for so long, and this was the first time I've had the chance to face it.

My chest puffs out for the rest of my walk. It was only a moment, but chasing that psycho gave me a taste of the old Hazel. The one who started her PI business ready to kick ass and take names.

The second I get to Jack's place, my chest deflates. I reach to put my key in the door and see that it's ajar. I'm happy I faced my fear once this evening. I don't need to do it again.

I pause outside the door and listen but hear nothing. I reach for my gun again and ease the door open. Is this where Face Mask went? To jump me at Jack's place? I flip the lights on. The town house appears empty. Nothing is out of place. The chairs line the dining room table in a perfect U. The throw rests on the couch back.

I step into the kitchen, and the refrigerator purrs, but silence permeates.

I climb the staircase and turn right into the bedroom.

A dejected voice calls from the front doorway, "Honey, I'm home."

My heart skips and then settles.

It's Jack.

I turn the light on in our bedroom, and it, too, is empty. I release a sigh and put my gun back in the holster.

"Are you okay? You look like you've seen a ghost," he says as I scurry downstairs.

I stop on the second step and wipe the sweat from my forehead. "Did you just get back?"

"Yeah, why?"

"The door was open."

"You mean, like, wide open?"

"No, not locked and loose."

"Huh." He corkscrews his mouth and looks to the ceiling. After a beat, he shuts his eyes and slaps his forehead. "I think I forgot to lock it on my way out to the debate. I'm so sorry, bubs. I was late and I forgot my notes—not that they did a lot of good. I blew it. The hits just keep on coming. "

I bite my lip. I love this man, but his absentmindedness will be the death of me. "It's okay, but please make sure you lock up. It's dangerous."

"I will. I'm sorry. But am I missing something here? 'Cuz I just got my ass whooped in a debate and learned that there's a serial killer on the loose, and you're worried about our front door. You expecting the Red-Letter Killer to pay us a visit?"

I pull him over to the couch, and we sit down. He throws his feet on the treasure chest coffee table. "There's something I've got to tell you. But you have to promise me you're not going to freak out."

His skin crinkles around his eyes. "After tonight's debate, I'm not sure what more you could tell me to freak me out."

"You know how I thought I saw someone watching us the other night?"

"Yeah."

"That same person followed me home tonight, and I think he's associated with the Kenneally and Tweed murders."

Jack's jaw clenches, and he breathes through his nostrils like a dragon. "I'm going to kill him. Who is it?"

"Is this you not freaking out?"

"I'm sorry." He takes a deep breath and speaks through gritted teeth. "Do you know who it is?"

"No."

He scratches the whiskers on his chin, and his leg shakes. "I bet that SOB Godo has something to do with this."

I place my hand on his leg to stop the shaking. "C'mon. I don't like Sandy any more than you do, but I doubt he's in league with a serial killer."

He grabs my hands, his eyes glowing with intensity. "I know it sounds crazy, but think about it. How did he know about all that Red-Letter Killer stuff?" He stands and paces the room. "Maybe he's involved in these killings. Before he ran Agra Pharma, he was a chemist. Maybe he's the one poisoning these folks."

As much as I want to dismiss Jack's theory as sour grapes, I have to admit, it's not totally crazy. I stand up and grab his hand. We make our way to the stairs. "Look, it's been a long evening, and both of us are a little cracked out. Why don't we call it a night and get some good sleep, and I'll dig into it in the morning? I've got a meeting with the archbishop first thing that will shed light on this."

We arrive on the second floor, and Jack undoes his tie and unbuttons his shirt. "The archbishop? I thought we were leaving him out of this."

"I wish I could, but we don't have a choice. He requested a meeting with me tomorrow."

"Lord almighty." He rubs his temples and releases a resigned sigh. "So, this Red-Letter Killer thing is real, huh?"

We reach the bedroom, and I shut the door like I'm shutting out the world. The blue-and-green tartan wallpaper makes me feel cozy and safe. I drop the blinds.

No one will watch me tonight.

I wrap my arms around him and put my head on his built chest. I feel his heart thundering.

"Yes. It's very real."

He puts his arms around me and kisses me on the neck. "Should we be scared?"

I nod into his chest. "Everyone should be."

24

At nine a.m., Mary and I sit in Archbishop Dinwiddie's office, waiting for answers. I'm wearing a red dress and black-checkered blazer. The archbishop is a formal man, and I need to extract the truth from him. Mary's sporting a hand-knitted sweater-and-skirt Sunday outfit. As we wait on the plush leather couch, I scan the pictures on the archbishop's wall. I've found, in business and in life, you can learn a lot about someone from the pictures they display. They reflect what is important to them. The last time I was here, I noticed what was on the wall: photos of the powerful—presidents, celebrities, athletes, business leaders, and popes. This time I notice what's not on the wall: children, working folks, veterans, the elderly, the people the archbishop should care about the most. This is a man who's forgotten whom he's supposed to serve.

Sister Teresa sits across from us, typing emails and answering phone calls. Every few minutes, she turns her craggy face from the computer screen to spy as though we're going to steal a trinket from the office. She reminds me of a pit bull on a chain leash. After another one of Sister Teresa's death stares, I look over at Mary and roll my eyes. She smiles, and I notice her cheeks are more rosy than usual. She spins her pendant necklace on her fingertips.

"You nervous?" I ask.

She drops her hands and locks them together in her lap, but you can still feel the energy. "Oh no. Well, I guess so. I'm a little starstruck by the archbishop, ya know?"

"Really?"

"Oh yeah. If my mom and dad, God rest their souls"—she crosses herself—"could see me now, meeting with the archbishop of New York, they wouldn't believe it."

"That's part of the reason I brought you here. I figured you'd prevent me from committing some irrecoverable social faux pas, like drinking holy water or picking my teeth with a cross."

"Oh, dear. Hazel, you're incorrigible."

The door to the archbishop's office opens, and he wheels himself out to greet us. Today, he wears his formal regalia. A bright-red cassock covers his shoulder and chest, and a red zucchetto rests atop his head. A glittering gold-and-diamond cross that could feed a family for a decade hangs from his neck. I wonder how he looks at himself in the mirror. He raises his palms and welcomes us with a kind smile. I notice the smile is considerably warmer than on our last visit. Dinwiddie knows how to turn on the charm when he needs something.

"Ah, Hazel and… I'm sorry, I've forgotten your name."

"Mary, Your Grace," she says. I've never seen that much blood rush to a woman's face.

"Mary. Such a lovely name." Dinwiddie looks to Sister Teresa for agreement, but she merely grunts in acknowledgment. I spy the tiniest smile underneath the grunt, though. I think Sister Teresa might be softening toward us.

"Thank you, Your Grace," says Mary.

He looks at me and gestures to his office. "Hazel, shall we?"

I rise from the couch and whisper to Mary to stay outside and wait for me.

He and I settle into his office. Sister Teresa brings in her customary tray with a pitcher of water, two glasses, and the archbishop's pills. He pours himself a glass, throws his pills back in one gulp, and then pours me a glass. The second Sister Teresa closes the door behind her, his face drops and his deep voice hardens.

"Thank you for coming, Hazel."

"It's my pleasure. What did you want to discuss?"

"I'm afraid I have some bad news."

"Oh?"

"Yesterday, I received a red letter."

The news hits me like a truck, but I try not to show it.

"May I see the letter?"

"Unfortunately, the police took it with them. But don't worry. I remember every inch. I'll remember it until the day I die."

He takes another sip of water. He puts on a brave face, but when he drinks, I see his hand is shaking.

"Okay, what can you tell me?" I pull out my notebook and take notes.

He pauses and strokes his mustache, every word chosen like a storyteller reading from an ancient tome, his deep voice purring. "It was a red letter in a red envelope. The address was typed and appeared to be composed on an old-fashioned typewriter. The kind we used to use around here in the eighties. You could tell by the spots where certain letters were worn and the ink didn't quite hold. The stamp was the portrait of Mary and the baby Jesus from Raphael's *Madonna of the Candelabra*."

I take notes as the archbishop speaks, but I can't ignore the tingle up my spine. Most criminals are erratic, uncontrolled. This is a methodical, disciplined creature. The same letters. The same typewriter. The same stamps. The way I crack cases is by exposing people's mistakes: when they hurry, when they rush, when they panic. This one never panics.

The archbishop continues, "The letter itself was also typed in the same font."

"Was there a drawing in blood?"

He coughs a few times and clears his throat. "I'm sorry. The water must have gone down the wrong pipe. What was I saying? Ah, yes, the drawing. Yes, at the top center, a sketch of one of the nine circles of hell from Botticelli's map in Dante's *Inferno*. It depicts souls violently tossed about in a storm for eternity."

"Which circle of hell was it?"

He licks his lips and takes another sip of water. Then puckers them together. "The second circle. For the lustful and adulterous."

"And what about the verse?"

Dinwiddie leans over in his chair and grabs at his chest. He releases a loud cough. "I'm sorry, I don't know what's the matter with me."

"It's all right, take your time."

"The letter said, 'Because thou sufferest the woman Jezabel, who calleth herself a prophetess, to teach, and to seduce my servants, to commit fornication, and to eat of things sacrificed to idols. And I gave her a time that she might do penance, and she will not repent of her fornication. Behold, I will cast her into a bed: and they that commit adultery with her shall be in very great tribulation.'"

"Any idea what that means?"

Dinwiddie puts his fingers to his lips and then grabs a napkin off the tray to wipe sweat from his brow. "Yes, I know what it means." He pulls out his Bible and pats the cover. "It's from the Douay–Rheims Bible. It's like the other letter you told me about. It's another red-letter verse, Christ's words. It's from the Book of Revelation, and it means Jesus will punish those who are seduced by Jezebel."

"Who is Jezebel?"

Dinwiddie loosens his priest's collar and clears his throat again. Perspiration gathers around his brow, and his dark skin pales. He looks like he's going to be sick.

"Jezebel is the biblical archetype of the wicked woman. The woman who seduces men to abandon the Lord."

"And how does that relate to you?" I know exactly how that relates to him, but I want to hear him say it.

Dinwiddie gives a quick, rough hack and grabs for his water glass. He takes a sip, but instead of gulping it down, he sputters, and the water spurts from the sides of his mouth. He coughs, then tries to speak, but his words come out slurred.

I rise from my seat. "Archbishop, are you okay?"

"Yes, I don't know—"

He tries to finish his sentence, but only a short, guttural noise escapes. His skin has gone from brown to tan to green. He attempts to wheel his chair away from his desk, but his hands slide across the wheels like the arms of a puppet manipulated by strings. His face transforms into a mask of terror.

I recognize that look. It's the same expression I saw on Father Kenneally.

I rise from my seat and run around the desk to help him. As I move, Dinwiddie vomits and bile drips down his chest.

I throw open his office door and shout to Sister Teresa, "Call an ambulance!"

Her face pinches. "Why, what's happening?"

"Call an ambulance now!"

I run back into the room. Mary leaps from the couch and follows me in while Sister Teresa dials. Dinwiddie now sits locked in his chair, groaning. He tries to lift his arms, but they move like limp rubber bands. He moves his mouth, but only clipped gurgling sounds emerge.

I tilt his head forward to prevent him from choking on his vomit. Drool and spit fall on his lap. I stare into his eyes. His pupils dilate to black, and his blood vessels swell with panic.

I want to do something, but my mind blanks. Mary slides in next to me and kneels down before Dinwiddie, her brow lined and her eyes focused with intensity. She grabs his wrist, checks his pulse, and then looks at me.

"He's got a pulse, barely."

"Stay with me, Archbishop," I say. He doesn't move. "Can you hear me? Archbishop, nod if you can hear me."

His eyes strain, and I can see him trying with all his might to move, but his body won't respond. Then I think I hear something, and I lean closer to his mouth. The smell of vomit overwhelms me.

Then I hear it.

"Be careful, H—"

The last of the oxygen escapes his lungs.

I wrap my arms around his torso, hoist him out of his chair, and lay him on the ground. I check his airway for obstruction. It's clear. I wipe his mouth with my sleeve to remove any poison and press my mouth to his. I blow into his lungs and pump his chest, maintaining the steady rhythm for the next minute or two, desperately trying to remember everything I learned in CPR class. My wrists burn as I pump. Mary holds his hand and stares into his eyes, willing him to keep going. I repeat the process over and over again until I'm exhausted. But Dinwiddie's body refuses to respond.

I turn to Mary, and she checks his pulse again.

Seconds pass before she shakes her head.

I dive back in to resume the CPR, but Mary grabs my arm. "He's gone, Hazel."

Sirens ring in the distance, but it doesn't matter.

Archbishop Milton Dinwiddie is dead.

25

stand in the hallway immediately outside Archbishop Dinwiddie's office in shock as the police investigate the scene. One officer strings yellow caution tape while another interviews Mary down the hallway to my right. They've separated Mary, Sister Teresa, and me so that we don't get our stories crossed. At the other end of the hallway, Sister Teresa sits on the beige carpet, crumpled and devastated.

I've seen a person die before, but I don't think I'll ever get used to it. It's different in real life from the movies. It's in the breath and the eyes. How that last breath pops from the lungs like a whisper, like death bidding farewell. And the eyes, the way they strain and flex in agony, unwilling to accept this is the last light they'll see. I'll never forget Dinwiddie's eyes. Like I'll never forget Kenneally's. Or Andrew's.

The conclusion I've been hedging and ignoring is unavoidable now. My theory of the case is wrong. This isn't someone exacting revenge for the church's failure to pay what it owed. This is a zealot with a bigger cause. A psychopathic serial killer stands at the center of all this.

I've never been involved in a serial killer case.

To be honest, ever since I took coursework in criminal pathology, I've always wanted to face a serial killer. To match wits with an evil genius like the great fictional detectives, Hercule Poirot, Harry Bosch, or Kinsey Millhone. But now that I'm here, I've realized it's not fun, it's not entertaining; it's terrifying.

The letters.

The depictions of hell crafted in blood.

The Bible verses.

The sense of dread.

It compresses my heart in a vise and won't let go. The little things around me I normally wouldn't even notice now seem fraught with danger. The slam of a door, a crooked glance, the flicker of fluorescent office lights.

And that's the power of the serial killer.

Putting fear into the mundane.

Tears roll down Mary's face as she recounts the story of Dinwiddie's death to the cop. He's young and still has genuine empathy in his eyes. The city hasn't beaten it out of him yet. I view Sister Teresa down the hallway. I've never seen her vulnerable. It's jarring.

I turn back to Dinwiddie's office. I still can't accept that a man died here moments ago. As I play the scene over again in my mind, I feel the space closing in on me. Suddenly, the hallway feels smaller and stuffier. I can't catch a deep breath.

That same feeling that gripped me in Shavali's office, and the catacombs, returns. All I want to do is leave. Maybe if I move fast enough, I can sneak out with no one noticing. They can call me if they want me to answer questions.

As I'm about to exit, Detective Marcos's voice freezes me. "Funny seeing you here, Cho," he says.

Why couldn't it have been any other detective? I close my eyes and reopen them, hoping this is a bad dream. But as I look at his leathery skin and Cro-Magnon forehead, I know that it's not. I'm not going anywhere. He rolls up the sleeves of his black button-down with too many buttons undone, showing off his tattooed, meaty forearms. He's inside, yet he keeps his aviators on. Every move he makes intimidates.

I stifle my anxiety and put on a brave face. You can't show weakness to this man. "Why's that, Marcos?" I ask.

"I don't know. I keep running into you, that's all." His voice carries a whisper of a Spanish accent.

I scowl and say nothing. I figure, the less I talk, the quicker I can get out of here. Farther away from Dinwiddie's corpse.

"I'm going to need to interview you."

I nod.

The police have cleared out the entire floor, so he drags me into one of the empty conference rooms and gestures for me to take a seat. I collapse into a tan faux-leather swivel chair and swing back and forth, surveying the room. A fake cactus plant sits in the center of the table. A whiteboard with a church fundraising thermometer in red ink stares back at me. The periwinkle-blue walls hold Bible quotes that are a lot nicer than the ones I've been reading lately. "Love is patient, love is kind," "You are the light of the world," "For what will it profit a man if he gains the world, and loses his soul?" The last one reminds me of the archbishop.

Marcos checks his body camera and then sits down and groans like he's still recovering from leg day. An unappealing mixture of sweat and pine body spray emanates from him. He removes a pad of paper and a pen from his back pocket in a slow, methodical movement and traces the other end of the pen over the scar on his lip. He can sense my desire to leave and wants to make this as painful for me as possible. After listing off my name, the date, and the time, he begins the questioning.

"Why don't you tell me what happened in your own words?"

He uses his tongue to clear out something from his teeth—probably a raw pork chop he ate with his bare hands, and makes a smacking sound. The idea of being interviewed by Marcos right now nauseates me. But I remind myself that he's just doing his job.

I give him the full story of the red letter Dinwiddie received, of our meeting with him, and of his death as quickly as I can.

"What do you think killed him?" he asks.

I snort. "Poison, obviously."

He crinkles his forehead in feigned curiosity. "Why do you say 'obviously'?"

"Please, spare me the routine. It's pretty straightforward. He received a red letter. The next day, he's dead in a violent spasm that matches all the symptoms of tetrodotoxin poisoning that killed Father Kenneally."

"And Fred Tweed." He raises a thick eyebrow. "You seem to know a lot about tetrodotoxin."

I note Marcos has linked the Tweed killing with the Kenneally killing, finally. Sam might be off the hook. "Yeah, I do. It's my job. It's called doing your research. You might…" I pause and look at the camera. Insulting a cop will not get me out of here any quicker.

"You might what?"

"Nothing."

"You know that poison's found in Japanese sushi, right?"

"Yeah?"

He raises the other eyebrow and tilts his head.

"I'm Korean, not Japanese, Marcos." I can now add *lazy stereotyping* to his list of accomplishments. I think of Momo and thank God I brought Mary here instead of her. He squints at me, and I can tell he's considering pushing the Asian angle further, but then he glances at the camera behind him and lets it go.

"Sister Teresa mentioned you had a contentious meeting with the archbishop the other day. Is that true?"

"I wouldn't call it 'contentious.'"

"What would you call it?"

"A typical interview. I asked him the same questions you would ask if you were doing an investigation. How he knew the victim. When was their last contact. Did he know of any reason someone would want to kill Father K."

"So why did Sister Teresa call it 'contentious'?" He refers to his notes. "She said she heard the archbishop become agitated and ask you to leave."

I close my eyes and search for patience. This is the problem with Marcos. He gets one piece of evidence and chases after it like a dog playing fetch. Then another piece of evidence arrives, but he's already gone to chase after the first piece, so he doesn't even notice. He doesn't analyze and assess the complete picture.

"He was agitated because I asked him about the church's refusal to pay the legal settlement for the child sex abuse scandal."

Marcos scowls. "I can see why he'd be irritated. No wonder he kicked you out. I can't believe you asked the archbishop that. Don't you have any respect?"

The anger in his defense of the archbishop strikes me. I noticed the gold cross necklace hanging from his neck. "I have respect, but Kenneally died days after the church refused to pay the settlement. Don't you think that's curious?"

"Not really."

"'Not really'? Well, if nothing else, it was a red flag and it would be malpractice for me to disregard it. It doesn't matter, anyway, given some of the information we've discovered about the victim and Father Kenneally."

"What information?"

"I'm not at liberty to discuss that. I'm sure you'll hear all about it from Shavali in due time."

He sneers and scratches his chin. "How would you describe your feelings toward Archbishop Dinwiddie?"

I shake my head. He's run out of factual questions and is fishing now. "Are we done here?"

"No, we're not done. A man was murdered today, Cho, and I need to find out who did it. We're on the same team. I don't get why that's so difficult for you to understand."

"If I knew who did it, I would tell you."

"Would you? Because between undercutting me on the

Sampson case and stonewalling me today, you seem hell-bent on making sure I don't ever clear a case again."

"And you seem hell-bent on making false accusations. It's not my fault you tried to cut corners and pin it on Sam."

"Cut corners? We had video of him dropping off a threat letter and his prints on the letter. What did you expect me to do, throw him a party?"

"I'm not having this conversation." I stand up and start toward the door, but he grabs me by the arm. His fingers drive into my forearm muscle. I snatch it away.

"What aren't you telling me?"

I grab my bag. "Can I go now?"

"I think you should come to the station for an interview."

"No, thanks."

He rises from his seat and points his pen at me. I feel his size. "You know I could arrest you."

His threat freezes me. Technically, he's probably right. I was the last person in the room before a murder. It's enough probable cause for an arrest. But Marcos is smart enough to know that if he arrests me, I'll lawyer up and he'll be stonewalled. "You could, but I wouldn't recommend it."

He sneers and puts on a mock-sympathetic face. "Of course, Cho. I wouldn't do that to you. You've had a rough day. But do me a favor and stick around town, will you? I'm probably going to have some more questions for you later on."

"I'm sure you will."

He takes down my information, and I feel my face flush. Marcos is dead set on making my life more difficult, payback for me blowing up the Sampson case. I'm not a suspect yet, but it won't take much for him to change his mind. The last thing I need right now is more pressure. I burst out of the room and grab Mary, who's wiping tears from her eyes and snot from her nose. She looks like I feel. I grab her by the arm and walk her down the hallway.

A beat cop lifts the caution tape. As we enter the elevator, I spot Marcos poking his head out, watching me leave. I punch the button for the lobby while Mary sniffles. The elevator doors close, and both of us release a breath.

Mary's chest heaves as she speaks. "I'm sorry, Hazel. I can't stop crying."

I put my hand on her back and rub it. I'm terrible at affection, so a back rub is the best I can muster. "Don't apologize. That was awful. There's no other way around it."

She sniffles again, and her voice quakes. "At the funeral home, I see corpses all the time, but seeing someone die in front of me like that. The way his body spasmed and then froze. I don't think I'll ever forget that, ya know?"

I do know. It's that very thought that's driving me out of this building.

"I understand," I say.

The elevator doors open, and my heart sinks deeper as I look across the lobby out the glass doors of the archdiocese's headquarters. News trucks are parked out front, and media members pace and look at their phones, waiting for the action. Mary and I keep walking past the cops who are securing the lobby, but we slow our pace like we're walking the plank. Lights from news cameras rip through the glass and bounce off the shining lobby floors.

My phone rings, and I see it's my mom on FaceTime. She has impeccable timing. I decline the call. She calls again. I run my fingers through my hair and then answer.

"Mom, I can't talk now."

"Are you okay? I saw the archbishop died." I made the mistake of telling her over the phone that I interviewed him a couple of days ago.

"How did you hear that?"

"It's on the news."

I remember my mom watches the news twenty-four hours a day now. If she knows, everybody knows.

"Yes, Mom, it's true. The archbishop is dead. But I'm fine."

"Is Jack okay?"

I rub the spot between my eyebrows. "Of course Jack is okay."

"This won't be good for his campaign, huh?"

"Mom, I can't talk about this right now. I'll call you back."

I hang up the phone.

Now it's Mary's turn to put an arm around me. Except, unlike my mother, she knows how to hug.

"Sounds like my mom," she says.

We reach the exit doors, and I see five sets of cameras pointed at us. Reporters stand out front, mics in hand, like wolves ready to feast. I stop Mary before we walk outside. "Now, so you know, when we exit, the media will fire a bunch of questions at you. Some of them will be aimed at generating a reaction. Stuff like, 'Did you kill the archbishop?' et cetera." Keep walking regardless of what you hear.

Mary's eyes widen, but she nods her agreement. "Gotcha."

We step onto the First Avenue sidewalk, and it's exactly like I predicted. The lights from the cameras blind us. The news truck generators roar in the background. Pedestrians stop and gawk, trying to decipher what's happened. The reporters follow us and shout questions. "How did the archbishop die? Was he murdered? Are you two suspects?" It feels like the sidewalk is shrinking, but we ignore them and keep walking. My hands tremble as the reporters close in on us and push microphones closer and closer.

I shove my way through the horde and frantically wave my arm to hail a cab. The cab driver squeals to a halt in front of us, nearly taking out a journalist. Mary and I dive inside. The reporters tap on the roof of the cab and the windows.

"Go!" I shout to the cab driver.

He tears into the street and merges into traffic. He looks at us in the rearview mirror. "You ladies celebrities or something?"

I shoot him my fiercest glare.

"No," I say.

The cab driver gives us a second look but seems satisfied, then turns his attention to the road ahead.

As we roll back to the office, Mary looks at me, determination in her eyes.

"This is going to get a lot worse before it gets better, isn't it?"

I watch the hurried New Yorkers tromping down the sidewalk, unaware that the Red-Letter Killer has struck again, and consider telling her it's going to be okay, that it's not as bad as it seems. But sometimes the truth is so inescapable that lying is an impossibility. I look her dead in the eye and nod.

"Yeah, it's going to get a lot worse."

26

spend the rest of the evening cuddling and decompressing with Jack over a bottle of wine, then organizing the Kenneally file while he prepares his speech to the League of Women Voters. His arm drapes around me, and I absorb his crisp smell. He sports blue-striped pajama pants and a white formfitting V-neck T-shirt that is a little too distracting. Cute black horn-rimmed reading glasses rest on his face, giving him Clark Kent vibes, and I watch as he reads his speech silently to himself, mouthing the words and practicing the gestures. I clench my teeth together. It makes me want to drop what I'm doing, toss his papers in the air, and jump him. But now is not the time. I need to get my head around this case. With Dinwiddie's death and my friendly neigh-borhood stalker, I've barely had a moment to think.

I stare at the painting hanging over Jack's mantel and ponder. It's a print of Van Gogh's *Wheatfield with Crows*. At least, I hope it's a print, or we should both quit our jobs immediately and retire. I'm not really an art buff, but I love Van Gogh's work. It's both powerful and peaceful, like staring at the ocean. The painting depicts three paths diverging through a wheatfield set against a dark-blue sky. Crows fly overhead.

It reminds me of the killer's drawings and how much further I must go to find him. I envision a case as a series of paths. One path leads to the perpetrator, but you must walk each path before you discover the right one. So far, every path I've walked has been a dead end.

I've looked into the letters themselves. There's no DNA on the first two letters other than the victims' and Sampson's. I'm confident the letter the killer sent to Dinwiddie will be clean as well. The killer typed the letters, so there's no chance of a handwriting sample. The typewriter and stationery are common, so we can't glean anything from that. Video evidence on the Kenneally killing shows nobody unusual on the day of his death.

At first I thought the blood on the letters might be human, which would allow us to trace it, but because it's animal blood, it's worthless. I'm still waiting for Bobby to give me the data on where the killer mailed the letters, but if the killer's as smart as I think he is, he will have sent them from a series of mailboxes in random parts of town. We still don't know how the killer obtained the poison. Maybe Momo can gather meaningful intel from the puffer fish purchases. And so far, known acquaintances have been worthless. Father Kenneally was beloved. Sister Teresa said the archbishop didn't have any obvious enemies and didn't receive any threats besides the letter he received the other day. My only hope is Arika Tweed.

The following morning, I stand across from Prospect Park in Brooklyn by Grand Army Plaza, a few blocks down from the opulent home of Arika Tweed, wife of the deceased Frederick Tweed. Bobby and I have an appointment to interview her this morning. I'm doubtful she'll give us much, but I'm looking forward to seeing Bobby's friendly face after what happened yesterday with Dinwiddie. I talked to Jack about it last night, but it's hard because he can't really relate. Bobby's been there. He understands.

I cinch my violet car coat around me to trap in the body heat. The sky is blue, but the winter chill that's been cutting through the city remains. A billow of steam rises out of the public library, and the sun crosses the sky along that sunken autumn path, where you know dusk isn't that far behind dawn. The bite of another gust of wind unsettles me. It reminds me of the early scenes in a horror movie where everyone looks happy but the music tells you they won't be for very long.

While I wait for Bobby, I sip on my Red Bull and glance over at the newsstand on the corner. Beneath the bottles of Yoo-hoo and packs of Extra rest a few stray newspapers for the few people that still read them. I see the headline of *The New York Times*. "Archbishop Murdered. Police Suspect Serial Killer." The *New York Post* headline is even worse. "Better Dead than Red: Red-Letter Killer Terrorizes the City." The more publicity this case gets, the harder it will be to solve. Once the crazies come out of the woodwork, determining the factual information from the fake becomes exponentially harder.

"You checking to see if you made the papers?" says Bobby.

He holds a cup of steaming-hot coffee in one hand and a cigarette in the other. He flashes me his chip-toothed smile and takes a drag. Something about this guy makes me feel at ease. How he and Marcos can work in the same profession boggles my mind.

I smile back at him and then slug the rest of my Red Bull. "More like hoping I *didn't* make the papers." I try to look cool by shooting my can at the recycling like a basketball but end up missing and then awkwardly picking it up and depositing it by hand. After Bobby laughs at me for several seconds, we walk up Prospect Park West toward the Tweed residence. The neighborhood is gorgeous, lined with multimillion-dollar turn-of-the-century townhomes, but Prospect Park has always seemed foreboding to me when compared to Central Park. Whereas Central Park is open and accessible, a thicket of trees and bushes surrounds Prospect Park so that only the persistent can enter. There's even a statue of a lion guarding the entrance.

"Yeah, we're in the shit now. My captain is already on my ass about solving this. Twenty-four hours ago, he couldn't have cared less." He drops his voice an octave. "He was like, 'Who gives a shit about Tweed? That guy was a scumbag. He deserved to die.' But now that it's a news story, it's priority one."

"I get it. Is your captain okay with me riding shotgun with you on this interview?"

He takes a drag, twists out the cherry on his cigarette, and puts the butt in his pocket. "Ah, no. This will be our little secret."

"Got it."

We reach the Tweed townhome, which is more of a mansion. A black wrought-iron gate surrounds a massive yard that looks like something you'd expect to see in the suburbs, not in some of the most expensive real estate in New York. I did a little research before I left. The house used to be owned by the Brooklyn Society for Ethical Culture before Tweed bought it for $30 million. How ironic.

I stop in front of the home and whistle. The three-story brick structure presents more like a history museum than a home. Hand-carved cream stone surrounds the first floor and bends in stunning arches over the front door. The rest of the building is brick, but on the second floor, bay windows surrounded by more stone jut out, overlooking the park, with a stone-carved balcony resting on top for good measure. The pièce de résistance is the set of curved parapets surrounding the roof, extending up to the sky like a church.

Bobby tilts his head at me as if to say, *Impressive*. I can't help but be impressed by the gorgeous architecture, but I wouldn't want to live here. There's no warmth, no family, no heart. And as I inspect the outside of the building more closely, I immediately sense that something's wrong. The ivy along the outside runs rampant. The plants in massive marble vases have dried up. The grass on the lawn and the bush out front are overgrown. The curtains are drawn. It's as though the house has retreated into itself.

Bobby finishes his coffee, tosses it into the nearest trash can, and gestures to the front door. "She's really let the place go," he says as he rings the bell.

Arika Tweed opens the door to reveal an opulent entryway cloaked in darkness. Dust specks float through the light from the door.

One look at Arika and I notice that the condition of the

house reflects the condition of its owner. She was clearly beautiful once. She holds herself like a model, nearly six feet tall and lithe. Her face carries the hallmarks of traditional beauty: small nose, high cheekbones, sea blue–green eyes. But like the house, Arika has fallen into disrepair. Dark circles sink underneath her eyes. Black hair roots corrupt her dyed-blond hair. Her lips are so enlarged and her leathery skin is pulled so tight across her face that she resembles a wax figure. She wears a floral silk robe that reveals two age-spotted breast implants perched preposterously high on her bony sternum. A Bloody Mary sloshes in a crystal lowball between her thin fingers. When she moves, her robe flutters behind her gaunt frame. She reminds me of a queen who's been deposed but no one had the heart to tell her.

She places a hand on Bobby's chest and lets it linger. "Good morning, Officer…?"

The smell of vodka chases every word. Bobby offers a closed-mouth grin and gently removes her hand from his chest.

"Riether, ma'am. Detective Riether. You may remember I interviewed you a few months ago. And this is Haz—"

But Arika doesn't stick around to hear my name. She walks through the living room and into the kitchen, her long, bony finger bending in the air, beckoning us to follow her. I shut the door behind me, plunging the house into darkness. I inhale the stale, dusty air. From the smell of it, Arika hasn't opened the house in weeks.

Bobby and I follow the sliver of light seeping through the shades and join Arika in the kitchen. I have to squint to see through the darkness, but I scan the living room and spot a plush, curved orange crushed velvet couch, a coffee table made of the glazed stump of a tree, and what looks like an original Picasso hanging from the wall. Of course, Arika doesn't acknowledge any of it. She's too busy pouring more vodka and Bloody Mary mix into her glass.

"Have a seat," she says, gesturing to the hunter green-and-white-striped breakfast banquet. "Would either of you like a Bloody?"

"No, thanks," say Bobby and I simultaneously.

"Ah, you two are no fun." A slight hiccup escapes her throat. The way she devours us with her eyes, I can't help feeling like a mouse dropped into a snake's cage. "Well, you must have something to drink. You can't leave me to drink alone." Her voice is nasally and whiny, like a teenager angling for a late curfew on a Saturday night.

"We'll have water," I say.

She sticks out her bottom lip and grabs two crystal highball glasses, then fills them from the polished-brass refrigerator-door faucet. I think about Tweed's demise and watch to make sure she doesn't poison our water. She drops the glasses in front of us.

"What can I do for you two this fine morning?" She says *you two*, but her eyes never leave Bobby, and she plays with the gold necklace that dangles in her cleavage.

"Well, I know we've already spoken, but I wanted to follow up on our earlier interview." Bobby pulls out a recorder and places it on the banquet table.

"Fire away, Officer." She lets the word *officer* dangle on her tongue. She takes an olive out of the drink and bites down on it while she stares at Bobby. I'm not sure she even knows I'm here at this point.

He clears his throat and turns on the recorder. I catch him blushing. He states her name and the interview details, then prepares himself to drop the bomb.

"Mrs. Tweed, we're here because we now believe that your husband's death may not have been an accident."

She shrugs and takes another sip of her drink. Her hands quiver as she tips the glass back. "I saw that online. The Red-Letter Killer. Rolls right off the tongue, doesn't it? I can't say I'm surprised."

As she says it, I think I hear a noise upstairs—almost like footsteps, but faster and lighter. Is there someone else in the house? Bobby doesn't seem to hear it. If he does, he ignores it.

"Why do you say that?" he says.

"My husband was not a well-liked man, but I don't have to tell you that."

"Of course." He takes a sip of his water. I don't touch mine. Nothing about this woman seems safe. "We, um, we believe he was poisoned intentionally."

She runs the toothpick from her olive against her lips. "Seems reasonable."

"Prior to his death, do you remember if he had any visitors?"

"When didn't we have visitors? Frederick and I loved to throw parties. We were voted the 'it' couple of the year, you know."

"I notice you have security cameras out front. Do you know how long that footage is stored?"

She laughs. "No more than a week. Frederick was notoriously cheap about certain things. He said, 'If somebody robs us, it's not going to take us a week to figure it out.'"

Bobby glances at me and scratches his head in frustration. "That's a shame. Before he died, do you recall him eating or drinking anything unusual?"

She pauses her drinking for a moment and stares into her glass, twisting it and watching the minimal light reflect off the crystal. She pauses for so long that I wonder if she's forgotten the question. Then she snaps out of it.

"No, and I'm quite confident of that." Her words sound slurred, but her certainty is clear. "I remember. I was in bed watching *Real Housewives of New York*. I'm close with the women in the show. It's my guilty pleasure." She winks at Bobby. "He came home from dinner late. Around eleven. I asked him how his night was. He said he was exhausted. He'd spent the day with his attorney, strategizing about his legal...troubles. Then the two of them went to dinner and drinks to unwind. He mentioned they ate sushi, as I told you before, but he ate nothing else after that. Then he took off his clothes, brushed his teeth, and laid down with me."

I turn to Bobby. "I'm assuming you checked out the attorney."

"Yeah, there was nothing there. An old friend of Tweed's. Seemed genuinely devastated by his death. No connection to Kenneally, Dinwiddie, or Old St. Patrick's." He returns to Arika. "Did Mr. Tweed seem sick at all when he joined you in bed?"

"No, he seemed fine. He took one of his sleeping pills. Then he read his book, and the two of us went to bed. Next thing you know, I wake up and he's writhing next to me. It was terrifying. I didn't know what to do. Then he was gone."

My mind jumps back to the archbishop. *He* took a pill and then *he* was gone.

"Did your husband take a sleeping pill every night?" I ask.

"Every night. He couldn't sleep without it."

I look at Bobby. "Dinwiddie took baby aspirin every day." The tetrodotoxin is definitely in the pills. And they're pills that the victim takes daily, so he knows that if he replaces all the pills in the bottle, they'll take them. But how? Why? Again, I hear a sound from upstairs.

"Mrs. Tweed, is there someone else in the house?"

She squints and raises an eyebrow. "No."

"No one else lives with you?"

"No."

Bobby gives a discreet cough and shoots me an irritated glance. "Mrs. Tweed, what was your husband's affiliation with Old St. Patrick's?"

She rolls her eyes. "Ugh, he loved that damn church. He was on the board and on various committees. And still they wouldn't pay a dime to those child abuse victims. Bastards."

"I noticed you posted about that on Facebook."

"You're damn right I did. It was an outrage. I swear, if I hadn't reined him in, he would have given all our money to those bastards." She takes another sip of her drink. "Of course, I guess it's only fair, given he lost all their money."

I lean forward in my seat. "I'm sorry. Did you say he lost all their money?"

She looks at me like I asked her if the earth was round. "Of course. Don't you read the papers? He lost everyone's money." She hiccups again.

"You mean Mr. Tweed was managing Old St. Patrick's money?"

"Yes. He was managing the entire archdiocese's money." She slurs a bit when she says *archdiocese's*.

Bobby and I kick each other under the table. He shifts in his seat before he speaks. "Did Mr. Tweed have any enemies?"

Arika snorts and nearly spits out her drink. "Of course he did. That's what happens when you run a multibillion-dollar Ponzi scheme. But regardless of what he did, the fact is, my husband was a prick. Everybody, including me, loved him when he was riding high and making them a bunch of money. But the second word broke that he was a fraud, everyone turned on him."

Her eyes water and she flutters her oversize fake eyelashes. "You can't imagine what it was like for me." As she says it, her tone changes. Venom coats every syllable. I've seen this in people with drinking problems before: a switch flips and things go dark. She stands up and paces around the kitchen island in the near blackness. She waves her glass in the air like a blade. "I used to be the queen of this city. I served on the board of the Met. I was on *Page Six* every other week. I was in the most exclusive clubs. People would beg me to attend their parties and events. Then Fredrick runs into a bit of trouble, and suddenly I'm a pariah. The clubs ask me to leave. The invitations dry up. All these bitches who were supposedly my friends wouldn't even return my call. You ask me if anyone hated Frederick. Hell, *I* hated Frederick." She slams her drink against the marble island. A chip of the crystal slides across the surface. The sound rings through the silence.

I hear a rumble from the floor above. Footsteps flying across the landing, down the stairs. A figure bursts from the shadows and hurdles down the steps, but the house is so dark, I can't tell what it is. Bobby and I snap up from the banquet table to see what's coming. It looks like a dog but moves like a cat. I peer through the darkness and can't believe what I'm seeing.

Two amber eyes glow back at me.

The eyes of a Siberian tiger.

I grab Bobby's arm and blink to make sure I'm not hallucinating.

But it's real. A three-hundred-pound tiger stalks toward me.

"George! Sit!" snaps Arika in a searing tone.

Bobby and I flinch.

The tiger pauses for a second, looks at Bobby, then me, licks his lips with a tongue the size of a rib eye, and lies on the floor. A massive yawn escapes his mouth.

"Jesus, you keep a tiger as a pet?" says Bobby, his voice cracking like a pubescent teenager's.

Arika pours more vodka into her glass and a splash of Bloody Mary mix, unconcerned with the fact that the bottom of her glass is chipped and her pet Siberian tiger nearly mauled us.

"Yes, sorry about that. George is very protective of me. He probably got upset when I slammed my glass down. What were we talking about?"

Bobby and I sigh and exchange glances that say, *Rich people.* He sits down, but I walk over to her. I can see that underneath her drunken, careless facade, she's a woman in pain. I put an arm around her. She feels like a bag of bones. Her entire being emanates vodka. That she's drunk makes the substance of this interview difficult to use in court, but she's given us good information. I grab a bottle of water from the fridge and hand it to her. At first, she looks at it like it's a foreign substance, but then she takes a sip. George the tiger keeps a watchful eye.

"Arika, I know your husband wasn't everyone's favorite, but was there anyone in particular who might have wanted him dead?"

She dabs a tear from her eye and shakes her head. "No, not that I can think of. Well, there was this one—" She stops herself.

I ease in closer to her. "One what?"

"You're going to think it's ridiculous, but in the weeks leading up to his death, Frederick thought he was being followed."

My mind flashes back to Bleecker Street, and my heart pounds. But I try not to show it. "By who?"

"I don't know—and truthfully, I assumed he was being paranoid. I figured it was a paparazzo following him for a cheap, unflattering picture. But then one night, we were strolling home from a benefit at the library, and there was this person—"

Bobby interjects. "Did you get a good look at him?"

Arika walks away from me and sidles in at the banquet next to Bobby, excited that he's giving her some attention.

"No, that was the odd thing about it. It was dark, and whoever it was, was far away and never moved closer. Just kept following us from the same distance in the shadows. Part of me thought both me and Frederick were being paranoid. The only thing I noticed was that they wore a Yankees cap and a black medical mask."

27

nease grips me as I slouch on the sidewalk in front of Arika Tweed's townhome. Bobby and I spent another half hour interviewing her after she dropped the bomb on us that Frederick was being stalked, but she was lost to the liquor. Even if she had told us something meaningful, I wouldn't have heard it. I checked out when I heard *Yankees cap* and *medical mask*. There's no debate now. Whoever followed me the other night is the same person who killed Kenneally and followed Fred Tweed before he died, and presumably poisoned him.

I bend over at the waist and put my hands on my knees. I breathe in the crisp air to find calm. Every time I think I've got a grip, my darkest memories come rushing back.

Five years ago: Waking up in the morning not knowing where I am. The cotton taste in my mouth. The blood on my leg.

One year ago: The sound of Mia's song. The smell of Andrew's cologne as he held me down. The sharpness of Sonia's knife at my throat.

Two days ago: The face mask and Yankees cap following me home. The fear, the rage.

The images flick through my mind like subliminal messages, reminding me of one thing: you'll never be safe.

"Are you okay?" asks Bobby as he lights a cigarette.

I stand up straight and look at the clear sky hovering over the swaying sea of gold and orange lining the park. "Yeah. I'm trying to absorb all this."

"What do you mean?"

"It's nothing."

He rests a hand on my shoulder. "Hazel, if you think it's something, then I guarantee it ain't nothing."

I turn to him. He wears an expression of genuine concern, like I'm the only person in his world.

"Okay. You're going to think this sounds a little crazy, but the Red-Letter Killer is stalking me."

He backpedals and pulls his hair back, exposing his receding hairline. Like Jack, his first reaction is anger, and a desire to kick some ass, but he's smart enough to conceal it. "That's awful. How do you know?"

"He was wearing a Yankees cap and a black respiratory mask."

"Jesus." He bites down on the white cigarette filter. "So it was definitely a man?"

I close my eyes and envision the person watching me from the park, trailing me on the sidewalk. "I think so, but I can't say for sure. They were wearing a full-length black parka and a hat and mask, and it was dark. It's too tough to say. But I'm 90 percent sure it's a man. It would have to be a pretty big woman."

"I can call in a favor and secure some boys from the unit to watch your house for a week."

I'm tempted to say yes, but I know the NYPD has more important duties than babysitting me. "Thanks, but I can take care of myself." He raises an eyebrow and tilts his head. "I promise. I'll be fine," I insist.

He lingers on me for another second but then lets it go. "Okay. Well, this blows my theory out of the water. I thought Arika Tweed invented that whole stalker story as misdirection, but clearly that's not the case. Anything else she said jump out at you?"

I step to the side and lean against the black wrought-iron gate as a tour group plows by me and gawks at a bronze plaque on the historical building next door. "A few things. I didn't want to discuss it in front of Arika, but we can safely conclude the killer is using pills to poison the victims. Both Dinwiddie and Tweed took pills shortly before they died, and they were both taking pills they took daily. And Sam said Kenneally kept a daily pill case."

Bobby paces the sidewalk and shoots smoke out of his mouth in his signature blow-dart style. "I noticed that too. What that tells me is that our suspect likely has experience with chemistry or pharmaceuticals. Tetrodotoxin doesn't come in pill form."

"Not only that, but Tweed and Dinwiddie ingested different pills. Tweed took sleeping pills and Dinwiddie took baby aspirin. The killer had to know what pills they took and how to make similar-looking ones. They had to dye the pills and compress them into different sizes and shapes. Not a straightforward task." I think of Sandy Godo and his work in pharmaceuticals and wonder if Jack's theory isn't so crazy after all.

"That's good news, though. Because now we know that the killer had to get close to the victims beforehand."

Now I start pacing. The two of us look like lunatics pacing past each other. "Yes, they either knew the victims or got very close to them. Can you see if there is any available NYPD video footage from around Jack's house, the Tweed home, St. Patrick's, and the archdiocese in the days leading up to the murders? Maybe we can spot our suspect in the Yankees hat."

"Good call. I'll see what I can find. I doubt we'll have anything from the Tweed and Kenneally murders because they were so long ago, but I might be able to find something from the archdiocese and Jack's place. It will take some time, though."

"Yeah, that's the one thing we don't have."

"Switching gears, did you notice Arika drop the fact that she"—he raises his fingers in air quotes—"'hated her husband'?"

"Yeah, but I think that was drunken venting. I can't picture her being involved."

"I wouldn't put it past her to hire somebody, though. God knows she has the money."

"Does she though? The majority is tied up in Tweed's court battles."

"All I know is, she's still living in that house."

"Yeah, but why poison people when you can have your black market Siberian tiger kill them?"

Bobby laughs.

I continue. "Seriously, though, the other thing we have to

consider is the money trail. The archdiocese is battling the sexual abuse victims over payments. Imagine if the killer was pissed about getting shafted on his payment. You take that information and combine it with the fact that Tweed managed and lost the funds, and we've got a motive."

"Yeah, but how are Dinwiddie and Kenneally connected?"

"Who knows? Maybe they partnered with Tweed on the deal."

He shivers as the wind kicks up. He rubs the sleeves of his navy-and-white gingham button-down. "It's freezing out here. You want to go grab some breakfast? There's a solid diner on Seventh two blocks from here."

I look at him and catch the spark of hope in his eyes. I think he still wants to date me, and if I'm being honest, part of me wishes I had tried dating him. I love Jack, but there's an insecurity in him that makes me feel like I'm always trying to clutch something that's slipping away. That restless ambition attracted me to him, but when I contrast it with Bobby, who stands solid in who he is, it makes Jack look unsteady by comparison. Bobby's not asking me to have an affair with him. He's asking me to brunch. Still, I don't want to open the door. I love Jack too much.

"Thanks for the offer, but I should get going."

Bobby nods and takes a drag. "I understand." He snaps and claps his hands together to chase the awkwardness away. "I'll look at the video footage and let you know what I find."

"Sounds good. I'll look into the Tweed–archdiocese money situation and research how someone can go about making pills." I give him a hug and take a whiff of his unique blend of smoke and cologne.

Timing is everything, I guess.

We say our goodbyes, and I head up Prospect Park West toward the subway station, looking around to make sure nobody is following me. Fortunately, my stalker seems to be taking the day off. Before I descend the subway stairs, I stop at a bodega and order a breakfast sandwich. Bobby talking about brunch made me hungry. As I'm diving into a bacon, egg, and cheese on a bun, my phone rings. I look down at my screen: it's Shavali. I'm so famished, I don't have the discipline to delay the first taste before answering. I take a huge bite and then answer, "Hewo?" with a cheek full of egg and bacon.

It was worth it.

"Hazel, are you okay?" she says.

She must have seen the news about Dinwiddie. I speak through a mouthful of cheese and bun. "Yeah, I'm fine. Just a little rattled. It's tough to watch someone die right in front of you like that."

There's an extended pause. "Oh, yes. I heard about Dinwiddie, and that's dreadful, but I'm not calling about that. I'm calling about Jack."

I swallow my food but feel like I'm swallowing something more. "What about Jack? Is something wrong?"

"I…I'm sorry. I assumed you were with him and had heard. He's being investigated for campaign-finance violations. Someone in the DA's office leaked it to the *Post*."

All the sounds of the city—the horns honking, pedestrians chattering, cyclists whizzing by—fade to silence as I stand in Grand Army Plaza with my mouth agape, holding my breakfast sandwich like an idiot. Jack taking bribes? There's no way. He's one of the most honest men I've ever met. He doesn't even need the money. "Are you sure? There must be some kind of mistake."

Shavali sighs, and the way she sighs tells me she knows more than she's letting on. I think about Jack's luxurious townhome, about the tennis bracelet he gave me, about how irritated he got when I asked him how he could afford it.

"Shay, talk to me. I can handle it."

"I think it's true, Haze. I think he did it. I spoke with a friend of mine in the DA's office, and he told me off the record that they have him on tape. They have his bank records. Everything. The only reason they haven't charged him yet is that there's an election coming up, so they're navigating the politics of it all. I'm so sorry, Hazel. I hate to be the one to tell you."

I can tell from her voice that she means it. She sounds as sick as I feel. Still, I want to yell at Shavali. To tell her she's lying, that she's making all this up because she's jealous of me and Jack. But I know it's not her fault. She's telling me the truth. It's like that old saying, "A true friend stabs you in the front." I smother my instinct to kill the messenger.

"Don't apologize, Shay. I appreciate you telling me. I'd rather find out from you than the news." I toss my breakfast sandwich in the trash and head toward the entrance to the subway. I can't eat right now. "I gotta go. I need to talk to Jack."

"I completely understand, love. But before you go, I need you to know one more thing. My friend told me that one of the men who supported Jack, who gave him a sweetheart deal on his townhome mortgage?"

"Yeah?"

"Was Frederick Tweed."

28

When I watched that philandering priest squirm and choke out his last breath, I'd never felt so alive. I'd never felt so close to Jesus. When I summoned the Holy Spirit again and sent him to that gluttonous thief Fred Tweed, I walked on clouds for days at the thought of his heart ceasing in the Holy Spirit's presence. Of him choking on his own spit. Realizing that his selfishness and greed would finally be punished. The news showed footage of his corpse, drawn up and cold, and I smiled at the thought of him burning for eternity.

I have been patient.

Too patient.

Before the Father destroyed Sodom and Gomorrah, he gave Abraham a chance. He said that if Abraham's son Lot could find fifty righteous people, he would spare the city. When Lot failed to find fifty righteous men, God told him if he could find ten, the city would be spared.

There are no righteous men in this city.

Every day the world grows more sinful, more diseased.

And I sit and watch it rot.

Jesus will not tolerate that.

I must put an end to the evil. I must kill in his name. I must make every sinner scream with pain until there is no breath left in them. I must teach the world the price of their sin.

I must kill until all the sinners are gone and the few righteous ones see.

Then he will come back.

And I will sit by his side.

29

By the time I get to Jack's townhome, I'm in a full rage. Not because he took bribes, and not because he lied, but because I feel duped. Someone lying to you is rough, but being the last person to find out is ten times worse. One hundred times worse when it's someone you love.

Over the past few months we've been dating, I opened my heart to him. I told him about my hopes and dreams. I told him about my issues with my family. About my problems trusting men. About the darkest moments in my life. And I felt like he listened and understood. That because he has such a close relationship with his mom and sister, he might understand what it's like to be me.

I trusted him.

That he could lie to my face and hold a secret like this makes me feel like a sucker.

Like Andrew made me feel.

I throw open the door, and Jack's on the phone, pacing the hardwood floors, running his hand along the top of the sectional, defending himself with all the Texas charm he can muster. Fading sunlight flows in behind him. He's in full politician gear: navy slacks and a gray wool sport coat and a baby-blue dress shirt. He throws me a crooked smile and a wave, then rubs a hand through his sandy-blond hair. I expected to feel anger when I saw him, but I only feel disappointment. He let me down like every other man in my life.

I look at him and can't help thinking of my father. He was my hero, but he could never find time for me. There was always some excuse. He had to stay late at the market he and my mother owned. He had to play golf or cards, or bowl with his friends. He was too tired. I remember sitting down for my piano recitals, scanning the crowd, hoping that he would show, but he never did. I would come home, and he always waved it away with an excuse, but his sad eyes told me something different.

That he had no excuse.

My father's better now. As he's aged, he's learned what matters. But when I look at Jack, I see those same sad eyes.

Jack cajoles a reporter on the phone. "Lilly, these accusations are absurd. You know that. This is all a bunch of rumor and innuendo released by the Godo campaign to make me look bad. It'll all come out in the wash once they hear my side of the story. What you should really do is look at Godo and all this pharmaceutical money. His campaign is bought and paid for by the drug companies overcharging seniors and lining their pockets. You'll see—"

I snatch the phone out of his hand and hang up.

"Bubs, what—"

I shove him in the chest. It's an immature move, I know, but I can't help myself. I'm so tired of men and their lying bullshit. "How could you do this?"

Jack raises his palms, his eyes open wide. "Calm down, now. Didn't you hear me on the phone? I haven't done anything. This is all a big misunderstanding."

"Are you seriously going to look me in the eye and tell me you've done nothing wrong?"

His forehead scrunches in confusion. I must say, he's one hell of an actor. "What are you talking about?"

"I talked to Shavali, Jack. I know the accusations aren't just rumor and innuendo. There's a money trail. The DA is going to file a criminal complaint against you."

His soft expression turns sharp. His eyes squint, and his forehead creases. "So, what, you and Shavali are gossiping behind my back now? I wish you had talked to me first. I feel like I deserve a little benefit of the doubt."

His harsh countenance knocks me off-balance. The man standing in front of me now is not the Jack I know. There's a crack in the facade. But I've seen this movie before. The guilty trying to flip the attention from them to me. Trying to make me feel like the bad guy. That Jack would even try this on me only fuels my anger. "Don't pull that gaslighting bullshit on me. This isn't about me or Shavali. This is about you and the fact that you've been taking bribes."

He sulks into the kitchen and opens the refrigerator. He grabs a bottle of Lone Star out of the fridge and fiddles with the cap. I can tell he's buying time for his next excuse. His voice hardens. "Stop calling it a bribe, all right? I never took a bribe. I took donations and a home loan. I never promised anybody anything. Did they think they were buying influence? Sure. But I wouldn't give them anything once I got into office. You think I give a rip about those rich a-holes? They were the means to an end."

He takes a long swig of his beer, rests it on the counter, and then walks toward me. He puts his hands on my shoulders and softens his expression. "You know me, Hazel. You know why I'm doing this. I'm doing this for the folks who need an advocate. For the people who can't fight for themselves. Godo's got all that pharmaceutical money. He lives in his mansion and funds his own campaign. All those finance guys got politicians in their pocket. I figured, What's wrong with me bending the rules so that it's a fair fight and I can still pay my bills? So you and I can have a decent life? The life you deserve."

It's impressive how easily he's rationalized this. I wriggle out of his grip. "Don't you dare pull me into your choices. I never asked for any of this. I never wanted a diamond tennis bracelet. I don't need this townhome. You've seen where Kenny and I live. I walk four flights of stairs every day to get home. My wallpaper looks like a Rorschach test. I'll eat ramen all day if that's what it takes. You did this for you, not me."

"So that's how you're going to play it? When everything's going good and I'm on track to be the next mayor and own a nice place and give you gifts, you're on my side. But the second things get rough, you jump ship?"

I take a step back and assess his face, a portrait of selfishness and ego, and I realize that I'm seeing a piece of Jack that he's been hiding from me. The calculating politician lying beneath his *Aw, shucks* Texas routine. They say that power reveals; so does crisis.

"I'm not jumping ship. I'm asking you to tell me the truth."

He gulps his beer, hems and haws, and throws up his hands. He gazes into my eyes. His voice shakes. "I'm the only guy who's out there every day fighting for working people who are getting their butts kicked by the system. You think any of those other city council members give a damn about whether poor kids have a decent meal? About whether abused moms have a safe place to stay? Hell no. I'm the only one. But I can't do that if me and my campaign are as poor as they are."

I watch his face. This isn't an act. In his mind, he thinks he deserves this. He believes that if you spend your career fighting for underprivileged kids and single moms, you're beyond reproach. The question is, How far does he think he can go?

"I know that, but that's not what this is about. No one is saying you haven't done amazing things for people in need. That's why I fell in love with you. I remember our second date, when you derailed our dinner so that you could walk that homeless vet to the nearest shelter. I've never seen someone who cares so much about people he's never met. But that doesn't give you the license to break the law. Don't you get that?"

He flicks the beer bottle with his middle finger and leans on the counter. He scratches the stubble on his chin, probably pondering whether he should say what he's about to say.

"Yeah, I get it, bubs. But here's what you don't understand. You live in the regular world, where most people are going about their business, too concerned about their own lives to be worried about you or anyone else. A world where the vast majority of people play by the rules.

"I live in a world of professional politics. I don't talk to you about it a lot, because when I'm with you, I want to enjoy being with you. But you gotta understand that politics is a nasty, nasty game. These people don't play by the rules. This is a no-holds-barred war, and people will lie, cheat, steal, and stab you in the back if that's what it takes to win. And if you play it perfectly straight, you will lose. I guarantee it. And I hate that. I wish everybody would behave honorably and it was 'May the best man win,' but that ain't how it is. Every day, I've got a full-on money machine focused on one thing: tearin' me down. Assassinating my character. And it burns like hell."

He taps his chest and takes a sip of beer as if to douse the metaphorical fire. As he speaks, I see the frustration building on his face. I don't forgive him, but I understand him.

"Put yourself in my shoes. Imagine if everyday people were spending millions of dollars, running social media campaigns, television ads, direct mail pieces, telling everybody that Hazel Cho and C&S Investigations are trash. That you can't be trusted. That you don't care about this city. To where even your friends, your family, hell, your girlfriend, question who you are and what you're about. And you're sitting there thinking, *All I'm trying to do is make things a little better.* You're telling me you would sit there and take it? Bullshit. Don't you think you'd want to fight back? To let people know that everything they're saying is a lie. That you're not the person they're making you out to be? That you really can make the city better?"

I nod. "Of course, but—"

"Well, in this game, you don't get heard without money. And that's why I did what I did."

He slams the rest of his beer and sets it down on the counter. Blood rushes to his face, and a vein protrudes from his forehead. But as I watch him, I see that he's not angry—he's frustrated.

I step closer to him and study his movements as I ask my next question. "Jack, what was your relationship with Fred Tweed before he died?"

His eyes jump left and right, and his mouth twists to the side. He blows past me into the living room and gazes out the window onto Washington Square Park, his shoulders slumped, defeated.

"I'd like you to leave," he says without looking back at me. "I need some time to think."

"I'd like you to answer my question."

Jack turns and points his finger at me. I can see that it's shaking.

"Don't interrogate me like one of your suspects, Hazel." I flinch. He never calls me Hazel. I stare at him but say nothing, waiting to see if he'll break.

"Please go!" he shouts in a guttural voice I've never heard before, and hope I never hear again.

My face burns, and tears form in my eyes. I can't believe this is happening. Despite everything he's done, I still love him. That's the funny thing about love. It doesn't turn on and off; it brightens and dims. He's not an evil man. He's lost.

I turn away. My footsteps echo on the hardwood like the Doomsday Clock. I rotate the brass knob on the townhome I had hoped would one day be my future home. I can't stand the thought of returning to my crappy apartment right now. But it's like the bartenders say: *You don't have to go home, but you can't stay here.* As I walk out the door, I take one last look back at Jack. He's sitting on the couch, his head in his hands, crying.

30

The next morning I awake to a vicious hangover and the sound of gunshots. I snap up in my bed and yank my comforter tight to my chest. My stomach clenches, and my heart rate doubles. I listen closer. The gunshots seem far away, and button clicks accompany them. I release a breath. It's Kenny playing Call of Duty. One of these days I'm going to heave that PlayStation out the window.

I wipe the sleep out of my eyes and take a sip of water to wash the sticky alcohol taste out of my mouth. After my fight with Jack, I spent the evening polishing off a bottle of wine and venting to Kenny about Jack. It's one of those times when I thank God I have a roommate. If I had had to walk home and wallow in Nicholas Sparks's movies alone, it wouldn't have been pretty. I glimpse myself in the full-length mirror propped against my wall. I look like the lead singer of an '80s glam-rock band. I need a shower.

I check my phone. The screen shows fifteen missed calls from Jack, three from my mother, and two from my sister. Part of me was hoping I had dreamed the whole thing. Something about seeing the call log makes it real. My chest feels heavy, like when you're a teenager and you've done something wrong and you're afraid your parents might find out.

But I've done nothing wrong.

And when I think about it, it's not Jack that's bothering me. We can confront our issues, deal with them, hopefully resolve them. I realize what's really bothering me is that there's a serial killer out there who's getting closer to me, and the prospect of finding him seems further away than ever. My mind skips to the image of the killer sitting on the park bench outside Jack's house, frozen, watching me; to the red letter sitting on Father Kenneally's desk; to the twisted Bible verses typed meticulously on the paper; to the sound of "Danny Boy" ringing through the streets. Whoever is doing this, their sickness is infectious. It gets inside your gut like a worm, feeds on your fear, and grows with every minute.

My phone rings and I flinch. I curse myself for being so jumpy. One day, I'll be an action hero with nerves of steel, but that day is not today. It's my sister, Christina. I roll my eyes and answer the phone. Time to rip the Band-Aid off.

"Hello, Christina," I say.

"Oh my God, Hazel. Are you okay?"

I chew on my lip as I listen to her melodrama. I can tell she's battling two genuine emotions: concern for her sister, and joy at the drama of it all. I roll myself out of bed and walk into our living room slash kitchen. As I look down at my red pajama pants and Union T-shirt, I'm slightly impressed with myself for not sleeping in my clothes. "Yeah, I'm fine. It's been a tough couple of days."

"I'm sure it has. I mean, this is crazy. When I saw on the news that Jack's under investigation, I couldn't believe it. Is it true?" She asks as though she's hoping it's not true, but underneath you can tell she's wishing for the opposite. My sister and I have always been in competition. That Mom loves Jack so much has been a real thorn in her side. Me dating a felon would be a real win for her.

"No, it's not true. It's just political attacks," I say. I know it probably *is* true, but I can't give Christina the satisfaction right now.

She sighs, apparently disappointed that the cops won't be dragging Jack off to prison immediately. I give Kenny a wave as I enter the living room. A cold draft creeps through the gaps in our poorly sealed windows. He waves back and pauses his game as he sees me talking on the phone. He points to the kitchen table, and I can see a plate with a glass lid on top of it. He cooked me pancakes.

Best. Roommate. Ever.

I give him the heart sign as I grab a sugar-free Red Bull out of the fridge. I'll need liquid energy to survive this call with Christina. I grab a blanket off the couch and wrap it around myself to ward off the cold.

"And what's the deal with this archbishop dying? Mom said you saw it happen?" My sister's adopted a Kardashian-like upward inflection at the end of her sentences that grates.

I lift the lid off the pancakes and grin. Kenny made his

signature apple-cinnamon pancakes. My favorite. The scent of apples and cinnamon swirling together sends my stomach leaping. I take a bite, and all my troubles melt away. I shoot Kenny a thumbs-up and he smiles. With a mouthful of pancake, I say, "Christina, I can't discuss this. It's an active investigation."

"Are you eating? What are you eating?"

"Pancakes," I say with pancake stuffed in my cheek.

"Oh, Hazel, those are empty carbs."

I drop my fork and rub my eyes. I don't have time for this. "I can't do this right now. I've got work to do. I gotta go. I'll tell you all about it at family dinner."

"Okay, b—"

I hang up the phone and growl. My sister is the master of getting to me.

"That sounded like it went well," says Kenny as he rises from the couch and joins me at the kitchen table. He's wearing a black T-shirt and gray joggers, and I notice his biceps look a little juicier than normal. One day he's wearing suits, the next day he's getting ripped. What's happening to my Kenny?

"Yeah, my sister's a lot. I sometimes feel like she's cheering for me to fail."

"I guess that's one good thing about being an only child. I missed out on the whole sibling-rivalry thing." I nod my agreement as I take another massive bite of my pancake. Syrup drips down my chin. So sweet. So good. Kenny smiles and hands me a napkin. "So, you hate the pancakes, huh?"

"Mm-hmm."

My phone rings again. It's my mother. Another eye roll. I look at Kenny, hoping he's going to give me the green light to screen her call. Mary tells me I need to be nicer to my family, and she's right, but there're days when you—

"You should answer," he says. "She's probably worried sick about you." He gets up and pours himself a cup of coffee.

Damn him for being so nice. I'm living and working with my conscience. I take another bite of my pancake, the sugar and cinnamon compensation for dealing with my mother.

"Hi, Mom," I say with a mouthful of pancake in as chipper a voice as I can muster.

"Hanuel," she says. "Is Jack okay?"

And that pretty much sums it up. *Is Jack okay?* I repeat in my mind. I swallow my pancake and look up at our water-stained ceiling, searching for grace.

"Yes, Mom, Jack is okay," I say and side-eye Kenny. He smirks and shrugs.

"Hi, Mrs. Cho," he says, leaning toward the phone.

My mom ignores him. "The local news said Jack's in trouble. They said he stole some money. That's not true, is it?"

I drop my fork and rise from the kitchen table. I sip my Red Bull and pace the living room.

"No. Don't listen to that stuff, Mom. It's politics. It'll all be fine." It won't be fine, but if I tell my mom that, I'll never get off this call.

"And what about this serial killer I'm hearing about? The Red-Letter Killer, they're calling him."

"Yes, what about it?"

"I'm worried about you. Your father and I think you should come stay with us for a while."

I massage my forehead while I pace. I love the way she says

your father and I as though the two of them had an in-depth discussion about the matter, when in reality she probably suggested it while he was half paying attention, half playing dominoes with friends, and he absentmindedly nodded agreement. And it kills me how my mom somehow thinks that her home is an impenetrable fortress. As though the Red-Letter Killer is thinking, *Damn, I was going to kill Hazel, but now she's at Byung and Kyusil's house. I'm screwed. There's no way in that compound.*

"Mom, I'm thirty-one years old. I'm not moving back in with you."

Kenny laughs as he overhears what I'm saying.

For the next five minutes, my mom and I go back and forth, her peppering me with questions—"What happened with the archbishop? When will we get to see Jack? Who's this serial killer?"—and me doing my best not to answer them. Finally, I can't take anymore.

"Mom, I have to go."

"What? Why? What have you got to do that's more important than talking to your mother?"

"Well, you know that serial killer you're worried about? I'm investigating him."

"Oh." For once, I've caught my mom speechless. She pauses, and I can almost hear her thoughts bouncing around in her skull. She wants to tell me to quit the investigation, but she knows that will only provoke me. I was one of those kids who, if you told me not to touch a button, would touch it. She sighs. "You must be careful, Hanuel." I hear the genuine concern in her voice.

"I will, Mom. I promise."

We hang up the phone, and I take a deep breath. I look out our window onto Columbus Park across the street. It must be freezing outside, judging by how lonely the park looks. Normally, the tables would be jammed with old ladies playing mah-jonng and men playing Go, but today it's a ghost town. A gust of wind kicks up and whistles through our walls. I pull my blanket tighter over me. I'm about to say something to Kenny when my phone beeps, letting me know I've got three voicemails from Jack.

Part of me doesn't want to listen to them—I'm afraid that his honey voice and smooth drawl will make me forget what he did—but then I look down again at the three messages blinking at me. It's so unlike him. So desperate. I wonder if there's something more behind them than a simple apology. I press play on the first voicemail.

5:34 p.m.

"Haze, I wanted to say how sorry I am about tonight, about everything. I'm ashamed of myself, and I took it out on you, and you didn't deserve that. This whole thing is my fault, and I take full responsibility. I know you were only trying to understand the situation, and I should have shot straight with you from the beginning. I love you and I'm sorry. I understand you probably need alone time right now, but I hope you'll call me when you get a chance so we can talk more. I love you."

The voicemail punches me in the gut. A tear gathers in my eye. Jack has it so together all the time that I sometimes forget he's human. And human beings make mistakes. I heard it in his voice—the realness, the fatigue from constantly putting on a show. I love him. And I know part of loving someone is accepting them, warts and all. Is this a mistake I can forgive?

I hold my breath and listen to the next message. In this voicemail, Jack's tone sounds completely different. There's a desperation in his words. His voice quakes, and his breath sounds sharp and shallow.

7:22 p.m.

"Haze, I'm sorry to bother you with another call, but something's come up and you're the only one I can talk to about this. I just got the mail, and I found—" His voice cracks and he pauses. "I found a red envelope."

The phone drops from my hand and clatters against the floor. Kenny's forehead creases when he sees the look on my face. I pick up the phone and put a hand to my mouth. No, no, no. This can't be real.

Jack clears his throat, his voice barely above a whisper. I can hear him opening the letter, the paper snapping as it releases from the adhesive. I swear I catch the hiss of evil escaping as he pulls the letter from the envelope.

"It looks like the one you told me Kenneally received. It says… Oh no. It says, 'My house shall be called the house of prayer; but you have made it a den of thieves.'"

Terror rips through me. This monster is coming after Jack. My Jack. I snap at Kenny and point to his coat while I listen to the rest of the message. He jumps up from the couch, sensing something is wrong.

Jack continues. "There's a drawing on the paper too. It looks like blood. Naked people twisting in pain…and snakes. I'm a little freaked out here, Haze. I'm not sure what to do. I don't want to call the police with everything that's happening. I could sure use your help. Call me when you get this."

He hangs up, and I dial Jack's number. Every ring sounds like an alarm in my ears. His voicemail picks up, which scares me even more. Jack's a politician. He answers every call. I drop my phone to my side in disbelief. My brain fires with possibilities.

"What is it?" asks Kenny as he throws his coat on.

"Jack got a red letter," I say. I stifle sobs as I speak.

"Oh shit. I'll get a cab." Kenny throws open the door and runs down the steps. I lock the door, but as I do, I realize there's one more voicemail. I fly down the stairs and press play.

10:37 p.m.

"Hi, Haze. I promise this is the last voicemail. It's late, so I'm going to call it a night. I want you to know that I've locked the doors and windows and set the alarm, so I should be in good shape until morning. Whenever you get this, please call me. I understand I'm not your favorite guy right now, but I'm scared as hell and you're the only person who I can trust. I love you and I'll talk to you in the morning."

His words echo in my ears. *I'm going to call it a night.*

That means he went to bed.

That means he took his multivitamin.

If that fucking maniac broke into his place, he could have tampered with Jack's pills. I vault down the steps and dive into a cab with Kenny, terrified at what I might find.

31

This is an emergency. Go as fast as you can!" I scream to the cab driver. Sweat drenches my palms, and my heart strobes in my chest. I grab Kenny's hand and he grabs mine. We look at each other but say nothing. We both know what's at stake.

The cab driver weaves through traffic on Canal Street, honking his horn in rapid beeps to clear the other cars. The interior of the cab squeaks and groans as we shift left and right. Kenny and I hold on to the handgrips, knuckles white, in silence, both trying to envision every outcome and what we can do about it now. I try to think of the positive. Maybe Jack's out for a run. Maybe he took a morning nap. Maybe he's on a call with the media. There's a million reasons he might not be answering.

Then I think of that red letter.

Of what it means. Of what has happened to everyone who received that letter before him. I pray we're not too late.

I smack Kenny on the shoulder. "You call 911, and I'll call Jack."

He picks up his phone and dials 911.

I dial Jack again. The call goes straight to voicemail.

Kenny connects with the emergency dispatcher. "Yes, I need to speak with poison control, and I need an ambulance to 23 Washington Square North. My friend has been poisoned."

We don't know that Jack's been poisoned, I tell myself. He could be running errands. But it's the right thing to do.

The cab veers onto Sixth Avenue at full speed, engine roaring, but it feels like we're moving in slow motion. The city disintegrates around me, and I pray to God for one simple thing.

Please don't do this.

Please don't do this.

Please don't do this.

Kenny squeezes my hand tighter, and I feel my whole body shaking. But it's not fear; it's the realization that someone I love, someone I count on, someone I need, could be ripped away from me in an instant. A wave of nausea and fear rises from my stomach to my chest, then my throat and mouth. I realize how little in my life I have besides Jack. How few relationships I have that fulfill me.

He can't leave me.

He can't.

The cab screams onto Washington Square North and screeches to a halt in front of Jack's townhome.

What's supposed to be our townhome.

Park-goers stare at us as we exit the cab, but I couldn't care less. Kenny throws the driver a twenty, and we leap up the front steps. I turn the key and throw the door open.

The lights are off, and I immediately sense something's wrong. No one in here has moved since last night. The air is stale. There's no smell of food. No scent of Jack's cologne. No fresh air.

"Jack!" I shout as my eyes scan the living room for any sign of him.

The room sits empty.

The house is silent.

Kenny investigates the living room while I run upstairs, jumping the steps two at a time. "Jack!" we both shout simultaneously.

I reach the second floor, where the bedroom is.

"Jack," I say, softer this time, as though somehow that will make him appear.

No answer.

I step closer to the bedroom, and dread envelops me. Every hair on my body stands on end. My greatest hope is that the room is empty. That Jack has gone somewhere. That he's still in this world.

With each step and creak of the hardwood, I feel my hope sink.

I reach the doorway of the bedroom.

Then I see him.

Jack.

Splayed out on the rug.

He lies on his side in his white T-shirt and blue-striped boxers. A sickly shade of yellow runs through his skin. The muscles of his face are contorted in a visceral expression of agony. His body twisted, crumpled and broken. A pool of vomit rests beside him.

My heart shatters into a million pieces.

I drop to my knees and turn him onto his back. I place two fingers on his carotid artery, searching for his pulse.

His skin is ice cold.

His heartbeat is gone.

I place my palms on his chest and perform compressions. Pump. Pump. Pump. I breathe into his mouth and hear the oxygen swirl in his lungs. Pump. Pump. Pump.

I grab his face and turn it toward me. I shake his shoulders and shout his name.

"Jack, come back to me, baby. Please. I need you. I can't do this alone."

Pump. Pump. Pump.

I pump until my hands go numb. Until my shoulders feel like they'll come loose from their sockets. I kiss him, my tears running down my face and falling onto his. I press my cheek against his cheek, hoping my warmth, somehow, will bring him back to life. But it's not even Jack that I'm touching. It's a man-size doll made in Jack's likeness, cold and lifeless.

I pump again, looking into his eyes, willing them to look back at me. But they've drifted to another place. A place I can't bring him back from. The realization overwhelms me. I stop pumping and bury my head in his chest, overcome with the notion that I will never see him again.

Kenny's steps bang down the hallway, and he reaches the bedroom. He sees me, then he sees Jack, and he brings both hands to his face. He absorbs the hurt echoing from me and says, "Is he…?"

I sniffle and nod.

He kneels to the floor and resumes the chest compressions. Jack's body moves stiffly, like a CPR dummy. I appreciate that Kenny's trying, but I know there's no hope. Jack's been dead for hours.

I put my hand on Kenny's shoulder.

"Kenny, stop."

He ignores me and keeps going, pumping on Jack's chest and breathing air into his lifeless body.

I say it louder. "Stop."

He ceases and falls back to the floor. He runs his fingers through his black hair, like me, in disbelief at what he's seeing. For the next few minutes, he and I stay there, catching our breaths, sitting beside Jack, wondering how we can turn back time.

32

ime blurs, and my mind leaves my body, but I'm guessing
thirty minutes later, the police arrive. I sit downstairs alone
in the living room, staring out the window at Washington
Square Park. Street performers brave the cold. The central foun-
tain roars. But I'm not looking at them.

I'm lost in oblivion.

My entire body shakes and spasms, and I can't stop it. I'm not
even trying. My face is stiff from dried tears. Officers run up and
down the stairs, placing folded business cards on potentially relevant locations or objects. They brought Kenny up to the second
floor so they can interview us separately. Standard procedure.

I replay every moment from the last twenty-four hours,
drinking in the cocktail of regret and missed opportunities. I
never should have left him. I should have stayed with him, listened to his side of the story, talked it out. He told me to leave,

but I saw it in his eyes. He wanted me to stay. He wanted someone to fight with him, fight for him. But I was too chickenshit and ran away. What kind of person does that? You don't bail on someone you love when times get tough; you stand beside them. I know that Jack would have stood beside me.

I should have answered the phone instead of burying my feelings in a bottle of wine. While I sat in my apartment, bitching and moaning, the killer lurked and smiled, waiting for Jack to take the pill that would kill him. Why didn't I check the mail? One glance at the letters, and I would have seen it right away. That blood shade of red. That cold, lifeless type. The stamp depicting the Mother Mary. My insides twist from the knowledge that if I'd done any of those things, my Jack would still be alive.

The sobs force their way up through my chest, and I break down again. It's as though everything inside me—the regret, the self-loathing, the sadness—is trying to escape. Two cops watch me with sympathy in their eyes, trying to find the right words to say. But there are none, so they leave me in peace.

I hear the front door open and men's voices speaking in hushed tones. One of them sounds familiar. I wipe my eyes and look up as they enter. Then my face drops.

It's Detective Marcos.

It's not an exaggeration to say he is the last person on earth I want to see right now.

We make eye contact, and he adopts the phony pursed-lip look of sympathy that people do at funerals, but it's so insincere and condescending that it sickens me. He's not sorry for me. He's not sorry for anyone. He's here to do his job.

I prepare for him to head in my direction, but he ignores me and jogs upstairs. He wants to interview Kenny before he talks to me. That way he'll know the facts and might catch me in a lie. Twenty minutes later, he trudges down the stairs, his heavy boots against the hardwood sounding like gunshots.

He struts over to me, and I straighten up in my seat. I don't want to give him the satisfaction of seeing how broken I am. He kneels down beside me and looks me in the eye. His forehead hangs over his coal-brown eyes, casting a shadow, but they seem sincere. He scratches his coffee-colored stubble while he speaks.

"I'm sorry for your loss, Cho. I know we've had our differences, but I can't imagine what you're going through right now."

"Thanks."

"This is my least favorite part of the job, but as you know, I need to ask you some questions. Are you feeling up to it?"

Bullshit, I think to myself. This is his favorite part of the job. He's got me at the scene of two murders in two days. This is his lucky week. Still, I bury my fury. Right now, we're on the same team. We're both trying to find the villain who did this. "Yeah, I can answer questions."

We walk into Jack's office. Marcos shuts the door. I sit in Jack's cracked green leather desk chair, and my heart shatters all over again. I can smell his cologne. I can see the pictures of the two of us at his family's annual summer barbecue. He holds me around my waist, and I remember him tickling me as we took the picture. I swear I can hear his voice. I rub my eyebrows and cover my eyes to hide from Marcos.

He sets up a video recorder and presses record. He notes the date and time of the interview. I grab the throw hanging over the chair and wrap it around myself, stealing any piece of Jack I can.

"Why don't we start with you telling me what happened?"

My chest clenches so hard, I can barely speak, but if I don't do this now, I never will. I clear the phlegm from my throat. My voice is so hollow, I don't recognize it. "I, um…I woke up this morning and had a voicemail from Jack."

"Where were you?"

"I was in my kitchen."

"You didn't sleep here last night?"

"Correct." I answer his questions, but float outside myself. One part of my mind drifts in space, reliving every moment I shared with Jack, while the other responds to Marcos. I now know what it's like to be a ghost.

"Is there a reason you didn't sleep here?"

I shoot him an eyebrow raise with a knife's edge. "We each have our own place. I often sleep at my house."

"I understand that. But last night specifically, any reason you didn't sleep over? My understanding from Kenny is that you were here yesterday."

Now I see what he's getting at. He wants me to say Jack and I got into a fight. I probably should downplay the argument, but I'm too ruined to care. "Yes. I was here yesterday, but I left because we had an argument."

He adopts an expression of concern like a therapist. "What about?"

"You know what it was about, Marcos. The media reported that Jack had received illegal donations, and I confronted him about it."

For the next five minutes, he grills me about the specifics of our argument. What time did it occur? What did Jack say? How did that make me feel? After he's satisfied that he's painted the entire picture of yesterday, he moves back to today.

"I want to make sure I understand everything. You said that Jack called you last night. What time was that?"

"There were a few calls from about five p.m. to ten thirty p.m. But I didn't answer. He left voicemails. I'll forward them to you."

"And can I see that call log?"

It's his job to check, but the implication that I could be lying still stings. I show him my phone. He screenshots the log and sends it to himself before continuing the interview.

"And what did he say?"

"He said he had received a red letter, like the one Kenneally received."

"How did he know it was similar to Kenneally's letter?"

"Because I discussed the case with him. And because it contained a Bible verse."

"What was the verse?"

"I don't remember the exact verse, but it was about the den of thieves."

A knowing smile rises on his face. "'My house shall be called the house of prayer; but you have made it a den of thieves.'"

"You know it?"

His mouth crooks. "Yeah, twelve years of Catholic school." I nod casually, but in my mind, I make a note. "What did you do after you listened to the voicemail?"

"Kenny and I hailed a cab and came here."

"Why didn't you drive? You have a car, right?"

"Because there's no parking in this city, and my car is about five blocks from my apartment."

"You didn't call him?" As he questions me, I notice that his mask of sympathy fades and his interrogatory posture rises.

"Yes, I called him, but he didn't answer."

"What happened when you got here?"

"I went upstairs to search for him and found him in the bedroom, de—" I can't say the word. I feel like if I don't say it, maybe he'll come back to me.

"How did you know he was in the bedroom?" There's a barely observable smirk on his face, as though he thinks he might trip me up. That even a part of him thinks I might have killed Jack makes me want to claw his eyes out.

"I didn't. We didn't see him in the living room, so Kenny searched the first-floor rooms and I checked the second floor."

He sits back and crosses his meaty arms. "What did you do then?"

Something about the way he asks sets me off. The casualness of *When you saw the love of your life's dead body, what did you do then?*

"I gave him CPR."

"And then what?"

I stand up from my seat and point my finger in his Neanderthal face. "'Then what?' I fucking cried my eyes out, you heartless piece of shit. What are these questions, anyway? You think I would kill my boyfriend?"

"Easy, Cho. I never said that. I'm trying to understand what happened. And keep in mind we've found you next to two murder victims this week."

"I'm the one who called the police."

"It wouldn't be the first time a murderer called the police."

"So what's your theory, Marcos? That I murdered Kenneally and Tweed, then for kicks took the case to free the person wrongfully imprisoned for the killing and then went back on a rampage to kill the archbishop and Jack?"

"I don't know. You tell me, Cho. Maybe you missed your fifteen minutes of fame from the Dionysus Club bust and wanted another moment in the spotlight. Maybe you found out something you didn't like about the victims and decided to take matters into your own hands. All I know is, you've been present at two murders and have connections to the others."

"Connections? What are you talking about?"

"You knew Kenneally and Tweed."

It hits me that Marcos is no longer fishing. He's actually building a case against me. I stammer. "I...I...I met Kenneally once at his church, and Tweed approached me for work and I turned it down."

He parts his mouth to respond. The door opens, and Shavali bursts into the room. "What is going on here?"

"I'm conducting an interview," says Marcos.

Shavali runs over and embraces me. I smell her signature scent, and something about the comfort of it all guts me. When you're grieving, anything familiar that remains in your life serves as a gut-wrenching reminder of what was once familiar but is now gone.

I let the sobs roll onto her shoulder.

Shavali turns to Marcos. "We're done here." She grabs my hand and walks me out of Jack's office. The cops and EMTs stare at me like I'm a freak show.

"Let's get some fresh air," she says.

Marcos pops his head out of Jack's study. "It's your choice. But I wouldn't go too far if I were you. We have it on the record that you argued with both victims before their death. I'll be watching." The threat hangs heavy in the stale air.

The two of us walk outside into the gray. The air is crisp and bolstering.

"I'm so sorry, Hazel," says Shavali. "Is there anything I can do?" She pulls a handful of tissues from her handbag and gives them to me.

I wipe the tears from my face and blow my nose. I can barely muster the energy to speak.

"No, but thank you. I just want to go home."

"Of course. Why don't I go inside and grab Kenny, and the two of you can ride home together?"

"That would be good. Thank you." I put a hand on the black iron railing. I'm so gutted, I can barely stand.

"It's the least I can do. I'm sorry I wasn't here more quickly. I was at the office and didn't hear about it straightaway." She opens the door to return inside.

"Working on the Sampson case?"

Shavali stops and looks at me with a furrowed brow. "Oh, didn't I tell you? They released Sam two days ago. The evidence you found on Tweed, combined with the video, did the trick." She heads inside and closes the door behind her.

At first, I'm relieved that my investigative work freed Sam. But then Shavali's words catch in my brain: *They released Sam two days ago.*

Two days ago.

I feel sweat break out on my palms. My mind reels, and I start to shake again.

Sam left Rikers before Jack died.

33

The next few days fade in and out like a memory, a series of scenes that I watch from afar rather than truly inhabit. I know I should hit the streets and investigate Jack's murder, but I can't move. The grief hollows me.

I spend most of my time lying on my couch, staring out at the city through our spotted windows, listening to the radiator hiss and click like a snake is trapped inside and is trying to get out. A storm has moved in, so for the past few days it's been a gloomy gray outside, casting our living room in darkness. Hours pass, and I feel like I died too. Like I'm in some type of purgatory alongside Jack, floating in between life and death.

Every few hours, Kenny brings me something to eat or drink. He's substituted tea in place of my normal energy drinks. It tastes terrible but calms the sickness in my stomach. I don't know what I would do if Kenny wasn't here. Sometimes

I feel like he's the only thing standing between me and abject loneliness.

Jack is gone.

The first person I've ever loved, and who loved me, is gone.

I play clips from my memory of him in my mind. The crinkle around his eyes when he smiled. The high pitch of his laugh. The way he smelled when he held me. The scratch of his facial hair against my upper lip. Eventually, the memories overwhelm me like a bomb went off in my chest, eviscerating my insides. There's nothing left but smoke and rubble. My hands shake, the aftershock of the explosion.

Occasionally, I look at my phone. New York is now in full-blown panic mode over the *Red-Letter Killer*, as the news media has dubbed him. Even from inside my apartment, I can feel it. The city is so much quieter at night. I like to think that everyone's mourning Jack with me, but in reality they're all cowering in fear.

Marcos stops by to ask me follow-up questions. He still views me as a suspect, but I'm too devastated to fight. I share my suspicions of Sampson with him, but he quickly dispels them. He informs me the killer mailed the letter to Jack on Wednesday. Sampson wasn't released from Rikers until Friday. And he was in jail when Tweed and Dinwiddie were killed. There's no way he's the Red-Letter Killer, unless he has help on the outside, which I highly doubt.

My apartment turns into an unofficial wake. Despite my best efforts to be left alone, visitors stop by to pay their condolences. That snake Sandy Godo comes by with his entourage and puts on his best sad face, as though he's not popping champagne now that Jack is dead. To my shock, the archbishop's assistant, Sister Teresa, visits me and delivers two gifts: the archbishop's appointment calendar and a scarf she knitted for me. Her veneer of ice thaws, and she prays over me and begs me to find the killer. It goes to show you never really know someone until the chips are down.

Friends and admirers stop by and ask me how I'm doing and if I need anything. Jack's NYU interns are extremely dramatic, all tears and wails. They remind me of the girls in the black-and-white footage of Beatles concerts. I have so many white roses and floral arrangements that my house looks like a flower shop.

Momo and Mary visit. Mary carries a bouquet. Momo brings a fish tank with a puffer fish in it. Probably the worst gift someone could think of. She says it will give me motivation to find Jack's killer. As if I needed more motivation. She says she got it at one of the puffer fish vendors she talked to. Unfortunately, none of them had seen any unusual purchases. Another dead end. I think of her spouting off knowledge on puffer fish and tetrodotoxin and wonder if she knows more than she lets on.

Mary gives me one of her big, firm Midwestern hugs, asks me if I've made plans for the funeral, and offers to host it at her husband's funeral home free of charge. I tell her the Powells will probably want to host it at Old St. Patrick's. She gets it.

I watch the rain come down and seep through the cracks in our window sealant. I track the water as it creeps through every crevice and can't help thinking of whoever is behind these red letters. Of how he seems to creep through every crevice in my life. It's like he's inside my organs now, slowly tearing me apart until I cease to function.

My sister and my parents stop by. For once, my mom and Christina take a break from harassing me and support me. My mom cooks and my sister cleans. I think because they liked Jack so much and saw how happy he made me, and have husbands themselves, a part of them can understand the horror I'm experiencing. It's good to have them here. When you're broken, being with your family reminds you of what the whole you looked like. I don't know if I'll ever get back to whole, but maybe I can patch up the cracks enough to move forward.

It's my dad's words that have the most impact, though. He tells me to remember the *Chunhyangjeon*, a Korean folk tale he used to read to me and Christina when we were kids. In the story, a young man and woman fall in love. But his family takes him away and the woman is jailed and tortured. As she's on the verge of death, the man returns, saves her, and exacts revenge on his enemies. He tells me I can't give up on finding out who did this. That it's right for me to grieve, but I owe it to Jack to find his killer.

I sit up on my worn green Salvation Army couch, and for a moment, all I want to do is grab every person in New York City by the throat and shake them until they tell me who killed Jack. But then I'm thrown back down by the realization that it doesn't matter. Regardless of what I do, I can't bring him back. The hopelessness of it all paralyzes me, and tears stream down my face, and my body heaves.

I speak with Mrs. Powell, who's been up here for the campaign. She's the only person in the world who truly understands my devastation. Her pride and joy has been taken, and her pain reverberates in me. We set a date and time for the funeral, Friday. I picture Jack lying in a coffin, and I fall into darkness all over again.

One night, Kenny comes home with a fancy bottle of nongju, a Korean rice liquor. We toast to Jack and tell our favorite stories about him. We laugh about the funny Texas phrases he used to use: *That dog won't hunt. Gaaaaawly. Bless your heart.* We flip through the pictures on my phone and watch the videos of us together. Watching him in those videos tricks my mind into believing he's still alive, an insidious illusion. It fills me up and empties me at the same time. The donations to his campaign remain a mystery, but regardless, I know he was a good man.

I think of Sandy Godo. About how he knew about the Red-Letter Killer before anyone else. About how he worked in pharmaceuticals. About how he cited Bible verses. *An eye for an eye. A tooth for a tooth.* I think of Marcos. How he carried that Bible verse on the tip of his tongue. Everyone's a suspect, and everyone's responsible. If any one of us had been better, Jack would be alive today.

I see the way Kenny looks at me. The way Momo and Mary looked at me. They want me to solve this case.

Kenny and I make a toast to Jack and throw back another drink. For some people, drinking depresses them, but for me, it's like an accelerant, fueling my emotions for both good and bad. My mind swims in the rice wine. I make a promise to myself, and Jack. I won't feel sorry for myself any longer. I can't live in the past with Jack forever. His murderer remains free, and every day I wait is a day he might kill again.

Tomorrow, I fight back.

34

The following morning, I wake up with a thunderous headache but an even more powerful resolve. I slip on my comfiest slippers—the fuzzy ones with memory foam—and shuffle out to the kitchen. My temples pound like bass drums from last night's rice liquor. It reminds me of a phrase my grandma always said to me: *You play, you pay*. Well, Grandma, I'm definitely paying right now. Oddly, the hangover somehow makes me feel better about losing Jack. Like feeling physical pain gives me license to leave a small piece of the mental anguish behind.

I grab a Red Bull from the fridge and crack it open. The taste is truly horrifying, but I need it if I'm going to work today. I sense the tick of the clock. The thought of the Red-Letter Killer out there somewhere planning his next move has pierced through the fog of grief. If I do nothing, someone else will lose the Jack in their life. I can't have that.

THE RED LETTER

I open my laptop and research pill-making. I need to get a better understanding of how the killer's mimicking the victim's daily dose. The results are disheartening, to say the least. It turns out that there's a cottage industry online for pill production, another nasty side effect of America's drug epidemic. On Temu or Amazon, you can buy gelcaps of all colors and sizes, and a pill press and mold to compress any powder into any shape. For regular pills, add a drop of food coloring to the powder, and voilà. The food coloring will cost you five bucks, the pills ten, and the press about two hundred. No expertise needed. Not only that, if you ask ChatGPT, it will give you a step-by-step guide. AI will make serial killers of us all.

I'm interrupted by a groan from the other room. Kenny's feeling the same as I am. I fire up the coffee maker and put in his favorite blend of half-blond roast and half-caramel roast. I'm going to need my partner at full throttle today. I've never liked the taste of coffee, but you can't beat the smell in the morning.

Kenny shuffles into the kitchen. His hair stands in the rock-star-mohawk shape you get from sleeping on one side, then the other. He's wearing a faded-gray T-shirt, and one of his sweatpants' legs bunches at his knee. Throw some eyeliner on him, and he could be the leader of a Korean punk band. He rubs his eyes and gives me a limp wave.

"Whose brilliant idea was it to drink rice liquor last night?" he asks.

"Yours."

"Oh yeah. I'm an idiot."

I hand him a cup of coffee. "No, you're actually a genius.

It was exactly what I needed. I've decided I'm done moping around. Today, we go back to work."

"Really?" Kenny sips his coffee and then recoils from the heat. "Okay. I'm a genius, then. First things first: Where's the ibuprofen? Your partner isn't going to be very useful without it."

"There's a bottle in the medicine cabinet."

While Kenny goes to battle his hangover, I run downstairs to grab the mail. As I'm about to check it, I see Mrs. Yu from the bookshop. She gives me a wave and beckons me to come over. I wish I could avoid this conversation. I don't need any more people feeling sorry for me. But Mrs. Yu is a good egg, and she deserves my respect.

I step out of the lobby, checking the sky to make sure it's not raining, and then meet her out in front of her shop.

"Hi, Mrs. Yu," I say.

She gives me a hug and a kiss on the cheek, then grabs my shoulders with her frail hands and appraises my face. "My dear girl. I heard what happened. I'm so sorry for your loss."

"Thank you. That's very kind."

She puts her arm around me. "Come inside. I have something for you. I was going to bring it to your apartment this afternoon after the shop closes, but now you're here…"

"Okay, but I can't stay long. I have work to do."

She opens the door for me and nods. "I understand. Young people—always in a rush. It won't take a minute."

We enter her bookshop, which is everything you want a bookshop to be. It's a small space populated with books of all sorts and varieties displayed haphazardly. Warm yellow lighting glows from the ceiling. The smell of paper blends perfectly with the coffee aroma from the small café in back. I could picture losing myself here on a rainy day.

Mrs. Yu shuffles behind the counter and pulls out a package and a ceramic pot. She hands me the pot, and I glance through the glass lid. "You didn't," I say.

"I did," she says with a grin. "I said to myself, 'Hazel's so sad, she's probably not eating. She needs my dumplings.'"

Mrs. Yu's dumplings are the best I've ever had. She doesn't make them very often anymore because she's getting older and is battling arthritis. She makes them by hand, so this is a real treat. My stomach growls from the scent of ginger, dough, and meat.

"Thank you so much, Mrs. Yu. You didn't have to do this."

She ignores my thanks and hands me a package wrapped in beige kraft paper and twine. I tilt my head at her.

"Open it," she says. I undo the twine and open the paper. It's a book entitled *Wednesday's Child* by Yiyun Li. I've never heard of it. "It's a collection of short stories about grief. Read it when you're ready to let the sadness out."

My eyes water at her unexpected act of kindness.

"No, no, no," she says. "No crying in here. You go home and eat your dumplings first."

She turns me around and guides me out the door like a lost toddler. I'm carrying a pot and a book, and crying my eyes out. I look like a crazy person.

I exit the shop, thank Mrs. Yu again, and head back to the lobby of my apartment. As I'm about to trundle upstairs, I remember the mail. I put the pot and book down and unlock the mailbox.

I haven't checked it for days, so I'm bracing myself for a

landslide of unwanted catalogs and credit card advertisements. And that's exactly what I find. Pottery Barn, Wayfair, Amex, Visa, Discover—

I stop. A jolt of terror runs through me.

Underneath the pile of junk mail, I spot the corner of a red envelope.

I take a step back like I'm holding a live grenade.

I drop the junk mail to the ground and stare at the letter.

My name and address glare back at me in the same dated typewriter font as the other letters. The Mother Mary stamp is stuck to the upper-right corner. No return address.

I scan my surroundings. The lobby. The stairway. Outside the entrance to our building. Hoping to see Face Mask so I can chase him down once and for all. But Mulberry Street is empty except for an old Chinese man reading the newspaper.

I know I shouldn't open the letter. I should deliver it to the police so they can analyze it for fingerprints. But I also know that whoever sent this is too smart. They haven't left fingerprints before, and they won't slip up now.

My hands quiver as I pry open the envelope. A single piece of red stationery sits inside; at the top, a drawing of naked men and women crawling up an endless hill, trying to escape hell. Beneath it is a single phrase:

WHOSOEVER SHALL SEEK TO SAVE HIS LIFE, SHALL LOSE IT.

An icy dread fills my veins. I picture Jack lying on the floor. I picture Archbishop Dinwiddie taking his baby aspirin—

The pills.

Kenny. The ibuprofen.

My ibuprofen.

I drop the letter and spring up the stairs.

First level.

Second level.

Third level.

I burst through our doorway and into our bathroom. Kenny's drinking water.

I smack the glass out of his hand. The glass flies against the shower tile and shatters in the tub.

"What the hell?" says Kenny.

"Did you take the ibuprofen?"

"What?" he says, his eyes packed with confusion.

"Did you take the ibuprofen?"

"Yes, why?"

"How long ago?"

"I don't know. Ten minutes ago. Whenever you went downstairs."

I push him toward the toilet. "I need you to throw up. Make yourself throw up."

"What? Why? Hazel, what's going on?"

"I checked the mail and found this." I shake the red envelope in his face.

Kenny's eyebrows leap as the realization hits him. He immediately bends over the toilet and sticks his finger down his throat.

I run into the kitchen and grab my phone. I dial 911 and scream for an ambulance. As I talk on the phone, I hear Kenny gagging and attempting to bring the pill back up. I tell myself that it's probably ibuprofen, not tetrodotoxin. But we can't afford to risk it. The operator informs me the ambulance is en route. I hang up the phone.

Then the gagging sounds stop. I hear a weak cry, "Hazel?"

I run back into the bathroom.

Kenny's on the floor, writhing, panic in his eyes.

He tries to speak, but the words come out mumbled.

I flash back to the video of Father Kenneally losing his words. No, no, no. This can't happen.

I hoist Kenny onto his knees and support his body over the toilet. I feel the strength leave his body as the tetrodotoxin slithers through his bloodstream. His head drops over the toilet, limp like a newborn.

"I'm sorry, Kenny, I have to do this."

I stick my finger down his throat and pump his stomach with my other hand. He gags, and I see the pain in his eyes, but I don't stop.

Nothing comes up.

I keep going.

Kenny groans, and his body convulses. He touches his face, seemingly in disbelief over the fact that he can no longer feel his hands. His breathing becomes labored. I push my finger down farther and pump his stomach again as hard as I can. Finally, he spasms and vomits into the toilet. I set him down on the floor and then drop onto my backside, exhausted.

I take a moment to catch my breath and then assess Kenny.

His irises still spark with life. He tries to speak, but the words garble. He lifts his arms but can only manage a small flinch. I massage his neck and shoulders, trying to keep the blood flowing. I bend his legs up and down and stroke his hair. Sweat pours down his face.

I stare into his eyes, and with every ounce of certitude in my body, I say, "It's going to be okay, Kenny. We are going to get through this."

He squints and gives me the smallest sliver of a smile. I feel like my heart might break. I hug him and put my ear to his chest. His heart beats, but slower.

The door buzzer sounds. I leap up off the floor.

"The paramedics are here. I'm going to run and buzz them in. I'll be back in a second, okay? Stay with me."

Kenny blinks, and I sprint into the living room and buzz them up. I hear them stomping up the steps. Each footstep feels like an eternity.

The two paramedics reach my unit, and I tell them he's been poisoned. They throw him on a gurney and cart him out of the apartment. We run downstairs with Kenny on the gurney, his body shaking, his skin ghostly green. The paramedics load him in the ambulance, and I jump in back. I grab his cold, sweat-drenched hand and press my temple against his, silently pleading with him.

Please don't leave me.

35

sit in the shabby burnt-orange vinyl chair of the ICU, staring at Kenny, willing him to wake up. An IV is attached to his hand, pumping saline solution to clear the poison from his bloodstream. Cords of different shapes and sizes hang from his body. The heart monitor beeps with a steady rhythm. His face is no longer the sickly white that it was. There's color, and with it, hope.

The doctor says he'll be fine. That the poison needs time to flush out of his system. I want to trust her. But when you've lost the love of your life and your best friend is in a hospital bed, you've got to see it to believe it.

The TV news chirps in the background, featuring wall-to-wall coverage of the Red-Letter Killer. "Experts" with little expertise and even less knowledge of the case opine on who the Red-Letter Killer could be, who their next victim will be, their astrological sign, and anything else they can fabricate to provide content. They reference the Zodiac Killer, Son of Sam, Ted Bundy—none of whom bear any resemblance to the Red-Letter Killer. The program cuts to a clip of Sandy Godo talking about how devastated he is by Jack's death and how he will not rest until he finds the killer. My gut curdles, and I turn off the TV.

As I watch Kenny's chest move up and down, my thoughts jump to the Red-Letter Killer. He meant the poison for me. There's no question about that. But why? This case gets more bizarre by the minute. Me, Jack, Archbishop Dinwiddie, Father Kenneally, Fred Tweed. What do we have in common? At first, I was thinking it had to be the Catholic Church. Someone who was upset about the church refusing to pay the victims. Dinwiddie and Kenneally would certainly match that hypothesis, and the killer might implicate Tweed because his theft of the church's endowment made the settlement more difficult. It's a stretch, but this psychopath could even blame Jack for his dealings with Tweed. But me? Because I date Jack? That seems like a stretch. Especially when there's no shortage of Catholic Church members to target. Clearly, the killer views themselves as an instrument of God, but it's impossible to predict who their next victim will be. The motive is too broad. Unless it's merely a string of association? Tweed knew Kenneally. Dinwiddie knew Tweed. Jack knew Dinwiddie. I knew Jack. But that's worthless. Every person knows hundreds of people. Picking out the next victim would be a needle in a haystack.

I have to focus on the weapon itself. When you investigate a weapon, you have two avenues that give insight. The first is how the killer obtained the weapon. Kenny and the team have researched that already, and there are no obvious clues regarding how he's getting the tetrodotoxin. Given the lack of a paper trail, I have to assume it's being made in some type of home lab. Of course, with Godo's history in pharmaceuticals, he could easily have a stash, but there's no way he could move unnoticed. He would have to have an accomplice.

The second is how he wielded the weapon. We know the poison is being delivered in pill form, and more importantly, it's being snuck into pill bottles the victims use every day. For me, it was the ibuprofen in my medicine cabinet. For Jack, it was his multivitamin. For Dinwiddie, the baby aspirin. For Kenneally, his cholesterol medication. For Tweed, his sleeping pill. The killer replaces the nightly pills with poison pills so they can be sure the victim takes it. So the killer must possess some familiarity with the victims and access to their homes or offices. They must know what pills the person takes, and the color, type, and size of the pills so they can replicate them. The problem is, I can't know exactly when the killer replaced the pills. I have to assume it's in the days before and after the victim receives a red letter.

I think back to my bottle of ibuprofen. There's been a parade of visitors in my apartment over the past few days offering their condolences to me and Kenny. Any of them could have used the bathroom and replaced the pills. Sandy Godo visited. Sister Teresa visited. Detective Marcos. Shavali. Mary, Momo. My family. Somehow I don't think my mom's the Red-Letter Killer.

But there's something in that. Thanks to Shavali, Bobby, and Marcos, I have the logs of who visited Jack, Tweed, Dinwiddie, and Kenneally before their death. If I can find a common thread, that might give me a lead. I pull up my case file manager on my phone and reference the Sampson case file. I find a file of Father Kenneally's appointment calendar. I remember reviewing it when I first investigated his death, but at that point I assumed this was a lone killing. Now I may find a repeat visitor. I kick myself for not checking sooner. As I pull it up, my phone rings. It's Momo. Why is she calling?

"Hey, Momo,"

"Hello, Hazel. I'm sorry to bother you, but have you heard from Kenny?"

It's strange that Momo is calling me about Kenny. I look at him, and he's still breathing peacefully in his hospital bed. "Yeah, I have some bad news. I'm at the hospital with him right now. He's been poisoned." As I say it, vengeance boils in me all over again. "The doctors say he'll be fine, but I'm here monitoring him."

An audible gasp escapes from the other end of the line. "Oh no. How did this happen?" Her voice quakes.

"It was meant for me."

"What hospital are you at?"

"We're at New York Presbyterian. But I don't think you need—"

"I'll be right there." Momo hangs up. I look at my phone as though it can explain that exchange. Why was Momo looking for Kenny, and why was she so eager to see him? I think back to the morning they arrived at the office together. I shake my head and return my attention to the case file. I don't have time to ponder that right now.

I spend the next twenty-five minutes scrolling through pages of appointments in Father Kenneally's calendar. It doesn't help that Samuel Sampson wasn't the most diligent assistant. Half of the appointments don't even have full names. It says things like *Dave, the guy who wants to talk about his marriage*, or something like that. That is one of the most misunderstood aspects of detective work. In television shows and movies, people are always perfectly organized, and the evidence is in immaculate condition. The key players always save the video footage, and it's in 4K-quality resolution. The appointment books are pristine and comprehensive. In reality, the video is usually auto-erased after forty-eight hours, and if it's not, it's black and white and grainy. And people's calendars are only half-filled or completed so sloppily that it's unclear what the appointment is referencing. I move on to Archbishop Dinwiddie's calendar and scroll through the appointments.

A knock on the doorframe shakes me out of my trance. Momo's face pops in the doorway. That was quick. Her eyes are red, and tears stain her cheeks. "May I come in?"

I stand up from my seat. "Of course. Come in. Are you okay?"

She bows her head and enters the room. Outside the office, her look is slightly different. She's done away with the grandma glasses, and, I notice, she's covered her neck scar with bronzer. At the first sight of Kenny, she runs to the bed and grabs his hand and kisses it. "Oh, my Kenny. What have they done to you?"

I stand and watch with my eyebrows at my hairline and my jaw to my chest. Part of me wants to laugh at her dramatic reaction, which would have been right at home in a Korean soap opera. The other part of me is in shock that Kenny and Momo are together. How long has Kenny been keeping this from me? That little scamp!

Momo sees my surprise and catches herself. Her face bursts with red, and she stands up and pats his hand.

"It's okay, Momo. Please, continue. I just had no idea. How long has this been going on?"

She grins but covers her mouth. "One month. Kenny didn't want to tell you until my internship was over, because he thought you'd disapprove of us working together and dating. We hung out whenever you were at Jack's house."

I sit back in my chair, stunned at the news. I'm not sure how to feel. He's right that I don't like office romances, but I'm happy that he's found someone. I can't believe I'm saying this, but I'm a little jealous. Kenny's never really dated anyone while we've been roommates, and I've grown accustomed to having him all to myself. It's not that I ever saw myself dating him, but I never pictured sharing him with anyone else either. And with Jack gone, I need Kenny more than ever.

I'm also stunned that he kept this secret from me. I thought the two of us shared everything, but now I feel like there's another part of Kenny's life he's kept from me. Everything I've relied on to bolster me this year is slipping away.

"You're mad, aren't you?" she says. "If you want me to quit, I understand." She turns back to Kenny and stares at him. Clearly, she couldn't care less about me or her internship with her boyfriend laid up in the ICU.

I raise my hands up in a peace gesture. "No, no. Of course not. I'm so happy for you both. Surprised, but happy. Where's Mary?"

"She wanted to come, but I asked her to stay at the office in case someone stopped by." She answers me, but her attention points toward him. She strokes his hand and rests her head on his chest.

"I'll give you two a minute," I say and rise from my chair.

I walk into the hallway, thunderstruck. I expect to see doctors and nurses rushing through the halls to another emergency, but it's quiet. I pace the hallway. The stark white of the linoleum floors and clean walls only highlights my loneliness. The fluorescent lights hum and the hospital machines beep, and I've never felt so alone. I walk down the hallway in a daze, trying to process the earthquake that's shaken my life. As I walk, I flip through Archbishop Dinwiddie's calendar entries in my phone, not really absorbing them but too scared to be alone with my thoughts.

As I'm scrolling through meaningless name after name of visitors, something catches my eye.

It's a name I know.

I open up the guest list from Tweed's fundraiser and scroll through page after page of unfamiliar names. Then I see the same name.

It's not possible. This makes no sense. I double-check the handwriting to make sure I'm not hallucinating.

My stomach spins as I read the name.

Shavali Patel.

She attended Tweed's fundraiser.

She visited Dinwiddie five days before his death.

She's been to Jack's house.

She visited me to "offer her condolences" two days before I received the letter.

Could she be involved in this? I think of the figure watching me from the park. No. There's no way. It makes no sense. If she was, why would she defend Sam when he was headed toward a life sentence? Why would she ask me to investigate the case?

It can't be. She's one of my best friends. She'll be at Jack's funeral tomorrow, for God's sake.

But why did she attend the Tweed fundraiser? Why was she visiting the archbishop? Why wouldn't she tell me? Why would she keep it secret?

36

Men and women dressed in black fill the pews of Old St. Patrick's Cathedral. I sit in front with Mrs. Powell and Jack's two sisters. I try to be strong for them, to hold my head high, my jaw firm, my hands still. But the weight of Jack's absence crushes my insides. It's hard to look at them. Jack had his mom's eyes.

I hear the sniffles and quiet whispers of those who knew Jack behind me. I realize now that when you attend the funeral of someone close to you, the funeral isn't for you. It's for those on the outside. The people who think they knew him but really didn't. This is their chance to say goodbye to someone who touched their life but never inhabited it. I don't need to attend this funeral, because I'll never say goodbye. He'll always be with me. Even here in this church, I can hear his Southern drawl. I can smell his ocean scent. I can see his profile in the darkness as he sleeps.

Father Ricardo speaks, but I don't listen. The pain distorts the sound. I remember the priest who should be here: Father Kenneally. The one who actually knew Jack and might capture a glimmer of his light. But he's gone too. And he wasn't the man I thought he was. I replay the video of him dying steps away from where I sit, struggling as that evil poison wormed through him. I think of the cold, stale catacombs beneath us, and the dead bodies they hold.

I scan the attendees in the pews behind me. It's strange to see the place so full. I see friends and colleagues. Bobby, Momo, and Mary. Kenny's still in the hospital. I wish he were here. I see Jack's many adoring interns bawling their eyes out. I see Sandy Godo staring up at the sculpture of Jesus on the cross that hangs from the ceiling, playing the part of the grieving opponent. I see Detective Marcos, who's watching me as though at any minute, I'm going to rise from the pew and declare myself the murderer. Sister Teresa stands in the rear, her arms crossed, her face dour, making sure everything runs smoothly. She's a tough old woman, but it's nice she's on Team Hazel now.

And then I see Shavali.

She sits a few rows back with a couple of other law school friends, dressed in a silk black dress, which highlights her dark hair and smoky eyes. She looks like a villain again, and for the first time, I wonder if she is.

Her eyes meet mine, and she gives me a sad wave.

I size her up, watching to see if she'll look away or fidget or somehow reveal she's involved in this. But she doesn't. She simply looks sad, torn up. But then, why the visits? Why go to Dinwiddie and Tweed? Why keep it a secret? I hate that Jack's death has made me question everyone around me, even my friends.

The funeral ends, and most of the attendees exit the rear of the chapel. As the doors open, I hear the media shout and see the lights of cameras outside the door. They're looking for anything they can find on the Red-Letter Killer. I've never realized how little our society cares about the victims of crime. We only care about exacting revenge on the perpetrators or wallowing in the shared drama. To the media, Jack Powell is yesterday's news.

I follow the Powells to an anteroom in back, along with a small group of close friends. We've arranged for an intimate reception for those who were close to Jack in order to let the media storm subside. It's a typical church reception room: simple and boring, musty rust-red carpet, white walls with pictures of Bible scenes, a teak table stocked with cheap refreshments. The church staff set up coffee and pastries, but my insides are too destroyed for food.

Shavali strides toward me and buries me in an embrace. She's several inches taller than me, so my face gets pushed against her boobs like a baby. I wriggle free. As I assess her, I feel the red burning on the edges of my eyes from the tears.

"We need to talk," I say.

"Okay?" she says, her eyebrows pinched in the middle.

I pull her up against a wall, away from the other mourn-ers. "What were you doing at Fred Tweed's fundraiser the week before he died?"

"What?"

I shoot her a raised eyebrow and let it speak for me.

"Oh, nothing. I knew it was going to be a who's who of New York, so I went for the networking."

She says it with total polish and assurance, but I've known Shay long enough to know she's holding something back. I want to shout at her, but I keep my voice barely above a whisper. "And what about Dinwiddie? I know you visited him before he died as well."

"What is this about?"

"You know what this is about."

"What? You think I'm associated with these murders?" She whispers the word *murders*, crosses her arms, and props her weight on one hip. "Hazel, Jack was my friend."

"I want to know why you visited all the victims shortly before they died."

"What about you? I could say the same thing about you."

"Don't give me that shit. I was investigating a case you asked me to investigate. And the fact that you didn't tell me about this makes me wonder."

She bites her lip and looks over my shoulder. People around us gather and chat quietly, but our conversation has garnered attention.

"You want to do this here? Now?"

"Yes. Ever since this started, I feel you've been holding back on me."

"Fine. I was hoping to be appointed to a judgeship if Jack got elected. I figured if I had the support of Jack's biggest donor, the archbishop, and some other community leaders, I'd be a shoo-in."

I feel a giant vein pulsing through my forehead. "Why didn't you tell me?"

"I was going to tell you about Tweed, but when Dinwiddie died and the media became involved, I panicked about the optics of it. I was afraid I'd get sucked into the scandal. Plus, I didn't want to recuse myself from the Sampson case. I couldn't damage my reputation."

"What about my reputation, Shay? I've got Marcos, the cops, the media on my ass because I tried to help you out."

"I'm sorry, Haze. I really am."

I open my mouth to tell Shavali what to do with her *sorry* when I feel a gentle grab on my arm. I whip around to tell the person to buzz off but stop when I see it's Bobby. He's wearing a black suit that's two sizes too small and a black tie. He's clearly uncomfortable, but I appreciate he tried.

"I'm sorry to interrupt, but, Hazel, can I borrow you for a moment?" From the way he bites his lip, I can tell it's important.

"I'm not done with you," I say to Shavali. "We'll talk later."

We walk past the other mourners to a corner of the room.

He gives me a hug and a kiss on the cheek. I take in his familiar scent. For the first time since Jack died, I feel a spark of warmth inside.

"I wanted you to know how sorry I am for your loss. He seemed like a good man."

My eyes crinkle, and the tears break free. Right now, my brain seems capable of only toggling between two emotions: anger and sadness. "He was."

He pats my shoulder while I grab a tissue from my bag and blot my eyes. He removes a folded-up piece of paper from his pocket and hands it to me.

"Look, I know this isn't the time or the place, and you're

probably too broken up to even think about this, but last time we spoke, you asked for it, so here it is. You can't tell anyone where you got it, though."

I've been so consumed with Jack's death and Kenny's near death that I don't even remember what I requested. I open the page and scan the room to ensure no one is watching.

A list of zip codes and towns stares back at me. "Are these the locations the Red-Letter Killer mailed the threats from?"

"Yeah, we tracked them using the USPS barcode. I plotted them on a map to identify any discernible shape or pattern but found nothing. To me, it looks like a bunch of unconnected towns, but I thought maybe you'd see something I didn't."

I look down at the paper again. He's right. It is a series of random locations scattered around the state of New York. Syosset. Manhattan. Middletown. Millbrook.

And then I see it.

A chill crawls up my spine.

Wappingers Falls.

Why do I recognize that name? I know I've heard of it. Such a funny name for a town.

Then it hits me.

The convent where Sister Teresa lived.

Could she be connected to this?

I feel a bony hand on my shoulder and jump out of my skin. I turn and see Sister Teresa staring back at me as though she sensed I was thinking about her.

"Oh, I'm so sorry, dear. I didn't mean to scare you," she says. There's a detachment in the way she says it that crawls across my skin like an icy wind.

I crumple the paper in my hand and paste on a smile. "No, I'm sorry, Sister. I've been a little jumpy lately."

She glares at the paper and frowns. "Of course. That's completely understandable. I wanted to say how sorry I am. I feel awful about how I treated you at the church and in the archbishop's office. I was protecting the archbishop, and I took it out on you. And now this happens. You don't deserve any of it. Nobody does."

"Thank you so much. No apology needed. You were doing your job."

She wipes a tear from her eye and lowers her head. I didn't think Sister Teresa was capable of crying. "We worked together for twenty years. I travel to the office every day, hoping he'll be there. I can't imagine what you must be feeling. Jack was such a wonderful young man."

"That's very kind of you." I know I'm behaving strangely, but the paper that Bobby's given me feels like it's burning a hole in my hand. The two of us stand in awkward silence for another ten seconds.

"Well, I have some church matters to attend to, but if you need anything, please don't hesitate to call."

"I won't. Thank you for coming."

I watch her as she shuffles out of the room. So unassuming, but so stiff. I turn back to Bobby.

"I need to ask you one more favor."

"Name it."

"I'm sneaking out of here, and I need you to cover for me. Tell people I was overcome with grief and went home."

"Where are you going?"

"To Wappingers Falls. Believe it or not, I think we might find our answer in a convent."

37

slam down the pedal on my Tesla SUV as I merge onto I-87 north toward Wappingers Falls. The sky turns dark and rain breaks loose. Water from the highway sprays the sides of my windows. It's a hefty drive, and I need to get to the convent before it closes. Do convents even close? This is a first for me.

As I rip down the highway, blurring past cars, the charcoal sky hovering over me, I try to process this new information. I don't want to get too far ahead of myself. Just because the killer mailed one letter from Wappingers Falls, and Sister Teresa was a nun at Poor Clares, doesn't mean that she's the Red-Letter Killer. She hasn't lived there for years, after all. But if nothing else, it is one hell of a coincidence. Especially when you consider the size of Wappingers Falls.

Raindrops tap against the roof of my car, and the back-and-forth of my wipers lulls me into a trance. I run through the standard checklist regarding a murder suspect. Did she have a motive? She might have. We know that the Red-Letter Killer is driven by religious fanaticism, and Sister Teresa certainly has the hint of a fanatic about her.

Did she have the opportunity? Yes. She knew Kenneally and Dinwiddie personally. I checked the log before I left, and she attended Tweed's fundraiser with Dinwiddie. She visited me in the wake of Jack's death. The only thing I can't explain is how she accessed Jack. But Jack was notorious for leaving the door open at his place. She might have simply watched us and walked right in while we were out. Maybe the night of the debate? Or she could have attended a fundraiser at his house without me even knowing.

Did she have the means? This is a major question mark. Whoever is committing these killings possesses an intimate knowledge of chemistry and pill production. She could have been self-taught. You can learn anything on the internet these days, but something doesn't fit. And there's one other thing: she definitely wasn't the person who's been following me, unless she was on stilts. So if she wasn't following me, who was? Maybe the nuns at Poor Clares can fill in the missing piece.

An hour later, I arrive at the convent. It's different from what I expected. I imagined a stone building set on a remote hill in the countryside, surrounded by rolling fields, a few cows, and chickens. What I find is quite different: a modern brick building that looks more like a house than a religious institution. A long circular driveway leads up to the home. At the driveway's center stands a statue of the Virgin Mary, head bowed. In this weather, it looks as though she's sheltering herself from the rain.

Next to the house, a small chapel gives the only hint that you're at a convent instead of a Christian household. A single light shines from inside.

I bolt from the car and dodge puddles as I scamper to the front door. The rain falls in sheets now, so I stick close to the overhang to stay dry. Mist floats out of my mouth from the cold. Winter is at the gate. I knock on one of the walnut double doors and pray that someone answers.

A petite older woman with pale skin and sunken eyes answers. Her white hair rests in a tight bob, and she wears a nun's habit with a gold cross hanging from her neck. She hunches, and her eyes dart upward to inspect me. Her mouth falls open in confusion.

"Hello, can I help you?"

The wind shifts, and the rain pelts my back. "Hello, Sister. My name is Hazel Cho. I'm a private detective, investigating a homicide in New York City. May I come in?"

"Oh my. Yes, of course. I'm Sister Agatha." She offers her warm, frail hand for a shake. "You're drenched. Come in."

I note she didn't seem surprised. It's like she's been expecting me. She opens the door, and I step inside. The door groans as she closes it and locks it behind me. The house smells stale. You can tell everything in it, from the people to the furniture, has a long history.

She ushers me into the kitchen and offers me a seat at the worn teak kitchen table. I notice the floral square-paneled flooring is peeling off at the edges.

"I was making tea. Would you like some?" She smiles, but her eyes are dead. Two sharp, oversize incisors peak out from her smile like fangs. She closes her smile, self-conscious.

"No, I'm fine. Thank you."

Something about this woman unnerves me. I've just told her I'm investigating a murder, and she offers me tea like it's the most normal thing in the world. She fills an ancient steel teakettle with water, then lights the gas stove and places it there. I watch her every movement as she prepares it, in case she makes a cup for me anyway. I don't trust anyone serving me these days.

My eyes scan the mustard wallpapered kitchen, which is dark from the sky outside. A picture taped to the white refrigerator shows Sister Agatha with the other nuns in the convent. She joins me at the table and picks a speck of lint off her black skirt.

"It's really coming down out there, isn't it?" she says, her eyes evaluating my all-black funeral outfit.

"Yeah. I arrived in the nick of time."

"Did you say you drove all the way up from New York City?"

"Uh-huh."

"Well, if you need to stay until the weather subsides, you're more than welcome."

"That's very kind of you. Where are the other nuns?"

She gives me another dead smile. "Oh, they're over at prayer in the chapel. I stayed behind to work on dinner." I inspect the counter but don't see a meal.

"Where's the food?"

"Oh, we're doing leftovers. All I need is five minutes and a microwave, and huzzah. We eat quite simply here. Vow of poverty, and all that."

"I see. I'm sorry to bother you, but the reason I'm here is to gain some additional information on a nun who I believe stayed at this monastery years ago."

"No bother at all. Who would you like more information on?"

"Sister Teresa."

She folds her hands in her lap and sighs. "Hmm, I can't say I'm surprised."

My breath catches in my throat. The teapot whistles, and I wriggle in my seat. "Why do you say that?"

"Sister Teresa was a troubled soul when she was here. There was an…incident."

"What sort of incident?"

She rises from her chair and pours the water into a gray mug that says LOVE IS PATIENT on the outside. She steeps the tea and stares out the window as the wind rips through the boxwood bushes out front. "Follow me," she says. She grabs her tea and flips on the hallway light, then opens the door to a steep flight of stairs. I follow her and look up. They lead to an attic. I can see the exposed beams and insulation. "We keep our records up here."

The wind screams through the cracks in the house. I picture Sister Teresa giving us a tour around the catacombs, a sick smile pasted to her face, and part of me feels like there's a fifty-fifty chance there's a dead body in this attic. But then I think of Jack, and I'm propelled forward by his memory.

Sister Agatha eases her way up the stairs. Each step creaks louder than the one before.

I breathe in and out slowly, like I'm giving birth.

We reach the attic.

Gray legal boxes fill the room, each with names of nuns who

have come before. I have to give the Catholics credit. They are serious about their recordkeeping.

She points to a box. "Would you be a dear and lift this one for me?"

I bend over and lift the box. As I do, a howl of wind shakes the attic. The light flickers, but I see a name: Sister Teresa.

I turn to Sister Agatha and point at the lid. "May I?"

She nods, and a pained expression crosses her face.

I open it.

Handwritten letter after letter fills the first half of the box. I pick up the first one.

Dear Sister Agatha,

When I was in town yesterday, I witnessed Sister Roberta having intimate conversations with a man.

I could tell from their body language that the conversations were salacious and untoward.

Sister Roberta has broken her oath of celibacy and is a sinner. She should be punished.

"Now the Spirit manifestly saith, that in the last times some shall depart from the faith, giving heed to spirits of error, and doctrines of devils."

The letter goes on, becoming increasingly strident, but I flip to the next one.

Dear Sister Agatha,

Sister Roberta continues to sin. How have you done nothing about it?

Especially since we know she sins with Father Kenneally from St. Mary's. I can't sleep due to the stench of lustful rot in this place.

Has the devil gotten his hooks in you too?

So that's why she went after Father K. She knew about his sexual proclivities from her days up here. I flip to the next letter.

Dear Sister Agatha,

This monastery has become a den of thieves and liars...

I hear Jack's voice reading the letter in that voicemail. *A den of thieves and liars.* I turn to Sister Agatha, whose countenance carries a grim expression, as though she still remembers the poison of Sister Teresa's words.

"Are they all like this?" I ask.

"Yes, and I'm afraid they get progressively worse." She nods at the documents, encouraging me to read further.

I pick up a letter closer to the back.

Dear Sister Agatha,

I can no longer live in such wretched sin. The Lord demands justice. If you do not expel Sister Roberta from the monastery by the end of the week, she will feel God's wrath.

"In a flame of fire, giving vengeance to them who know not God, and who obey not the gospel of our Lord Jesus Christ. Who shall suffer eternal punishment in destruction, from the face of the Lord, and from the glory of his power."

"What happened to Sister Roberta?" I ask. Although I already know the answer.

Her voice catches. "She died."

"How did she die?"

She brushes away a piece of hair that has fallen in her face and strokes the cross around her chest. "The doctor deemed it a heart attack, but I could never shake the feeling that Sister Teresa was behind it. She always loved chemistry and had a small laboratory in her bedroom. She used to teach kids at the local school. I always wondered if she concocted some type of potion for Sister Roberta, but the police found nothing conclusive. We asked her to leave Poor Clares after that incident." Her voice cracks, and a tear falls from her eye. "It breaks my heart because when she came to us, she was such a bright-eyed, innocent girl."

I have trouble imagining Sister Teresa as ever being *bright-eyed*. As if she can read my mind, Sister Agatha moves toward me and digs into the box. She pulls out a picture and looks at it.

"Tell me. Is this the face of a murderer?"

She hands me the picture, and I brace myself to see a younger, sweeter version of the curmudgeonly Sister Teresa that I know.

But it's not that version.

It's not Sister Teresa at all.

It's my assistant, Mary.

She's younger, and her face is thinner, but I'd recognize those North Dakota grass-green eyes anywhere.

The picture falls from my hand, and I take a step back.

Sister Agatha places a hand on my back. "Is something wrong? You look like you've seen a ghost."

I snatch the picture off the ground and squint. A smiling, innocent Mary looks back at me. She must have been in her twenties when the photo was taken. I shake my head to make sure I'm not hallucinating, but it's real. My stomach twists with dread.

"Are you sure this is Sister Teresa? I was inquiring about another Sister Teresa who worked for Archbishop Dinwiddie. I know this woman, but her name is Mary."

Sister Agatha points a finger into the air. "Ah, yes, Sister Teresa Angelica, she was here as well." She lifts the lid off another box, pulls out a similar picture, and hands it to me. "Wonderful woman. Truly one of God's children. A bit cold at first, but solid through and through. Always there for you."

The second photo is of the Sister Teresa I know as Archbishop Dinwiddie's assistant. Even in her younger days, her face was made of steel. "As I'm sure you know, many nuns choose to change their name when they join the order. The woman you know as Mary chose Teresa. We've hosted many Teresas over the years."

Another gust of wind rattles the attic. The cold cuts through me. I bring my elbows tight to my sides for warmth, in disbelief at what I've been told. It feels like an earthquake. It can't be Mary. I look at those eyes. They're not the eyes of a killer; they're the eyes of a friend. She's been by my side from day one.

She's never lied to me, that I know of. She's never let me down. There must be some mistake. I scan the dusty attic, hoping that if I keep searching these old boxes, I can find some piece of evidence that tells me something different.

Sister Agatha's eyes meet mine.

She says nothing.

She looks at the picture in my hand, memories of her troubles with Mary carved into her face.

Her head slowly nods as if to say three simple words.

It was her.

38

speed back to the city, vibrating with adrenaline. As the Tesla hurdles down the freeway, my chest thumps and my stomach coils. The black-and-white image of the younger Mary pulses in my brain. Or should I call her Sister Teresa?

How can it be?

I hit ninety miles per hour and hammer the horn to clear traffic from my lane. The white Honda in front of me seems oblivious to my struggle. I turn on the radio to calm myself, but all they can talk about is the Red-Letter Killer. They make up theories about Jack. Was he having an affair? Could it be a jilted lover? Was he working with the Mob? Did his Asian girlfriend, Hazel Cho, do it? They take particular glee in saying *Asian*. It's not enough that Jack's dead and I'm alone—they have to dance on his grave and bury me with him.

I accelerate, swerve, and brake my way down the Taconic State

Parkway. My mind won't accept that Mary could be behind all this. That she could have taken Jack from me and nearly taken Kenny. I try to rationalize it all away. Maybe this is a big mix-up. Just because the killer sent a letter from Wappingers Falls doesn't mean Mary sent it. Just because she was a little fanatical in her youth and wrote letters quoting Bible verses doesn't mean she's a serial killer doing the same thing now. If I brought this in front of a judge, he'd throw it out in a second.

But the more I consider it, the more it makes sense. Mary was a nun. She's familiar with the Catholic Church and its players. She has a background in chemistry. My mind flicks to her rattling off the chemical composition of tetrodotoxin. She visited the archbishop's office with me days before he died. She could have used his bathroom and snuck the pills in then. I think of her in my home after Jack died, telling me everything was going to be all right. My skin prickles, and my heart beats faster.

She had access to me, to Jack, to my files, to Kenny.

I roar down the highway. The wind blows so hard that I have to fight to stay within the lane. Fear runs through my bloodstream like an illness. She meant those pills for me. But next time, they may be for Kenny.

Kenny.

He's not safe.

I'm not safe.

No one's safe.

I call Bobby.

The phone rings, and I tap my hand against the steering wheel, willing him to pick up. "Hello?" he answers. As always, hearing his reedy voice calms me. Bobby's like an old sofa.

I swerve onto the shoulder and rip past traffic. "Bobby, I need you to do me a favor." I try to keep my voice calm so as not to sound paranoid.

"Yeah, what's up?"

"Can you get somebody to guard Kenny's room?"

"Sure. It probably won't be until later this evening, though. Why? You think that sicko is going to take a shot at him?"

The thought of it sends my foot crashing down on the accelerator. "I don't know. But she murdered Jack and then tried to murder me, so I feel like no one around me is safe."

"'She'?"

"Yeah, I have an idea who the killer is."

He laughs. "Don't tell me you think it's a nun."

"No, it's not a nun."

"But it's a woman? What about the man following you? You think that's somebody different?"

"I never said it was a man." My tone is more defensive than he deserves. "I said it was probably a man. It could have been a taller woman. But I couldn't tell because of the face mask."

"All right. Who are you thinking?" I can hear the exasperation in his voice.

"I think it might be Mary."

"Your assistant?"

"Yeah, I know it sounds crazy. I don't have any hard evidence, but hopefully I can find some tonight."

His raspy voice cracks. "Hazel, you're not going to do anything stupid, are you?"

"No, just a little research."

He sighs, and I can hear him thinking. He's spent enough

time with me to know when to pick his battles. "If you say so. But there's something you should know."

"Oh God. What now?"

"The letters are spreading. Two different people in Brooklyn have reported receiving them. Two more in Manhattan. I talked with Marcos, and you're a person of interest."

I zoom past cars, weaving in and out of traffic. Horns blare behind me. I can't help feeling that the entire world is against me. I want to scream, but I bite my lip instead. "Seriously? He can't possibly think I'm involved in this."

"I know. It's ridiculous. But detectives go where the evidence takes them. And it doesn't help that every time a dead body shows up, you're there."

I want to blurt out, *That's because my assistant is a psychopath!* But it's not Bobby I need to convince. Instead, I say, "Okay, thanks for telling me."

"If you need anything, let me know."

We hang up the phone, and I feel my sadness and disbelief condensing into rage.

I call Momo at the office. "Momo, it's Hazel. Is Mary still there?"

"Yes, let me get her for you," she says in her soothing voice.

"No, there's no need. I wanted to make sure you guys made it back to the office from the funeral okay."

"Oh, yes. It was a lovely service. Thank you for allowing us to attend."

I block the thoughts of the funeral from my brain. I don't have time for grief. "I'm glad you could be there. I need you to do me a favor. Will you go check in on Kenny? A friend of mine is sending an officer later, and I want to make sure he's okay in the meantime."

A tremor passes through her voice. "Oh, yes. Do you think he is in danger?"

"No, he'll be fine, but it's better to be safe than sorry."

"Okay. What about my work?"

I need to hire Momo permanently. Her boyfriend's in the hospital, and she's still worried about her job. "Don't worry about your work. I'm giving you the day off."

"Should I bring Mary?"

"No. You can tell her to cut out early and go home and relax. I think we could all use a break."

"Yes. I will do that."

"Thanks."

I end the call and turn onto FDR Drive toward Lower Manhattan. My lips creep upward.

Mary's been hunting me for a long time.

Now it's my turn.

39

sit in my car fifty feet east of Mary's home on West Forty-Third
Street, still sick at the thought that she could be involved in
this. Night has fallen, and the streets sit empty on account of
the Red-Letter Killer. Even the leaves in the maple trees sound
scared and restless. The building stands in the center of the
block. A dark stone facade on the first two floors separates the
funeral home business from the offices and residences atop the
structure. Two underpowered lights shine on a green awning
over the entrance that says Donahue Funeral Home and
Crematorium in a cursive country club font. As I observe the
building, it's like I'm seeing it for the first time. What used to be
a quaint four-level with a modest funeral home now resembles
the entrance to a dungeon.

I wait and watch. I make out two silhouettes in the rooms on
the fourth floor. Presumably Mary and Brian. Part of me wants

to kick down the door and shove a gun in her face until she admits she's a murderer, but I need more evidence than an old photo and a couple of creepy letters.

I used to love the thought of stakeouts. In the movies, the detective slinks down in the driver's seat, drinking coffee, smoking a cigarette, with his fedora pulled down low over his face. It all seems so mysterious and riveting. In reality, surveillance is the worst, a vicious cocktail of boredom and tension. You watch and eat awful food and nothing happens, yet your stomach tangles itself in knots because you know at any moment, you could be thrust into action. I've had times where I sat in front of a house for hours to find out later I was watching an empty house or even the wrong house.

It's Friday night, so I'm hoping the Donahues will go out. She and Brian do date night every Friday. From the back-and-forth movement in the windows, it appears they're getting ready. I turn on the stereo and listen to my bossa nova mix to shake the tension. I figure it's hard to get too stressed out when "The Girl from Ipanema" is playing.

My phone buzzes. I open a text from Momo.

I'm at the hospital. Kenny's awake! He looks so much better.

Followed by a parade of emojis and GIFs, half of which I don't know the meaning of.

Thank God. I release a breath that's been trapped in my chest for two days. Now that Jack is gone, Kenny is my only remaining anchor.

Jack is gone.

The thought stabs me in the chest.

That's grief in a nutshell: your heart gets blown to bits, and the second a couple of pieces come back together, you think of the one you lost and you're obliterated all over again. I look up at the house, at Mary and Brian, laughing and putting on perfume and cologne, and a vein rises on my forehead.

My phone buzzes again. It's Bobby.

Officer should be at the hospital in fifteen minutes. Need anything else?

I survey the cold, empty street. I need a lot of things. I need Jack. I need a partner. I need a hug.

I consider asking Bobby to provide backup, but I can't do that. I've already asked him for so much. I can't ask him to help me with a B and E. If he got caught, it could destroy his career and ruin any chance of getting a conviction.

I have to do this alone.

I have to know.

The black-cherry front door of the funeral home opens, and Mary steps onto the sidewalk with Brian in tow. She wears a mauve coat, brown heels, and her dusty-brown hair styled in a bun. Brian sports jeans and a blazer, which disguises his oversize gut. I wonder whether he's been assisting her in this madness or is an idle bystander. She takes a long breath of the chilly fall air, and a self-satisfied smile crosses her face. I watch her in astonishment. How she disassociates from everything mystifies me. I search her face for anything that might show a human connection to what she's done—guilt, nervousness, anger, sadness, fatigue—but there's nothing. She conjures up any other middle-aged woman spending a lovely Friday night with her husband. It's enough to make me question whether I've got this whole thing wrong. I haven't forgotten Godo, and Shavali has some explaining to do, but through the cold lens of rationality, Mary is the only realistic suspect.

Brian steps out, and I watch to see if he sets any type of alarm on the entrance to the funeral home. He doesn't. He locks the door behind him and plants a kiss on her cheek. The couple strolls west down the street, holding hands and laughing. Brian runs his hand over his balding head and puts his arm around her to shield her from the cold. I remember when Jack used to do that. The memory of him sparks something in me. I'm no longer nervous or afraid; I'm enraged.

They turn the corner, and I grab a screwdriver and my lockpick kit from the glove compartment. I step out of the car and put on my black leather winter gloves. A pebble crunches under my heel. I'm still in my funeral outfit: a black car coat, black sweater and skirt, pearls, and black heels. Not ideal for a break-in, but oddly appropriate for a funeral home. I survey the street, but the block is quiet. I cross the slick pavement and jog up to the front door, evading puddles from the earlier storm.

The external lights pouring down on the entrance shine a spotlight on my lock work. Fortunately, I don't think there are a lot of small thirty-one-year-old women breaking into funeral homes these days, so even if someone walks by, they'll probably think I'm fumbling with the key.

At first glance, I can tell this is a pin-tumbler lock, so it shouldn't be too bad. I pick a bump key and shove it into the lock as though I'm returning home and unlocking the door. The key wiggles out a notch, and the tumblers move. I give it a whack with a screwdriver and turn the lock, expecting the door to open. But it doesn't. I'm getting rusty in my old age.

I'm about to whack it again when a voice from behind interrupts.

"Everything all right over there?"

My body hitches.

I slip my bump key into my inside coat pocket and slide the screwdriver up into my coat sleeve so that only the bottom is in my palm. I half turn to see who's speaking to me.

It's a cop.

He's standing ten feet away on the sidewalk with his hands on his belt. His round face is kind but inquisitive.

I give him a big, flirty smile. "Oh, yeah. Everything's good, Officer. These old-building locks are stubborn sometimes. You know how it is."

"I hear that. You need a hand?" He takes a few steps toward me.

If he tries to help, I'm screwed. He'll see that I don't have an actual key. I raise a hand at him. "No, I've got it. Thank you."

His nose wrinkles, and he looks me up and down. "You sure?" He walks toward me.

I'm screwed.

I have to open this door before he reaches me.

I turn, grab the bump key from my pocket, shove it in the lock, and whack it with the screwdriver butt in my palm like I'm hitting it with my hand.

A bolt of pain runs through my wrist. I bite my lip to stifle a yelp.

The key turns.

The lock clicks. I push the door and, in the same motion, slide the screwdriver up my other sleeve.

"You got it!" he says.

I smile and laugh, sweat beading around my hairline. I flex my biceps. "Sometimes you got to give it a little muscle. Thanks, Officer." I slip inside and give him a wave.

He waves back. "All right, then. Have a nice night."

"You too."

I cross the threshold and collapse against the door as I shut it behind me.

I'm inside.

40

t's dark.

They've drawn the curtains.

I can barely see my hand in front of my face.

I pause for a minute to ensure the cop has had time to leave. It's so quiet that I hear my heartbeat thundering in my ears.

I turn on my phone's flashlight and look around the room. I stand in the entryway to the funeral parlor. Aged Oriental rugs rest on the floor in the foyer and lobby. The walls are painted a tasteful shade of green. A sign that says THE LIEBOWITZ FUNERAL sits on a tripod stand. Behind it is a room filled with chairs and a small stage and casket base. Flower arrangements dot the perimeter. The scent of old wood, dust, and Pine-Sol fills the room. To my left, I spot a staircase leading to the basement, where they perform the dirty work of the burial and cremation business. I don't even want to know what's down there. To my right, a staircase reaches up to the second level and, hopefully, the living quarters.

I double-check the first floor to make sure I'm alone and then climb the staircase. Sweat pours from my armpits. I take long, slow breaths through my nose to steady my pulse. The place is old, so each step creaks so loudly, it's almost obscene. It reminds me of when my sister and I used to sneak out when my parents were asleep, finding the right spot on the steps to avoid a creak. But these creaks are ten times more terrifying.

The staircase leads to an open entrance to the second floor. I enter and glimpse a reception area with an old-fashioned bar and draped high-top tables for post-funeral events. To my left, I view another door with a sign that says Do Not Enter. This must be the entrance to the Donahues' apartment. It also seems like a warning sign.

Do not enter.

I turn the knob with a gloved hand.

My fingerprints won't be found anywhere near this place.

It's unlocked.

I enter the cramped staircase. The air is warm and stagnant, and it feels different from the funeral home, as though you've shifted from the shine of Mary's public persona to the rot behind the curtain. With each step, my stomach cinches tighter. My mind knows the Donahues are away, but my spine senses something still lurking in this place.

I reach the top and am greeted by another door. I listen for any movement, but the house is quiet. The only sound is the occasional car puttering down West Forty-Third Street. I turn off my camera light and enter.

The first thing I notice is the odor.

A poisonous mix of death and chemicals. Like when exterminators kill mice in the walls. It's not overwhelming, but it's there, signaling to your brain that there's something wrong here. The next thing I notice is that I've stepped back in time.

Yellow street light filters in through the windows, and I notice that every piece in the apartment is antique. I'm standing in a living room stuffed with 1920s furniture. A velvet armchair rests beside an ivory settee. The tables perch on bentwood legs. A small chandelier hovers overhead. A floral porcelain teacup sits on a saucer on the end table.

These people live in the past.

They refuse to accept the modern world.

I check the tables and cabinets for any evidence. Papers on poisons. Receipts from a chemical firm. Red envelopes and paper. Stamps of the Mother Mary. The quicker I find evidence and leave, the better. But there's nothing.

I move to the bedroom, and the theme persists. A four-poster bed. An antique dressing table. A gold mantel clock ticking at the bedside. It's as though Brian and Mary have built a private world, apart from society. A fantasy land from a hundred years ago. I check their bedside tables, the bathroom cabinets. Empty except for the necessities of everyday life.

Returning to the living room, I notice that the mysterious smell grows. My cheeks flush and my body temperature rises as though whatever is making that smell is slinking into my immune system. The odor multiplies as I approach the kitchen. I pull my sweater over my nose to stifle the stench. I want to leave, but I know the truth lies here.

My gaze falls on the refrigerator. A light-blue 1940s beast with rounded edges.

A shiver runs through me.

I think back to all the serial killer cases I've studied, of the body parts in the refrigerator.

I don't want to open this door. I don't want to know what's in here. But I have no choice.

I snap open the refrigerator door and brace myself.

Again, there's nothing.

Fruit, vegetables, leftover pasta. Still, the stench persists. I close the refrigerator door and squint through the darkness.

Where is it coming from?

Then I spot it, tucked into the back corner of the kitchen: a weathered white door with chipped paint. At first it appears to be to a pantry, but I know something more lurks inside.

I turn the doorknob. The door sticks but then pops open.

The odor knocks me back, a sickening smell that conjures evil itself. I inhale through my mouth and hold it, pressing my sweater tighter to my nose. The room is windowless, but a giant aquarium sheds dim light on the space.

What I see disgusts me.

Japanese puffer fish fill the aquarium, packed so tight they can barely move.

On the other side of the room, two massive tables line the walls, filled with chemistry equipment, a spray dryer, pill kits, and other drug-making paraphernalia. A three-by-four portrait of Jesus looks down from on high. A long black coat hangs over the chair, and a Yankees hat and respiratory mask sit beside it.

But that's not what rattles me.

It's the dead animals.

Dissected frogs and squirrels rotting on trays, staring lifelessly into space. The victims of her sick experimentation. I move closer to look at them. Their bodies are contorted in the same way that Father Kenneally's was before he died. For a moment, I forget myself and let my sweater drop from my nose. The revolting stench rushes into my nostrils, and I feel the vomit rising in my gut. I try to stop it, but it's involuntary. I puke on the worn diamond-patterned rug.

I wipe the vomit from my mouth and re-cover my face, but the smell overwhelms me. It's inside me now.

Air.

I need air.

I run from the lab into the kitchen. As I do, I catch an object out of the corner of my right eye.

But it's not an object.

It's a person.

It's Mary.

She's holding a gun, a twisted expression on her face.

"Oh my," she says.

Before I can react, she slides behind me as I pass and cracks me on the back of the skull, and I fall to the floor.

I see stars.

I reach my hand to my head and feel sticky, warm blood rushing from my skull.

I peer through the fog and see Mary shaking her head. She holds up her phone and points to a motion alert from her Nest camera.

Then all goes black.

41

When I regain consciousness, I'm still dazed. The back of my head throbs. I have no sense of time or space. How long have I been gone? What happened to me? A blend of images whirs in my mind in the void between dreams and reality. I feel like I'm falling.

No.

I'm not falling.

Someone is carrying me and lowering me down. I sense small, muscular hands under my back and legs, supporting me like a baby.

A machine hums by my feet and gives off heat. I smell blood and a faint chemical scent. Pangs of pain ripple through my skull, and when I try to open my eyes, the bright light blinds me. I try to think, but my thoughts jumble. I must be in a hospital. What happened to me?

The nurse lowers me down with hard, unforgiving hands onto a narrow bed with cotton sheets. A hinge squeaks. I smell pine and lacquer.

Where am I? How did I get here?

A thick, rough palm shoves me down.

A faraway sense of unease takes hold of me. Something in my mind clicks, and I snap out of the fog. I force my eyes open and brave the light.

I flinch and flail when my vision clears.

Mary hovers over me, red faced and sweating like the devil herself.

"Oh, look. She's awake," she says. Perspiration beads along her hairline, and a deranged smile creeps across her face. Her emerald eyes flash with unspoken malice. Her rosy cheeks are aflame with fury.

I lift my head and look around the room.

Bright-white fluorescent lights hang from the ceiling, buzzing their unnatural buzz. Light reflects off the ivory walls onto a stainless steel slab in the center of the room. An army of metal tools stand beside the slab, shining. A bone saw. Scalpels of all sizes and shapes. Surgical scissors and thread.

I'm not in a hospital.

I'm in the crematorium.

And this isn't a hospital bed.

It's a cremation casket.

My eyes return to Mary, unable to accept what I'm seeing. This must be a sick joke. But all hope vanishes when I see her face. She revels in my terror, licking her lips with anticipation.

A fear unlike anything I've ever felt surges through me.

Sweat runs from every pore. The pulsing in my head screams like a siren. My temples feel like they might burst.

I force myself to squint through the blinding light and look at my feet. A massive metal cremation machine stands inches from my shoes, waiting to gobble me up.

Mary plans to burn me alive.

I panic and try to hoist myself out of the casket, but she's closed and locked the bottom half of the box and strapped my legs down. My hands remain free, but she shoves me down with a stiff left hand to my chest and points her pistol at me with her right. I sense by how she handles it that this isn't her first time with a gun. I remember her stories about hunting red foxes on the farm.

"Now, now. You stay put. I haven't got all night. Brian's waiting at Carmine's for me. You don't want to spoil date night, do you?"

She flicks the safety off, and her hand steadies on me. For a moment, I'm paralyzed, gripped by the sickness of everything around me: the cremation oven, the bone saw, the stench of chemicals and death. Part of me wants her to pull the trigger to end the pain, to end the horror, to free me from this hell. Then Jack and I could be together again.

But then I think of Jack. Of the way he held me. The way he looked at me. Of how she took him from me. How she smiled in my face while she gutted me. I can't let her win. I swear I will drag her into the fire with me if I have to.

I flex my stomach muscle to feel if my gun is still in my belly holster. It is. Mary didn't notice it when she was carrying me. I consider pulling it now, but she'll shoot me dead before I draw. I freeze and lie back in the casket, playing possum.

"That's a good girl," she says, a serpentine smile curling across her bloodred lips. She shuts the top half of the box, and I hear her turn the sealing key and remove it.

I'm locked inside the casket.

The cremation fire roars outside.

It's blackness, except for the slivers of light slipping through the cracks in the box. I see the white lining and wonder if I'm already dead. I'm alone, stuffed in here like a cadaver. The box closes in on me. My heart moves into overdrive, and my breath escapes me. I hear the familiar buzzing, whining sound in my brain. Panic takes over, and I bang my palms on the casket top.

I hear Mary's voice purr from outside the box. "Easy, dear. I don't want to have to shoot you." I can picture the sinister grin on her face as she glories in watching me burn. The thought of her sends me into a psychotic rage.

"Why don't you just fucking shoot me, Mary? You've come this far." I kick my legs and slam my right fist against the roof.

As I flail, I feel my pistol come loose from the holster. I keep shouting and banging, using the distraction to grab hold of it.

"Hazel, you can bang all you want, but that won't change God's plan for you."

I hear a click as the cremation oven door opens. I picture the monster's mouth agape, waiting to swallow me whole. Even through the box, I feel the heat of the fire. Sweat pours down my face. I grip my pistol tighter. It takes everything in me not to panic.

"How do you know what God's plan is? Maybe his plan is for me to end you," I shout.

Mary sighs. "Violence is never the answer. Blessed are the peacemakers."

As she speaks, I tilt my ear toward the top of the box. I try to follow the sound with my gun, but the casket limits my movements. I need to bring her closer. I need to keep her talking.

I keep banging on the box to make her feel she's won and shout through the pine. "So burning me alive isn't violent?"

I hear a sinister chuckle as she eases closer, almost whispering through the box.

"No, heavens no. This is God's justice. Remember your Bible: 'The fearful and unbelieving shall have their part in the lake which burneth with fire and brimstone.' You are an unbeliever. I told you to go to church. This, my dear, is your fire."

42

hear a low grind and feel the box moving. The conveyor rumbles, pulling me into the fire. The heat sears my feet. The clock ticks in my skull. I'm going to burn alive.

I bring the gun to my chest and listen for Mary, but the furnace is too loud.

"What did you say?" I ask her. "I couldn't hear you."

The bottom of the coffin crackles at my feet. Blood and perspiration run down my neck. I fight the dizziness coming over me. I trace my fingertips across the wood. A bullet should be able to pierce it.

She speaks, and I can tell she's leaning closer. "I said, the fearful and unbelieving—"

This is my chance. I aim my pistol at the sound, then fire three shots in different locations, hoping to hit something. I hear a grunt and then a thud like Mary's body has fallen to the floor.

I freeze, praying that she doesn't get up. The wood beneath my feet catches fire. Burning heat and smoke rushes into the box. I rip off the leg straps and pull my feet up closer to my body. The fumes choke me.

The burning casket wood cracks again and again. A clock ticking down the seconds to my death.

Crack.

Crack.

Crack.

I spot the underside of the lock on the casket. I can't shoot it directly because the bullet might ricochet off it and kill me. I have to hit it from the side. The casket pins my arms to my ribs, but I wriggle to catch an angle. I aim at the crack a centimeter to the right of the lock and fire. The bullet splits the wood. I slam my palm against the top half, but it's still locked. I must have missed. Mary wails in pain, and I freeze so I can hear if she's coming, but from the sound, I can tell she's down for the count.

The smoke and heat invade faster now, trapped in this cocoon. Blood rushes to my face, and the pain in my skull is almost unbearable now. A spark jumps, and I smell my hair burning. My soaking hands can barely hold the gun. I reposition myself and fire again. Another miss. The lock still holds the casket shut. The heat stings now, and the smoke burns my eyes. I can hardly see. I can barely breathe.

I look at my gun. I've fired five shots in a six-round mag. Only one shot left. I wipe my palm on my sweater and hold my breath to steady my hand.

I aim at the other side of the lock. The keyhole stares back at me through the crack.

I pull the trigger.

The lock explodes in an ear-shattering clang, taking a chunk of the box with it. A splinter slices through my cheek. A ringing echo lingers in the air, and between the sound and pain in my face, I'm unsure what happened. But then I spot the light from the hole in the box and my heart leaps.

I throw open the top half of the casket and suck in the oxygen. The fresh air scalds and then revives my lungs. Still, my legs burn. I look down and watch the bottom half slide into the cremation oven. I lift my legs up to my chest to avoid the fire and hoist myself up with my arms. The heat is so strong, I have to cover my face.

I leap out of the casket and down to the floor one second before the cremation oven digests the box. The casket crackles and snaps as the fire devours it, and I imagine what could have been. My chest pounds with fury as I turn to Mary.

She lies on the floor.

A chunk of her ear is missing, and blood runs down her cheek and coagulates in her hair. Another bullet wound seeps from her chest. And another in her leg. Her gun rests a few feet from her. She's crawling toward it, her breathing labored.

I march over and stomp my foot on the gun before she can grab it.

I pick up Mary's gun and secure it along with my empty pistol.

She rolls over onto her back. A pink mixture of blood and spit coat her teeth and gums. She spreads her arms and laughs, a shrill, maniacal laugh mixed with wheezing. A hyena at sunset.

"Don't move," I say.

Blood pours from my cheek and the back of my skull. My vision throbs like a club beat. I see my phone sitting on the counter. I grab it and dial 911. "Yes, I need police to 445 West Forty-Third Street. Someone's been shot." I hang up the phone.

I glare back at Mary. She's staring at me, her eyes green with fire, her face crimson with hate. She laughs her hyena laugh and twirls her cross pendant on her fingers. "Oh, Danny boy, the pipes, the pipes are calling…" she sings.

As I watch her. Hate bubbles in my bloodstream. I see Jack, the only man I've ever loved, cold and lifeless on the floor of our bedroom. I picture Father Kenneally crawling along the church floor, reaching out to me to save him. I remember Archbishop Dinwiddie writhing in agony. I think of Tweed's widow destroyed by grief. I envision Kenny, shaking and spasming, fighting for breath. I stew on the destruction this woman has wrought. Of everything she has taken from me and so many others.

And she doesn't even care.

She laughs.

I don't know if I can let her go to trial. I step closer to her and release the gun's safety. My hand shakes, but Mary can see the resolve in my eyes.

The edges of her mouth curl upward in a clown-like grin. With one shot, I could erase that grin for eternity.

"What's so fucking funny, Mary?"

She cackles louder. "You."

I grip the gun tighter. "Oh yeah? Why is that?"

"Because you think you're the hero."

"I don't think I'm a hero."

"Yes, you do. You think you're a hero. And you know what? I thought you were a hero once."

"What?"

"That's why I applied for the job. Did you know that?" A police siren whines in the distance. "No, I didn't."

"Yes, sirree. I saw what you did for those girls at the Dionysus Club. I read about it in the paper, and honest to God, you were my hero. I thought, *Finally, someone who understands the amoral cesspool that this world has become and is taking action.*" She coughs and spits blood. "For the next few weeks, I read everything I could find about you. The more I read, the more I thought you could be the woman I've been searching for my whole life."

"Hmm," I say as I tighten my grip.

"I remember the day I interviewed with you. I was so nervous, I could barely breathe." She grimaces as pain ripples throughout her body. "But you were so sweet and kind. Then when you gave me the job, I thought I had died and gone to heaven." The maniacal grin on her face morphs into a sneer. "And then I worked for you and realized you weren't a hero; you were just another godless lost soul who cares about nothing but material things. What the office looks like. How much the clients pay. What the media says. I thought I'd be helping you put away child abusers or sexual deviants. Instead, I'm billing insurance companies. And that's when it hit me. I kept looking for others to do God's work—the convent, the church, you. But I didn't need anyone to do the Lord's work. I could do it myself."

"You think killing people is the Lord's work?" With every

word out of her mouth, my finger gets more comfortable on the trigger.

She chuckles, and a wheeze escapes her lungs. "I don't kill people. They kill themselves. If they were truly saved, God would keep them from taking that pill. But they never avoid the pill. Not that philandering priest. That greedy hedge fund thief. That debased archbishop. And worst of all, your lying, thieving, worthless politician boyfriend."

The more she speaks, the more poison she spills. Blood rushes to my face, and sweat chokes my pores. Every inch of me wants to pull the trigger—or better yet, drop the gun and strangle her.

She sees that she's getting to me and doubles down. Police sirens ring closer now.

"It was fun, you know. Watching. The priest slithering along the church floor like the snake that he was. And I could barely contain my excitement when I got to see Dinwiddie crumple on the ground right in front of me. I was a little worried when you called the cops so quick, but his old ticker never stood a chance. I never got to see Tweed die, but I'm sure a spineless weasel like him went quick.

"I like to imagine how God snuffed out Jack's life. How his pretty little body squirmed and shook. How his Captain America face pleaded. How impotent he must have felt when he finally found a situation he couldn't smooth-talk his way out of. He must have—"

"Shut up!" I scream. It's one thing to lose someone, but to watch someone delight in it is something I wouldn't wish on my worst enemy. I aim the gun at her forehead and imagine the bullet splitting her skull. The police and paramedics are almost here. If I kill her now, I can say it was self-defense. No trial. No jail time. Only justice.

Her eyes light up as she sees me aim. "Do it, Hazel. Send me to heaven."

I steady the pistol. I close one eye and burrow my gaze into her forehead. I ease the trigger forward. I envision her brain going dead, her eyes stilling, her voice ceasing.

But then I pause. And I think about the people still in my life. I remember who I am and who I want to be.

A pounding from upstairs, followed by the ring of the door-bell, breaks me loose of the trance. I hear the door snap open. "Police."

"We're down here!" I shout.

I drop the gun to my side.

"You're not going to heaven, Mary. You're going to hell. But first stop is a maximum-security prison."

EPILOGUE

I lie on the tan fabric couch in my parents' living room, watching the news while my mom, sister, and brother-in-law prepare our traditional Sunday-night dinner. Winter has arrived early. Tiny snowflakes flutter outside, and my dad has even started a fire to get us in the mood. The smell of firewood puts me in the holiday spirit. Let the Christmas-shopping season begin. My dad sits next me to me in his ancient leather recliner, wearing oversize faded jeans and a periwinkle sweater from the local golf course. My niece and nephew sport matching outfits of polo shirts and corduroy pants—my sister insists on it—and play with LEGO bricks on the cream shag carpet. Most weeks, I dread Sunday family dinners. There's a lot of questioning about my love life, my career choices, my fashion sense. But tonight it feels good. Sometimes you need the loving chaos of home.

The news returns from commercial break, chyrons fling

across the screen, and the anchor announces that Sandy Godo has won the New York mayoral election in a landslide. They show a shot of him in front of a podium, smiling his lizard smile while cameras flash.

"This isn't a victory for me. This is a victory for every New Yorker who's ready to take back their streets. The Red-Letter Killer is behind bars, and we saved six individuals who received the letter before they took her poison. Let that be a warning to every criminal out there... This is only the beginning."

I shake my head. He looks so proud of himself even though he had nothing to do with catching anyone and was essentially running against a dead man. When Jack died, people asked me to run in his place, but I declined. Politics isn't for me. The guy they eventually found was a poor substitute. Then again, measured against Jack, everyone is.

The next news story is an exposé on the Red-Letter Killer. Mary's mug shot flickers on the screen. I flinch in my seat. I still see her face in my nightmares. The psychotic sneer, the seething green eyes. Sometimes I kill her in my dream. I pull the trigger and watch her face go blank. In my dream, I don't regret it. I'm not sure what that means.

My dad fumbles for the remote and turns the television off. "I'm sorry about that, Hanuel."

I sit up on the sofa and put my feet on the ground. "It's fine, Appa. I just haven't gotten used to seeing her on TV yet."

His kind cocoa eyes carry pain. My pain. He takes a long, sad breath through his nose, and his wide jaw clenches. "I know. What will happen to her?"

I sit down on the floor and grab some LEGO bricks. My

niece, Aram, smiles a gap-toothed smile, while my nephew, Sung, fires me a suspicious glance through narrow eyes. I assemble a piece of the Death Star to put his worries to rest. "Shavali said the DA's asking for a life sentence."

"Do you think she'll get it?"

"I don't know. It could be tough if Mary puts on her whole Midwestern-mom routine."

"I see."

"But the good news is, she's over fifty, so there's a chance she won't be released in her lifetime regardless."

"And the husband?"

"Yes, they'll charge him since he was aiding and abetting. I'm sure the DA will go for less prison time, but he'll definitely serve time."

"That's good." My dad pauses and twirls his wedding band around his stubby fingers, an old tell for when he needs to ask me something personal. Our family doesn't do personal very well. "And how are you?"

I place another piece into the Death Star, which earns me a pat from Sung. "I'm doing okay."

My dad looks up at me, and his eyes are watering. Water from a stone. His long lashes flutter to beat back the tears. "No, I mean, how are you doing *really*?"

One look in his eyes, and I want to break.

I want to cry and tell him I'm a mess. That I think of Jack five hundred times a day, and every time, it feels like my chest is going to collapse. That I'm scared when I walk down the street because I can't shake the feeling that someone's following me. That I don't know if I can keep C&S Investigations going any longer.

But I can't.

Because if I don't keep fighting, who will? As Perry once said, *The world's going to try to break you. The only choice you got to make is if you're going to let it.*

"Really, Dad. I'm doing okay. I'm sad, but I'm okay." He raises an eyebrow that says, *You gotta do better than that.* But I know if I say another word, I'm going to lose it.

I get up and give him a kiss and hug to shut him down.

"Hey, you're taking the turret guns," says Sung as I walk away. Aram giggles and shows me a gummy grin.

"Oh, I'm so sorry, Lord Vader," I say, and return the pieces back to him.

The doorbell rings.

From the kitchen, my mom shouts, "Hanuel, can you get that?"

I look around. My entire family is here. Who else could this be? I swear, if my mom invited Dr. Lee over for another dating setup, I'm going to burn this house to the ground. I stomp over to the door and open it.

To my delight, it's Kenny, Momo, and Shavali.

"Hey, girl," says Shavali as she gives me a big hug. Per usual, she's dressed like she's dining at Cipriani: bright-tangerine skirt and a navy blouse that reveals far too much chest. The scent of orange blossom shampoo rushes into the house as she breezes by me.

Kenny follows her in and squeezes me tight. It's the kind of embrace that a friend gives you when you need that extra oomph. "Your mom invited us. She thought it might cheer you up. I told her that normally I annoy you, but she insisted." He's dressed to kill as well, sporting a white cashmere sweater and designer jeans. Momo has been good for him.

Momo smiles at me as if she can read my mind and hands me a cardboard box. Her curious eyes analyze my reaction as I open it. It's filled with cream puffs. "Kenny said this is a better gift than a puffer fish."

"It's perfect. Come on inside, it's chilly out there." As we enter the living room, my mom pokes her head out of the kitchen. Her cheeks turn upward, and then she returns to what she's doing. My mother mystifies me. She never says *Good job* or *I love you*, but then she does these incredibly thoughtful things that remind you she really cares.

I point Kenny, Momo, and Shavali over to the dinner table. "Grab a seat."

We all sit and chat while my mom and Christina scurry around, pots gurgling, steam flying. My brother-in-law, David, looks completely lost.

My mom brings out a giant steaming bowl of mandu, Korean dumplings. The heavenly scent of pork and garlic runs across my nose. They're not quite as good as Mrs. Yu's Chinese dumplings, but they're damn close.

"Byung! Dinnertime. Bring the kids!" she shouts at my father from the kitchen.

I roll my eyes. "Sorry it's a little chaotic in here. So, how are you guys doing?"

Kenny reaches in to grab a dumpling, but my mom slaps his hand away and wags a finger at him. "I'm doing good. Nobody's tried to poison me for over a week."

I laugh. "That's a good start. Yeah, I told my mom she should poison you as a fun prank, but she refused."

Momo straightens her plaid skirt as she settles into her chair.

"I also have some good news. I will finish my criminal justice degree program this spring, one year early."

My eyebrows jump. How she's completed her BS early while working at C&S, I'll never know. "That's incredible, Momo. I'm so proud of you."

She bows her head. "Thank you."

David drops off water glasses for everyone at the table.

"What do you think you'll do when you graduate?" I ask Momo.

She shifts in her chair and pulls her white blouse tighter to her neck. "Well, I was hoping I could work for you full-time." She glances at Kenny and then back at me with a plaintive smile.

"Are you kidding? That's fantastic. Of course. We'd love to have you."

I look at Kenny, who mouths the words *Thank you.*

Momo claps her hands quietly. "That's wonderful."

"I talked to Marcos today," says Shavali, clearly uncomfortable not being the center of attention.

"Oh, did you? He called me a couple times this week, but I couldn't deal with it. Does he still suspect I'm the Red-Letter Killer, or has he finally let that go?"

She crinkles her eyes, acknowledging my sarcasm. "No, believe it or not, he's moved on. And he asked me to tell you how dreadfully sorry he is for how he treated you."

"Wow. That's shocking."

She laughs her melodic laugh and flips her hair. There's something she's not telling me.

"And…?" I say.

"And…he asked me out."

I shoot a five-alarm look at Kenny and Momo, who simultaneously shrug.

"Oh, Shay, please tell me you said no."

"I told him I'd think about it." She giggles and twirls her hair. I slap my palm to my forehead. "What? He's kind of cute, in that bad boy sort of way. Have you seen those biceps? My, my, my."

Christina sits down with Sung and Aram in tow. "Ooh, what are we talking about? Some good gossip?" The woman possesses a sixth sense for rumor and innuendo. Mom, Dad, and David join us at the table.

"We're not talking about anything exciting, C. Just Shavali's poor life decisions," I say.

We all laugh until my mom clears her throat, her way of saying, *Be quiet.* I remember when we were kids and we'd hear that throat clear. It was like a gunshot. You froze.

She grabs my dad's hand, and when I look in her eyes, I see that she's holding back tears. Her round, age-spotted face bunches, and her voice quakes when she speaks. "Before we begin the meal, I want to welcome our guests and thank you for coming. This has been a difficult time for Hanuel, and we very much appreciate you visiting our home and supporting her." A tear falls from her eye, and she quickly wipes it away. "Hanuel, you may have noticed there is an extra chair at the table, and you may have wondered if another person was coming to dinner."

She pauses and stares at me. I feel my face scowl, uncertain where this is going.

My mom continues. "The answer is no. There is no one else coming to dinner. That chair is for Jack. Because he will always be with us, and he will always have a seat at our dinner table. You will never be alone."

I'm speechless.

I don't think I've ever seen my mother cry, and I never thought she was capable of such a heartfelt gesture. I feel like I could burst. The cacophony of emotions I've felt over the last year—grief, fear, anger, disappointment, pride, happiness, hope—crash together inside my chest until tears force their way out and roll down my cheeks. I should say something, but I don't know what to say. I open my mouth to speak, but nothing can encapsulate all that I feel.

As usual, Shavali steps in for me.

"That's so beautiful, Mrs. Cho."

Such a simple statement, but so true. It was a beautiful act.

"Thank you for that, Mom," I say. I want to hug her, but that's not really what my mom and I do. I reach my hand across the table and rest it on hers.

She smiles for a moment, and as our eyes meet, I glimpse all the things she's wanted to say to me but never could. I hope she sees the same.

She quickly recovers herself and pulls her hand away to grab a bowl. "Okay, enough of that mushy stuff. Let's eat."

We pass the incredible spread of dumplings, bulgogi, and rice back and forth. The kids tell stories of their Star Wars adventures. Kenny and Momo share that they're taking a vacation together—a big relationship step. Christina and my mom lecture Shavali on her dating choices while my dad looks on and chuckles.

Despite all the chatter and clinking of utensils around me,

I can't take my eyes off that chair my mom placed at the table. Because as crazy as it sounds, I can picture Jack sitting there, winking at me with that mischievous Texas grin.

His memory is something Mary can never steal from me.

And for me, at this moment, it's enough.

PLEASE ENJOY THIS SNEAK PEEK AT DANIEL G. MILLER'S NEXT BRAND-NEW WORK OF SUSPENSE, COMING SOON.

CHAPTER 1

'm twelve years old and I'm on top of the world.

I'm swinging around the Ferris wheel at the Minnesota State Fair with my best friend, Olivia. It's one of those incomparable late summer nights—warm with a hint of dew in the air and a gentle fall breeze that tickles your hair. The meteorologist says there's a supermoon tonight. From up here, it looks like if I stretched far enough, I could touch it.

An intoxicating scent of pronto pups, spun sugar, and fried dough rises from below. Our seat creaks back and forth as I watch families and hand-holding couples making their way through the fairgrounds: buying deep-fried Snickers bars, munching on giant turkey legs, inspecting the latest tractor models, hugging goats at the petting zoo, throwing darts at balloons. Occasionally I hear a bell ring from someone winning another overstuffed animal, but for the most part it's quiet—peaceful, even.

For a moment I wonder if I could sit up here forever.

I glance at Olivia, and I can tell she feels the same way. Her espresso eyes sparkle as she takes in the explosion of stars in the night sky. I can't help staring at her. She's everything I'm not but want to be. Her black hair shines and curls, unlike my stringy, fried blond locks. Her skin is a freckle-free brown versus my spotted white. As she crosses her legs, her perfectly proportioned body moves with grace and agility, in contrast to my lanky clumsiness.

Sometimes I wonder why she's friends with me.

The gondola swings through the bottom of its arc. Hordes of sunburned fairgoers wait to board the ride. I catch a glimpse of Olivia's dad, Adam, sporting a pink polo and driving mocs, nibbling on a chocolate chip waffle cone, talking to my mother. We breeze past him, and I take a moment to admire his toned arms and sea-green irises. He laughs at something my mom says, his eyes crinkling, dimples dancing. He's the kind of dad you see in TV shows—perfectly tanned, perpetually relaxed, the world orbiting around his easy charm. Something stirs in me.

Olivia catches me staring and smacks my arm. "Eww, stop looking at my dad like that."

Heat floods my face. "What are you talking about?"

She laughs and shakes her head. "It's so obvious you have a crush on him."

"Nu-uh."

"Yu-huh."

"Whatever."

"Whatever, whatever."

She shoots me a knowing look but mercifully lets it drop. As we fly back up into the night sky, her lips break into a huge grin, and she wraps an arm around me and squeezes. I catch a whiff of her coconut conditioner.

"It's nice up here, huh?" she says.

I tap my head against hers and sigh. "Yeah, it's nice."

The Ferris wheel groans beneath us, and I flinch, clutching the safety bar with taloned hands. I glance down at the people below who look like ants, which only worsens my phobia.

"OMG," says Olivia. "It's just the wheel turning." She places a hand on my back. "Relax."

I force a smile and lean into the seat. "Sorry. The noise surprised me. I—I really do like it up here."

She sits silently for a minute, giving me a chance to settle back in, then taps my knee and points to the glowing moon. "See, CharBar, I told you there was nothing to be afraid of. Aren't you glad I made you do this?"

I blush. "Yeah, it's pretty cool. Heights just freak me out a little."

"A little? I thought you were going to bail on me. Thought I was going to have to ride this thing by myself."

"Whatever. I'm fine."

She cocks her head. "Oh, so you're saying you weren't scared at all?"

I throw her a defiant smile. "Nope." If there's one thing I've learned, it's that you don't win an argument with Olivia. But I like to get a rise out of her now and then.

"Ha! You are such a liar."

Before I can respond, she slides her legs from under the

safety bar and stands on the cracked brown leather cushion. The gondola wobbles beneath her feet. The hinges screech.

I press myself against the back of the seat, eyes wide in disbelief at what I'm seeing. My chest tightens, and the muscles in my legs and arms cinch. "Olivia, what are you doing?"

She ignores me and stands taller, spreading her arms out like she's flying, her weight forward, face cutting the wind like a carving on the prow of a ship—proud and invincible.

But she's not invincible. I know better.

One shift, one wrong move, and she's gone.

"Olivia, sit down," I say, my voice cracking.

She closes her eyes for a breath, basking in the danger as we rise higher in the night sky and the supermoon closes in. A gust of wind kicks up, and she shifts her hips to find her center. I want to reach for her leg and grab her, but I'm afraid I'll knock her off balance. My stomach twists, and my eyes search for some type of emergency brake or switch I could pull to make this horrible machine stop.

She spots my terror and winks at me, spreading her arms wider. "I want you to admit you were scared and wouldn't have gotten on this ride if it weren't for your beautiful, funny, awesome friend Olivia."

I search the fairgrounds for help, but no one notices.

My fingers clutch my seat cushion, knuckles white, stricken with panic.

"Okay, I'm sorry."

She shakes her head and steps onto the safety bar.

The realization hits me.

She's going to balance on the bar.

The sounds of the fair fade to a low hum.

An impish grin crosses her face. "I don't want you to say sorry. I want you to admit you wouldn't have gotten on this ride if it weren't for your beautiful, funny, awesome friend Olivia."

Everything inside me tells me to grab her. *Just lean over and grab her by the waist, pull her toward you, and don't let go.*

But I can't.

I'm paralyzed.

My nails dig into the seat cushion.

I squeal, "Olivia, please come down."

Her smile grows so wide that it takes up half her face, a sea of ivory. The Ferris wheel groans and squeals beneath her. She wags her dainty finger at me and places her other foot on the safety bar, arms spread like a gymnast on a balance beam. The ride is reaching its apex now, and as mortified as I am, I can't help but be struck by the beauty of what I'm seeing: this girl dressed in white, lit like an angel by the Ferris wheel bulbs below, framed by a glittering night sky. Stunning and dangerous.

It takes my breath away.

A spark of jealousy runs through me, watching how effortlessly she performs feats I couldn't even dream of. I wish we could trade places for just one day.

The shriek of the wheel snaps me back to reality—to the fact that my best friend stands on the precipice of death. "I'm sorry!" I scream.

"Not good enough. You have to say 'beautiful, funny, awesome friend Olivia,'" she says and raises one foot off the safety bar, lifting it to her hand like a ballerina.

I frantically scan the ground for help. My dad and the

Parkers chat away, oblivious, but my mom looks up now. Her jaw is on the ground, but she does nothing—like me, frozen by what she's seeing.

I turn back to Olivia and clasp my hands together. I've been holding my breath so long I can barely speak. "Okay, I wouldn't have gotten on this ride if it weren't for my beautiful, funny, awesome friend Olivia."

She cocks her head, measuring my sincerity, waits a beat, then drops her raised leg, puts her foot down on the bar, and laughs. "That's all I needed to hear."

I release a breath and run my hand through my hair.

She begins to step down. "See, that wasn't so hard, was—"

The wheel shifts.

Her weight wavers. Her grin vanishes.

My mouth drops open and my breathing stops.

Her arms pinwheel.

She reaches for me.

I reach for her—but my limbs won't move. I'm frozen.

All I can do is watch.

Watch as her arms flail.

Watch as her eyes bulge.

Watch as her chest screams.

Watch as her body falls.

Watch as my best friend tumbles to the ground below.

READING GROUP GUIDE

1. Hazel initially resists taking Samuel Sampson's case. Why do you think that is? What about her past informs her choice?

2. Early on we see Hazel's interactions with her family. How do you think her relationship with her family affects her? How did it remind you of your relationship with your family?

3. A central theme of the novel is power and the things powerful people get away with. How do you see this theme play out in the real world?

4. Hazel says, "People think of trauma as a moment, a temporary visitor. But it's not. It's a lifelong companion." What does she mean by that? Does that match your experience?

5. What did you think of Jack? How did your opinion of him change as the novel progressed?

6. Kenny and Hazel's relationship undergoes subtle changes during the novel. What do you think is in store for them?

7. Hazel experiences grief for the first time in this novel. How did this remind you of your experiences with grief?

8. What did you make of the ending? Did you see it coming? Did you expect a different villain?

9. Despite Mary's actions, did you understand her perspective? Why did she do what she did?

10. Hazel faces a dilemma regarding how to handle the killer at the end of the novel. Do you think she made the right decision? What would you have done?

ACKNOWLEDGMENTS

Mark Gottlieb, my agent at Trident Literary Agency, for listening to my hopes and dreams and making them a reality.

The team at Sourcebooks and Poisoned Pen Press for introducing Hazel Cho to the broader world.

Mary Altman for guiding this novel through the publishing labyrinth on an extremely tight timeline.

Reed Soeffker for keeping me honest about the nitty-gritty of criminal investigation and sharing the telling details of investigative work that make Hazel come to life. Any errors are mine, not his.

Siobhan Jones for yet another brilliant developmental edit. You never pick the easy route, but it's always the right one.

Rachel Norfleet and Jessica Thelander for fixing my reckless use of homophones and incorrect capitalization and always knowing what I'm trying to say whether I do or not.

The team at Damonza for delivering yet another breathtaking cover that somehow captures everything I want to say in a single image.

My wife, Lexi, and my new baby boy, Dayton, for reminding me every day about the richness of life.

And finally, my family and friends, the ultimate cast of characters, from whom I draw much of my inspiration.

ABOUT THE AUTHOR

Daniel G. Miller is the bestselling author of *The Orphanage by the Lake* and the Tree of Knowledge thriller series. When he's not writing, he enjoys sipping sunset cocktails with his wife, watching NBA basketball, and singing off-key to his newborn son, not necessarily in that order. He currently lives in Delray Beach, Florida. He loves hearing from readers, so feel free to drop him a line at dan@danielmillerbooks.com.

danielmillerbooks.com
Instagram: @danielgmillerauthor
Facebook: facebook.com/groups/danielgmillerauthor
TikTok: @danielgmillerwrites